Cassy's Voice

Emily Clarke.

First published in November 2015
on Amazon as an e book.
This paperback edition published in January 2016.
Copyright 2016 Emily Clarke.
All rights reserved.

This is a work of fiction. Any references to real people, events, institutions, or locales are intended solely to give a sense of authenticity. While every effort was made to be historically accurate, it should be remembered that these references are used fictitiously.

Scripture quotation from The New International Version Bible. Photograph for Cover: Jay Carrieres.

To the memory of the 1,836 who lost their lives to

Hurricane Katrina

and to the 705 reported as still missing.

***

When you have Read this copy

Pay it forward

Emily Clarke

follow me on Instagram

to let me know you Read it.

emilyclarke.ie

"Daughter, your faith has healed you.

Go in peace and be freed from your suffering."

-Mark5:34

Chapter 1

It was eight in the evening on Saturday August 27, 2005. Cassy was safe in the parlor of her Creole cottage on the corner of Burgundy and Toulouse Street. She lived here all her married life, over fifty years with her husband Louis. Earlier today, she overheard the news report Louis watched in the family room. She listened to it from her room right next door. The French doors, which joined both rooms, were partially open.

"There is a storm approaching us. I strongly advise all citizens to evacuate the city."

Cassy leaned around the door to watch the news report. She saw the governor along with the mayor, stood side by side. They had the same worried look on their face she saw on her husband. He sat forward in his armchair. She disappeared behind the door. The phone rang. She could hear Louis walk across the wooden floorboards and pick up the phone off the table just next to her room. She stayed hidden behind the drapes.

"Hello, Le Blanc residence...Oh yes I watched

it...Do, leave...No...The store will be fine...It's not your job, but thank you. Did you close the shutters and put out the sandbags? Good job."

Cassy glanced out from her hiding place. Louis looked in the direction of the T.V. again.

"I'm watching it now. Yes, they keep playing it. The governor spoke yesterday."

Cassy saw him look in at her bed.

"She wouldn't be able. She needs familiarity. I have to go by the doctors...what...oh yes I know that, but we have sat out many a storm. What is one more? You too, take care."

Louis put the phone down. Cassy stepped out from her hiding place. He walked into her room.

"That was the bookstore on the phone. A parcel arrived there for you."

He led her back to her bed as he spoke.

"We will collect it together Monday, once the storm has passed."

She didn't answer him. Instead, she lay down as he tucked her into bed. He leaned over and turned on her stereo. He turned the volume up enough for her to hear. He struggled to get to his feet again.

"Who is the parcel from?" she asked in the darkness of her bedroom.

She watched him stop in the doorway. In the half-light, she recognized the man she married all those years ago.

Without turning around he answered, "It's an address on the River Road."

He walked back towards her and sat down so they were face to face. His light blue eyes hadn't faded over the years. He looked down at her bed sheets and didn't meet her gaze as he spoke.

"It's from my family. It's addressed from my family's plantation."

Cassy drew in her breath. A rush of memories flooded back and she found it hard to breathe.

"You were never there though Cassy that is why I find it strange. I'm right in thinking you were never there?"

She nodded. She couldn't speak. He stood up to leave the room again.

"We will find out Monday. Leave on the music it will drown out the storm."

"Louis?"

"Yes my love."

"Will you stay with me till I sleep?"

"You know I don't have to sleep upstairs any night. I know the plan was that you have this space by day to rest, but you don't need to be here on your own."

3

"I know that Louis."

"I promise this storm is going to pass and we'll go together to the bookstore Monday and find out what is in that parcel."

"Well you can't let me out on my own. Isn't that what the doctor said?"

He sat down in the chair and didn't answer her. He watched her as she settled down to sleep.

***

When Cassy woke, she heard the shutters bang against the house. She lifted back the drapes next to her bed and looked out. The storm had intensified. She saw the door of the outhouse blown open. Her stereo crackled. The signal was affected by the storm. She closed her eyes and listened to the words.

"I woke up this morning my baby up and gone. I woke up this morning from dreaming all night long. He only gone and left me, ain't nobody see? My baby only gone and left me."

She was transported back to 1961. The music hall was filled to capacity and the crowd clapped and cheered. They wanted more. They called out her name.

"Cassy, Cassy, CASSY."

She turned and looked to her manager. He nodded and held up his arms in resignation. No other act would get

4

on stage tonight, but it didn't matter.

He had a full house and it was all thanks to 'Cassy Shaw'. Her dress shimmied as she moved. She touched the string of pearls around her neck and brought them to her lips. She kissed them and buried her face in her palms. The crowd laughed along with her mock hesitancy to sing. She picked up the microphone and belted out another song as her papa accompanied her on the piano.

She returned from the past when the French door to the gallery blew open. The lace sheers rose, fell, and landed around her shoulders. She was shrouded from the bedroom and exposed to the storm. She felt the rain hit her face as it blew in sheets. She stepped out onto the gallery. The sky looked troubled. There was a yellow hue mixed in with the rolling black clouds. The words she overheard on the T.V. came back to her. "Anyone that can leave should leave."

The door back into her room slammed shut. She tried to open it, but the force of the wind was too strong. She re-entered the house through the French door that led into the family room. The T.V. was on, but the volume was down. A black and white movie flickered on and off on the screen. Louis wasn't there. She walked into the dining room. The chandelier lights over the table dimmed and came on again. All the rooms of the house were connected by adjoining doors, except the kitchen. Louis built that for her when they moved in. He built it out of one of the cabinets at the rear of the house, designed for storage. It managed to remain feeling separate from the rest of the house. The door to it led out onto Toulouse Street.

She felt someone behind her. She turned around and saw a man stood in the doorway. He was tall and practically filled the doorframe. His skin was white and he had salt n' pepper hair. When he walked towards her, she noticed he had a limp.

"I was looking for you Cassy," he said.

His voice sounded panicked, but his demeanor remained calm. The lights faded again. When they came up, he was gone into the other parlor. This was her bedroom now. Before she was diagnosed with dementia, she used to leave their bedroom at night and Louis would find her down here, either trying to turn on the stereo or wandering around the house. He worried about her using the stairs. There was only enough room in here for a single bed, so he stayed upstairs. She watched him turn off the stereo. He came back into the dining room and pulled out a chair for her. She hesitated.

"I probably fell asleep," he said. "You were in here all along."

She sat down and he went into the kitchen. She heard

him plate up dinner. He returned with two plates of steaming food. It smelled so good. Her favorite, gumbo. He set her plate down in front of her and poured her a glass of ice-cold lemonade. She relaxed a little. He sat down across from her. She waited until he ate and followed his lead. The storm still raged outside.

"Who was that singing," she asked.

He held his fork mid-air. Some food fell back onto his plate. He looked pained as he raised his eyes to meet hers.

"That is your voice my love," he said. He smiled softly. There was a familiarity to him. Something about his eyes, she felt she could trust him.

***

Cassy left the confines of her bedroom. She told Louis earlier she needed to rest. He was reading in the room next door. She looked out into the courtyard. The magnolia tree Louis planted for her, bowed under the force of the wind. It was under its branches she sat when she needed to find solace from the past. Next to the tree was a statue of a woman with her head eternally looking down into the water. Water poured from the jug in her hand into the fountain. At the rear of the courtyard was the outhouse. When they first moved in, they were to convert it into a living space for the children they would have. It was never renovated and was used for storage instead.

She walked across the cobbled stone courtyard. The statue took on an eerie demeanor. A memory from the past came to her. She was in the garden of the mansion and someone watched her. It was difficult to see in the rain now as she made her way to the outhouse. She pulled open the door. When she was safe inside, she closed the door. There was no sound. She couldn't hear the storm anymore. Louis had soundproofed it for her, so she could come here to sing. She looked around the large room. Her papa's piano sat proudly in the centre. She sat down on the stool and opened its lid. She ran her fingers across its ivory keys. She never played it. It belonged to him. She just came here to remember.

All of a sudden, the room seemed strange to her. She didn't know how she got here. She looked out at the courtyard. Beyond it, she could see a house with lanterns suspended from its gallery. They swung over and back from the wind. There was someone walking back and forth. He disappeared through one door and back out another. She turned her attention back to the sewing machine in the corner of the room. She lifted off the dust cover. It was her mama's machine. Louis took it from her family home after her papa died. She sat down on the stool and worked on the phantom dress under the needle.

8

"I must keep up with my workload. Madame needs this dress," she muttered.

She began to sew as if she was working on something. She ran the machine. She could hear it hum. There was a bang. He was in the room and was drunk again. Her papa sat down at the piano and tried to play. He slumped over its keys and fell asleep.

The door opened and the silence was replaced by a sucking noise. Louis came into the room. His clothes were soaked. He had a look of desperation mixed with relief on seeing her.

"Cassy, you can't..."

He was breathless. He held his chest.

"I didn't know where you were," he said.

She stopped what she was doing, walked away from the machine and stood at the window.

"Do you know who I am?" he asked.

She didn't answer.

"I'm Louis, your husband."

"When do you leave for law school Louis?"

He came to her and put his arms around her. She didn't pull away.

"I finished the dress Louis, just in time too. It looks like there is a storm coming."

She pulled away from him and began to wander

around the room.

"I need to find it. Will you help me Louis?"

"Of course what is it?"

She looked back at him.

"I don't know if I'm allowed to say. It's a book. I was meant to bring it back to the library."

She paced the room.

"I'll help you," said Louis in a desperate bid to get her to calm down and get her back to the house.

She was stooped down in the corner now and her back faced him.

She looked up and shouted out, "It's okay I found it. Can I bring it back now?"

"Give it to me, I'll take it for you later."

Cassy handed over the phantom book. She allowed him to lead her to the door.

"When we get out here the wind will be strong, hold onto me," urged Louis.

She looked out. The door banged back against the wall and nearly flew in their faces on its return. Louis held her tight and forced the door close. She leaned in against him as they returned to the house. The wind circled around them and the rain poured down. They made it to the gallery. It was only a short trip across the courtyard, but in these conditions, it was difficult to walk.

When they were safe inside, she asked him, "Can we go to the bookstore?"

Louis was gone to get towels for them and he returned to her room with a fluffy towel, which she allowed him to wrap around her.

"We will go together Monday, once the storm has passed." He didn't look like he believed that anymore as he helped her get undressed and into her nightgown.

"Who would you think it's from Louis?"

"I don't know. You need to rest now."

"I need to clean the kitchen," she said.

She went into the kitchen and pulled pots and pans from the cabinets and started to clean them.

Louis called in after her, "I'll check on you in a while."

He left the room and went into the family room.

***

Mayor Ray Nagin issued a mandatory evacuation of the city. Louis stood up when he heard this on T.V. Cassy was kneeling on the mat cleaning every pair of shoes they both owned. She watched her husband.

"Louis," she said.

She stood up and dropped the cloth she held in her hand.

"Louis that noise, it's so loud."

He went over to the phone. He dialed a number, but she could see he couldn't get through. They both looked back at the T.V. when the mayor said, "We're facing the storm most of us have feared.

This is going to be an unprecedented event."

"Can we go get the parcel now?" she asked.

Louis stopped what he was doing.

"I don't want to wait till Monday," she persisted.

He left the room. She followed him.

"This storm is not going away Cassy and I have to see about getting us out of here."

They had nowhere to go and no one they could go stay with until the storm passed. Even if they could go somewhere, they had no way to get there. They didn't own a car. There was no need for one living in The French Quarter.

"There is one option," said Louis. "My brother, but I haven't spoken to him in years. I don't even know if he is still on the family plantation. I presume he is."

"Your brother?" asked Cassy.

"Do you remember Robert and his wife Olivia? They had one little girl. Goodness she'd be a grown woman now. Sara Jane was her name. I never got to know her."

Cassy tried to take in everything he was saying, but she couldn't remember his brother.

12

"I think it is the best solution. We'll leave early in the morning. The buses are still running I'm sure I heard that on the news report. There has to be still a way out of the city."

"What about going to the bookstore together on Monday?"

"That will have to wait now Cassy. It is more important we leave here."

Cassy couldn't settle. She didn't know where Louis was planning to take them to in the morning. However, that didn't matter now. She had to get the parcel and get it tonight. The doctors said she had dementia and ever since then Louis only tells her so much of what he's thinking. It's as if he thinks she could break at any moment. Cassy didn't feel she had dementia at all. Surely, someone with it wouldn't know they suffered from it. She knew something happened to her each time she got confused and couldn't remember things, but she didn't think she was sick. They had stayed in this house during countless storms. She didn't want to leave to go to The River Road. She wondered was Louis only saying they were going to go. Maybe they had no one to go to stay with until the storm passed. She didn't want to wait until tomorrow to find out. She must leave tonight.

Louis had left two sleeping pills beside her bed. The

doctors advised she take them. They would stop the nighttime wanderings, which they felt put her heart at risk. Cassy didn't agree with them. After all this was her home. She looked at the little yellow and red pills. She rolled them between her finger and her thumb. Instead of washing them down with the water Louis left for her, she put them under her pillow. Before she gave it another thought, she shoved some clothes from her closet into her bed. They formed the shape of her body. She took an old coat from her closet, one she barely wore and put it on.

She looked out through the French doors. It was dark now. She turned off her lamp beside her bed. When she got into the kitchen, she looked around for the keys to the bookstore. She pressed the side of her head as if somehow that would trigger a memory of where they were. The memo board above the sink had a message on it from Louis. Everyday household items listed to help her find them. Where the broom was, where her apron was, the cutlery drawer. Everything, except where the key was. There were no hazardous items listed. If she needed a scissors, she had to ask Louis or a knife. He had them all stowed away.

She spun around out of sheer frustration from searching for the keys. Her eyes landed on his coat on the back of the door. She reached into his inside pocket and pulled out his set of keys. There was a red tag attached to the bookstore one, so she separated it from the rest. Surely, he wouldn't notice one key. She opened the door and stepped down onto Toulouse Street. The wind had somewhat lessened, but it was still difficult to walk. She stayed in by the gallery of her house. When that ended, she was exposed to the elements again. She decided to keep in under the gallery of the houses to help her walk. As she passed her front door, she took one last look and kept walking up Burgundy Street. Everything looked different to her. Most of the windows and doors were boarded up.

She needed to leave this place and go home to where she was safe. She needed to see her mama and papa. The moon was veiled by the clouds, which formed like dark water in the Mississippi River and weighed down the sky. The wind made her nightgown whip around her legs and showed the form of her aged body. She was soaked in sweat. Her long dark hair fell loose down her back. She stole through The French Quarter and looked more ghost-like than human. Older than her years; a frail black woman alone in the streets of New Orleans.

Chapter 2

Cassy drew in her breath as she walked. She turned off for Treme, to where her childhood home was. Her parents, Hannah and Amos Shaw, raised her here. She walked down Essence Way until she came to the shotgun house she knew as home. It was derelict, not just abandoned because of the storm. When she looked in through the family room, she remembered all the times they had together. Even though she knew her parents were gone, memories came to her with such clarity that they felt real.

The house lay empty after her papa's death. Her Aunt Rosalie considered moving in, but she never did. Amos never managed to buy it, so it returned to the renter's market. There was a layer of mud on the window, which streamed down the glass from the rain. Cassy looked around the small family room. Only a few things looked as they did when they lived here, like the crack that ran up the wall behind the sofa. She remembers her papa filled it with talcum powder numerous times and painted over it, but after no length, it would reappear again. The pole that held up the drapes, which divided the living space was still there. She pictured her mama's sewing table just behind that floor to ceiling drapes. Her papa painted three birds across the surface of the table for her mama. Hannah kept it covered with a cloth as she sewed. Cassy didn't know back then why her mama kept those birds covered. She had the sewing machine in her house now, but the table went missing after her papa passed. The house lay idol for a while, Cassy couldn't bring herself to clean it out after her papa's death. The looters got here before her.

Amos lost his job through no fault of his own, while he worked on the sites. He was injured which left him incapable of work. She remembers the day the accident happened in 1955. She was twelve. At least that is what the papers called it, an accident. However, Cassy overheard her mama talk about it to her aunt Rosalie. A fellow employee of her papa drove his truck into the scaffolding. Amos was buried under a pile of rubble. 'Lucky to be alive' was how the papers worded it. They tried to free him, the other workers, but it took the emergency services to rescue him.

17

It was weeks before Cassy saw him. Her mama visited him every day.

Cassy saw him buried beneath all that rubble. Her mama was called to the scene. She had no one to stay with Cassy at the time so she brought her. His body was partly covered. Cassy bent down to touch his hand, but he didn't hold hers back. There was a question mark over whether it was an accident for a long time afterwards, but nothing was ever done about it. Essentially, there was a lot of jealousy over him getting the job, when some of his neighbors didn't and were looking for work. Before he got the job there was a lot of talk about this new development that was coming to the area and the employment it would bring. Everyone wanted to be in on it, but there was limited amount of positions. Only the lucky ones got work they said and now her papa was lucky to be alive.

Cassy and Hannah ran through Congo Square when news reached them of Amos' accident. Cassy's feet barely touched the ground as she clung onto her mama's hand. Others ran too, but nobody spoke. Each had their own loved ones on their mind. More than her papa was injured that day, but afterwards Cassy learned her papa was the only one not to walk away from it. Rosalie, Cassy's aunt met them on the far side of the square.

"Hannah I heard…Ebony is minding the kids. I'm

coming with you."

Cassy looked up at her mama, who suddenly stopped running. She was out of breath.

"Hannah, come on we'll walk. It will make no difference to Amos if we walk or run," said Rosalie.

Hannah threw her sister in law a look.

"I'm going to get to my husband as soon as I can," she said breathless.

"I'm sorry of course," said Rosalie quickening her own pace.

Rosalie was small and heavy, but she managed to outrun both Hannah and Cassy. Cassy knew she could keep up with her aunt, but she couldn't leave her mama. She walked beside her. Rosalie reached the site before they did, but they didn't need to get any closer to hear her wails from where they were. Hannah ran the last bit with Cassy beside her.

"Mama, is papa dead?"

"Hush now. Come on baby girl he's going to be fine," said her aunt.

Rosalie ran to Hannah and smothered her in a hug. Hannah broke free and screamed. Cassy looked to see where her mama ran to. Her papa lay under a pile of rubble. She can't remember much after that. There seems to be a whole chunk of time missing from when she took those last steps to where her papa lay and to when she saw him again. It was months before she saw him again. Life took some a new sort of normality for them afterwards.

When Amos returned to them, the big burly, laughter filled man that Cassy knew and loved was replaced with a quiet, weak stranger. He came home with a limp.

He sat and stared out the window a lot. When he wasn't doing this, he disappeared for hours on end. In the months, that ensued Cassy can remember her mama became the sole earner. Initially Amos couldn't work. As the months turned into years, he just wouldn't work. He turned to drinking and gambling. Cassy and her mama hardly saw him anymore.

They still had good times. Cassy loved when Mardi Gras rolled around each year, because in the months that led up to it, her papa gained work on the floats. He painted them. She remembers her mama and her stood on Bourbon Street waiting for him to pass on the float he had worked so hard on. He played the harmonica atop of one of them. Cassy used to her his tunes above the roar of the crowd and all the other musicians. When the parade finished they all went home together. Cassy loved those days. Once Mardi Gras ended, it was back to no work and he returned to "The Sugar Club" his usual haunt to drink and gamble.

Hannah wasn't happy about the late hours Amos kept. He played the piano in joints at night. These places ran as brothels. She knew this. She watched from the parlor of their shotgun house as he stumbled home. Sometimes she was thankful it was dark when he got back, so the neighbors couldn't see him. Treme had such a sense of community, but it knew no boundaries. The same people, who rallied round by day to help her at the start, now peered behind their drapes at night. Cassy often wondered was that the reason her mama became so private or was she ashamed of her papa. The police raided the joint Amos played at; one of those neighbors told Hannah and asked her did she wonder where Amos spent the night. Hannah lied, that she knew her husband's whereabouts. He stayed with his sister Rosalie not to disturb her and Cassy. Cassy was young at the time, but she remembered her mama came into the house crying.

Every night when Amos staggered in home, he promised Hannah it will be different soon. Cassy heard him stagger in home each time. Sometimes he'd bang the kitchen table and throw a wad of cash across it. The bang was a celebration, but it always made Cassy jump as she waited in expectation of what would happen next. Her mama would yell that she didn't want his gambling money. She'd hear her papa go into the family room, turn on the

T.V., and fall asleep. The next day the cycle continued. Hannah continued to be the sole earner. There were times he'd arrive home covered in blood and bruises from a bust up at one of the gambling dens. Cassy heard her mama cry and ask what happened to him. He'd explain he lost a bit, to which her mama would reply that she wasn't just talking about that night. As Cassy got older, she tried to understand it from her papa's point of view. It was difficult to get work, especially that he couldn't get work on any of the new sites with his disability. She saw the struggle and heard the arguments. The arguments got less. Often Hannah was gone to bed, ready to get up and work the following day.

Hannah was a seamstress and a good one. She sewed for all the women in the neighborhood, even though many of them could sew themselves. However, it was different she had an eye for design and could turn an old dress into something beautiful. Word of mouth spread through some of the help that worked at the mansions over in The Garden District, the women wanted to avail of her skills.

In those days, Cassy spent a lot of time on her own. Sure, she had friends on the street, but she preferred to be in home helping her mama sew. Cassy watched her work from a distance. The very thread she worked with somehow held her mama together. In the evening she always stopped sewing and cooked an evening meal for them. She still set a place for Amos. Cassy knew she did this for her benefit. She never served up his food. It wasn't as if he was going to come in the door at any moment. After the meal, she read to Cassy. As she got older and no longer needed to curl up next to her mama, they talked. She looked forward to the day rolling round so they could talk. She filled those moments with stories she heard from the neighborhood. She kept her mama up to date with the news, because she was so busy across town. Cassy told her about school. She liked how happy this made her mama when she spoke about school. Her mama told her an education is so important. Cassy wanted to make her proud.

When Amos left each morning, he went to "The Sugar Club." It was here he got in with a gambling crowd. He started to play piano there, but it was known as a gambling den. Cassy thought of her mama's reaction when he told her this. Hannah said she couldn't be happy for him pursuing his dreams while lining the devil's pocket. Amos always dreamt of playing the piano in a club someday. Cassy wanted to tell him she was so proud, but he stopped coming home at night. After a few weeks, they heard from a neighbor that he got in a fight at the club. Her mama didn't even answer the gossip this time; she had no fight left in her to protect him.

Music was the one connection Cassy felt she had left with her papa. On her way home from school, she changed route so she'd have to pass the "The Sugar Club." It took a few evenings until she coincided with him leaving.

"Papa...papa...wait it's me," she called.

She dropped her schoolbag to catch up with him.

"Cassy, baby girl what are you doing here?" he said and looked around anxiously.

"I heard about your job papa."

"You did, huh?" He smiled at her.

He looked older than she remembered and had thinning hair. He wore a moustache that moved when he spoke. He wore a grey suit. No matter how hot it was outside, he wore a suit. She was sure he owned two, that one and a brown one. She preferred the grey. The brown trousers were frayed at the ends and the sleeves stopped above his wrists.

"Your bag Cassy," he said and doubled back to pick it up for her.

"I have something to tell you papa," she declared.

"When did you get so grown up baby girl? How old are you now?"

"I'm nearly thirteen. It's my birthday soon."

"Thirteen, phew. How did that happen? Wait I know it's your birthday tomorrow."

Cassy felt so happy he remembered.

"Well aren't you in for a treat. I have something to show you," he gushed.

He started to walk. She had to run a little to keep up with his stride. They walked in the direction of Congo Square.

"I want you to meet some of the other musicians."

He looked around as if he was looking for something.

"Has Eli been here today already?" he asked one of the men, busy tuning his guitar.

"Haven't seen him."

Cassy saw the look of disappointment on her papa's face.

"Oh Cassy I really wanted you to meet him."

"Elijah. He's my cousin isn't he papa?"

Her papa hesitated.

"He's a fine musician that's what. He plays the double bass. He is a good kid Cassy. You'd like him."

Amos sat down on the bench and took out his harmonica.

"What did you want to tell me Cassy?"

She shuffled from one foot to the other.

"I sing Papa."

25

His eyes lit up with these words.

"You can sing here with me. Heck you can be part of the band."

He was so enthusiastic he practically lifted her in the air.

"Mama doesn't want me to sing papa," she said.

"It's not that she doesn't want you to Cassy, but you know she's afraid."

"She hasn't given up on you papa, you know. I hear her crying at night."

He took her by the hand and led her away from all the other musicians.

"I promise you Cassy I'm through with all those places. I have lost too much to them. This is where I belong now here playing music. I'm going to keep that job at the club too, wait you see."

He ruffled her hair. She wanted to say, her mama needed to hear him say that, but it felt so good to be here with him. Just like, it was before his accident. Even just being here in Congo Square was enough. To share with all the musicians who came here to play music. On Sundays, it became one big celebration of music. Despite Hannah's loathing of Amos's life now, there was a time when she loved nothing more than to come here. She got talking to the other wives as the men played.

"How about a song for your papa?" he asked. He started to play the harmonica. All the others had left. It was just the two of them. She sat down next to him and began to sing.

Tonight Cassy looked at her papa's former workplace. There was still the outline of the foundations on the ground, but it was overgrown in places and hid any evidence of a building. A fire burned the entire building to the ground about ten years after his accident. Even though all these years have passed, she can remember the panic in everyone that day, especially her mama.

Chapter 3

Finally, the day came when Cassy met Elijah. Eli as her papa called him. She went to the jazz club "The Sugar Club" where Amos played piano to a full house most nights. She waited for her papa to finish. All the other musicians had finished up, but her papa still had a full set. Though it was the end of the night, some people stayed around to hear him play. The bar staff called out last orders and the floor emptied and the bar filled. Cassy remained at her table. She wasn't supposed to be in here, but she always managed to go unnoticed. She came in from the stage, took a seat up near the front, and didn't move for the night.

"This seat taken?"

Cassy jumped with the sound of a deep voice coming from behind her. She was afraid to look around.

"Relax, I won't bite," said the voice again.

It was hard to see in the smoke filled room and the lighting was low. A spotlight shone onto the stage, though it didn't quite encompass her papa. She looked up to see who had spoken. A boy not much older than herself beamed at her. His hair tied back in a low ponytail. Some loose tendrils framed his brown eyes. His skin was darker than hers.

"I'm Eli. Your papa may have mentioned me, I'm your cousin."

He nodded towards the stage at Amos. Amos nodded back with a grin.

"I'm Cassy. Nice to meet you."

"Cassy Shaw. Your papa tells me you sing."

Cassy didn't know how to answer. Her papa had told her how good of a musician Eli was. She didn't want to claim to be a singer in front of him.

"Modest I see," he said and pulled out a chair for himself.

"And how would you know, I have anything to be modest about. For all you know I can't sing."

"You're a Shaw of course you can," he smirked at her.

"Well what's your excuse then," she said, surprised at her quickness.

She thought she saw a hint of darkness in his eyes, but maybe it was the light in here.

"Are you any good would you say then?"

He wasn't giving up. She didn't answer.

"Well little Cassy, I'm going to make a career out of music. The old man is good isn't he?"

"Papa...yes he is," she said and sat up in her seat. "He loves to play the piano. He played the harmonica for years, but the piano is his..."

"First love," offered Eli.

"Favorite," she said and folded her arms. He had a charm about him, but his directness irritated her.

Amos finished his set and joined them. He clasped hands with Eli.

"I see y'all have met. Eli, do you want to play?"

Eli looked nervous for the first time.

"I doubt they'd allow..."

"Oh hush come on, you're with me now. Come, play."

Cassy watched them take to the stage. She listened to them talk.

"How is your mama Eli?" asked Amos.

"Oh she's away on the cruise ships. A long stretch this time, but at least she's singing."

Even though he didn't even look at Cassy when he said this, she felt that comment was directed towards her.

"So you're on your own then?" asked Amos.

"Careful now Uncle you sound like my pops or something. Though I don't have me one of them," he winked at Cassy.

Amos stared at him with a faraway look in his eyes.

30

They began playing. She longed to be up there singing.

"Cassy, why don't you join us for this one," her papa called as he started to play.

She recognized the tune. Eli began to play the double bass, completely absorbed in the music. She took to the stage and took the microphone in her hand. A small crowd gathered around them. The bar staff looked in her direction. The audience clapped along. Her throat felt dry. She was sure she'd forget the words. The spotlight was on her. She found her voice, her place on stage. She pictured the room was empty just her and her papa playing together. Eli stopped playing. It was just her accompanied by her papa. She closed her eyes lost in the song. When she opened them, she realized she hadn't even left her seat.

One day Cassy went to Congo Square to meet her papa after school. She was told by one of the other musicians there that he left with Eli. Another one of them said he saw them over on Basin Street headed to "The Sugar Club". She went home and vowed not to tell her mama why she was home early. Hannah didn't like the fact she went to Congo Square to sing with him after school, but would certainly be disappointed that he wasn't there to meet her. Her mama reacted strange when she told her about meeting Eli. She went silent when she mentioned his name. Cassy figured it was because she fell out with Eli's mama, her sister, when they were young.

They hadn't spoken in years.

Once again Amos returned to the company he kept before. Cassy learned that he lost his job down at the club for having Eli play with him most nights. The neighbors told her mama that he got in a fight over cards. Cassy wanted to defend him and say it was because of Eli he lost his job, but her mama wasn't to know she was at the club. She waited for her mama in the family room.

"Mama, I need to talk to you."

Hannah sat opposite her with an anxious look on her face.

"I sing with papa, mama."

"You told me this already, Cassy," she said and went to stand up.

"Mama, wait...sorry mama...but I have been at the club when papa was playing."

"I'll kill that..."

"I've met Eli mama, my cousin. What happened with you and his mama?"

"That is nothing for you to concern yourself with. I can't believe your papa bringing you to them places. Well I was going to spare you this Cassy, but he's drinking again."

"Mama, no he wouldn't," she cried.

Her mama took her into her arms. "I'm sorry child.

Hush now. It's going to be okay."

"Papa loves us mama and he is really trying."

"I know child. I know." She looked down into her eyes and wiped the tears from her cheeks. "Stay away from Eli. He will get you into all sorts of trouble. He was in a gang."

"He told me mama."

"He did?"

"Well okay papa did. Papa told me he's a good kid and with his mama away it's hard for him."

She saw her mama's eyes glaze over when she said this. She held Cassy close.

"I'm going to lie down for a while Cassy. Could you get me a glass of water?"

"Are you okay Mama?"

"I will be child. I just need to rest a while."

***

She didn't expect to see Eli again, but she saw him a few days later in Congo Square. "There was a fight at the club. Only it didn't concern your papa," he said.

She listened to him speak.

"It was to do with me Cassy. Nothing to do with him, but he stuck up for me you know."

He spoke so fast, she tried to take in what he was saying.

"So it was nothing to do with my papa, but he lost his job anyway."

He looked away. "There is so much you don't know Cassy. You're so young you're only thirteen. It's not my place to tell you."

"Does it concern my papa?"

He shook his head.

"It must. Otherwise, why did he lose his job for you? Eli, please tell me."

"Do you want to join the others with me? I'm going to play for a while. I need to."

Cassy looked across the square. Sure enough the other musicians were set up and playing.

He called back to her, "It'll be okay soon Cassy. I'm going to leave for New York. Get out of everyone's way."

***

Cassy noticed a change in her mama. Every night she sat down a lot sooner. She spent less time sewing in the evenings. When Cassy asked her was everything okay, her mama said the light was better in the mornings. She was up early sewing and just liked to relax at night. Cassy couldn't help but notice her mama's persistent cough. She was always tired. One day she reached for a glass to pour some lemonade and the glass slipped from her hand. She had to reach out for the kitchen counter, but she couldn't save herself on time and collapsed to the floor. Cassy heard the thud. She ran into the kitchen. That was the start of her mama's illness, which slowly took her. She spent most of the day asleep and when she did wake, it was to take her medication and drift off to sleep again. At night, she used to call out for Cassy. She would wake up soaked in sweat. One night Cassy found her on the floor and had no strength to pick her up. Her aunt Rosalie had just called to the house and helped her. After that incident, Rosalie was at the house more often.

"Your Aunt Rosalie is going to help me more with the workload, so she's going to be here a lot. Ebony is eighteen now. Can you believe that Cassy?" She didn't wait for an answer. "So she's running the house, minding her brothers and sisters. Their papa works all the time."

"Did you want more children mama?"

"Why child what makes you ask that?"

Hannah tried to busy herself with something, but there was nothing to hand. She dropped her arms down by her side and sat down.

"We did, your papa and I, but it just wasn't to be."

She shook her head.

"I guess you're old enough to know for some women it's just not that easy."

"Did you lose a baby mama?"

Hannah looked at her suddenly as if pulled back from her own thoughts.

"Why would you ask me that?"

"Sorry mama. It's just Beth told me her mama did."

"Beth. Is that Chloe's girl?"

Cassy nodded and felt her cheeks flush red.

"Well Beth shouldn't discuss her mama with you like that. I'm sorry Cassy. I'm tired that's all."

"I'll let you rest Mama."

"Did I tell you that Beth is working over in one of those mansions in The Garden District?"

"No mama. What does she do?"

"Well her mama boasts that she has a high position. I presume she is one of the help like anyone else working in them parts. I see her passing by here on her way home at night. She puts in the hours let me tell you."

"So do you mama."

"Oh lately I'm just so tired Cassy."

"Should you see the doctor mama?"

"You don't be worrying now you hear. I'll go see the doctor. The Le Blancs, that's who Beth works for over in The Garden District. They own a law firm over on Canal Street. That house probably the grandest in those parts was passed down through the family."

Hannah bent over; such was the strength of the

cough that overtook her. Cassy handed her the glass of water.

"Off to bed now…Cassy I love you."

"I love you too, Mama."

"You're a good girl, Cassy Shaw."

Cassy watched her mama from the gap in the doorway. She pulled the blanket around her and waited on the sofa for her papa to return.

Chapter 4

"I'm upset to hear you're still friends with him", said Hannah.

"But Mama, you never listen to neighborhood gossip. She was the same one telling you about papa all those times."

"Yes and as much as I didn't want to hear it, wasn't she right?"

"Listen to your mama," said her aunt Rosalie.

Cassy was used to Rosalie being around for every interaction she had with her mama now. She'd not only take over her mama's sewing machine, but the entire working of the house it seems.

"Why did you tell her?" Cassy yelled at Rosalie.

She couldn't take out her frustration on her mama.

"There is something I need to tell you about Eli," said her mama.

"No Hannah, this is not the time," interrupted Rosalie.

"Cassy come into the kitchen, you can help me."

"Stop it Rosa." That took all of Hannah's strength.

No one spoke and waited for her to regain her breath.

"Cassy what your mama is trying to say is, though he's your cousin, he's not good company for you. You've enough with your mama sick, without any trouble from that boy."

"Fine, but why is it everyone else, even papa has been told about you been sick mama?"

"Cassy, come sit with me."

Rosalie disappeared into the kitchen. Cassy sat next to her mama. She was snuggled under a throw on the sofa.

"I am sick Cassy and the doctors said I won't get better."

"But mama your medicine, I have seen you take it."

"Hush now child and hold onto your mama."

Cassy knocked over a glass of water as she reached out for her. The sound of glass breaking caused Rosalie to rush in from the kitchen. She busied herself with mopping it up. It was as if she didn't know what else to do.

***

The following day Hannah was up before them. Cassy heard noise come from the family room. She presumed it was her aunt up early. She was surprised to see her mama.

"Mama, what are you doing?"

Hannah had fabric laid out across the sofa and had

matched up some of it to patterns.

"Good morning Cassy. Come here and I'll show you."

Just then, Rosalie came into the room and gasped, "That's not what I think it is?"

"What?" asked Cassy and Hannah at the same time.

"Nothing. Good morning sorry don't mind me none."

"Now Cassy, I should have shown you this a long time ago. I'm going to show you how to sew."

"Don't be ridiculous Han. I'll show her."

"Rosa haven't you anything better to do this hour than fuss me," said Hannah and smoothed her hair to calm herself down.

Rosalie looked hurt.

"Maybe you both could show me," offered Cassy. "I mean Rosalie no one cuts patterns like you, but you got to admit mama has a keen eye for detail."

"Well the cheek of you, but she's right," laughed Hannah.

It was the first time Cassy heard her laugh in a long time. Her breath came in short gasps as she composed herself. So it was Rosalie showed Cassy how to cut, while her mama waited for her by her sewing machine. Cassy carried one of the garments over to her .

"Now I have something special to show you. It's a signature of sorts and whenever you sew a garment from scratch for someone, you can sew your signature into the hem. Cassy watched as her mama sewed H.S. into the fabric. Hannah paused half way through to cough. It pulled at her chest so much it caused Rosalie to run to her aid. Hannah doubled over with the cough. There was no blood this time. Whatever way she sat back up, helped by Rosalie she managed to push the sewing machine and the cloth underneath slid to one side. The three birds Amos painted for her on its surface were revealed. Hannah was okay again and Rosalie stood back so as not to fuss her.

"Mama, there are birds painted on the table. I never saw them before."

"They didn't come with the table. Your papa painted them on for me."

Cassy detected that she looked to Rosalie when she said this.

"Do they mean anything?" Cassy ventured.

Rosalie answered for her, "Why it's you, your mama and your papa of course."

"But they are tiny birds, like baby birds," Cassy pressed.

Neither of the women answered her. Hannah asked Rosalie to take her to bed. She muttered something back to her daughter, about that being enough for today.

Hannah is so weak most days; she spends much of the day in bed. The sickness had taken over her so much, that Cassy can't remember a time when she wasn't sick. Any hope of her been restored to the fullness of her health was dashed by the doctors. They said she'd be doing well if she saw Thanksgiving. It's May now and not far from Cassy's fourteenth birthday. Even in her sickness she worried for her daughter and encouraged her into the sewing business. With the guidance of Rosalie, Cassy learned to sew, but her mama taught her all the tricks of the trade.

Rosalie did as much as she could to help Cassy, but also had to mind her own family. Her daughter Ebony gave up school and minded her younger brothers and sisters and in the evening Rosalie helped her, but the workload was too much for one young girl. Similar to the workload Cassy tried to keep up with. Her aunt did the deliveries for her, well along with her eldest boy Leroy Jr. This allowed Cassy to concentrate on the workload. She always saw her mama work on different garments, but when she handled the fabrics herself, she gained an appreciation for the finery the women of The Garden District were accustomed. It was a whole other world. A place she knew nothing about.

Once when she was a lot younger, she rode the

streetcar with her mama up towards First Street where
Rosalie worked at the time. Rosalie did so much talking
about where she worked; Hannah wanted Cassy to see it.
Cassy never rode the streetcar again. Slowly she made the
transition and became not only the neighborhood
seamstress as her mama was before her, but sought after
for her work by the women of The Garden District.
Rosalie always came back to her with the compliments of
her work. It didn't really touch Cassy. The further she got
into this world, the more it separated her from her singing,
her voice.

Rosalie lived with them full time now. Cassy didn't
ask how her own family coped with that. She needed her
help. The doctor didn't call as much. There was very little
he could say that could change the situation. Her mama
failed fast. Cassy didn't miss going to school. Though she
saw the women of the neighborhood, she never saw any of
her friends. With Rosalie doing all the deliveries for her,
maybe she wasn't in a position to see them, but she
couldn't help but feel that they in turn stayed away from
her. It didn't matter. With her aunt, pretty much living with
them she could spend more time with her mama. When
she finished her sewing, she was able to sit with her mama.
Initially she tried to do it all, give her the medicine she
needed, fetch her water, rinse out a fresh towel for her

head if she was too hot, but she saw she needed her aunt's help.

"I hear Eli has got in with a wrong crowd," said Rosalie to Cassy when they were alone.

"That's nothing to do with me aunt," snapped Cassy.

Rosalie looked around at Hannah's room.

"I know your mama asked you to stop seeing him."

"Seeing him? The way you said that…"

"Cassy, don't speak that way to me. I thought you'd want to know that's all. He's back with those boys over on Basin Street."

"So what you're really saying is he's like my papa, a drunk and a gambler."

Rosalie bit her lip and continued to fluff up the cushions on the sofa.

"All I'm saying is he's a talented kid. I've heard his music you know. Leroy Sr. took me one night and he's very good. More than, he's talented."

Cassy set down what she worked on at the machine. "And papa?"

"Your papa is very talented. Even when we were kids he always played so well."

"That's not what I mean aunt and you know it."

"Cassy that mouth of yours is going to get you into trouble. Your papa hasn't played in a while has he? Not since he lost the last job in I can't think of the name of the bar now. Anyway it don't matter none."

"That's just neighbor's gossip. I heard he still plays. Maybe the work just dried up in The Sugar Club."

Cassy hoped her aunt wouldn't come back with a comment to that. She didn't.

***

It had been a long time since they heard from Amos. Then one night he threw the front door open. He shouted and demanded to see Hannah.

"Why didn't you tell me she was so sick?" he demanded of his sister.

"Hush now, keep your voice down Amos Philip Shaw, don't be shouting at me."

"This is your house now is it sister?"

"Papa," cried Cassy when she saw him.

"Cassy baby, I'm sorry."

He slumped down on the chair next to where she sat.

"How long were you sitting there? I didn't think you'd be up, it's late."

"Rosalie and I are working."

"I'll go make some coffee," said Rosalie.

Amos settled back into the chair.

"You're drunk papa."

Amos hung his head.

"What happened at the club papa? You were getting on so good. I have been lying to everyone saying you still work there."

She could see out of the corner of her eye that her aunt was ready to come back into the room, but she stalled in the kitchen.

"Cassy, it wasn't my fault. The work dried up that's all. They weren't doing so good no more. I am looking though and I'll get something soon."

He hung his head again.

She couldn't stand to see him like this.

"Papa, you should be kinder to aunt Rosa, she's helped so much with mama. I'd be lost without her."

"When did my baby girl go and get so grown up on me?"

She wanted to say that she had no other choice. Instead, she pulled the throw from the back of the sofa and covered him with it. He moved over to the sofa.

Rosalie stood over him and he took the cup of coffee she offered him. He touched her arm with his other hand. Cassy knew this was his way to say sorry. She looked at her aunt who smiled.

"Rosalie I'm here now, why don't you go home? Leroy is surely talking about how we, I've kept you away from your own family."

"I don't think that's a good idea."

"Rosa, come on you know I'll be okay in the morning."

"Okay, well if it's okay with y'all I'll stay tonight. It's late now."

"Whatever you want, sis."

With that, he turned over and fell asleep. Rosalie stood over him for what seemed like forever.

"Cassy, I think we'll call it a night. Is it okay with you if I do go home tomorrow?"

Cassy saw a softness in her aunt she had never seen before, a need to see her own children perhaps.

"Oh course aunt. I love you. Goodnight."

Rosalie hesitated at the door as she went to turn off the kitchen lights.

"I'll leave that lamp on for your papa, in case he's to get up in the middle of the night. I love you too child."

For the first time in a long time, Cassy's family was all under one roof.

From that, night on her papa returned home. He was gone every day, but he told her he was trying to find work and she believed him. He played with the other musicians in Congo Square on the weekends. Cassy didn't go with him anymore; she stayed at home and worked. Rosalie told her to go that the orders were under control, but Cassy was afraid they'd fall behind. Truthfully, she didn't want to leave her mama.

Hannah had days when she left the bedroom and sat in the family room with her. One such day when she had more strength than she'd known in months, she asked Rosalie to bring her a chair for the courtyard. Cassy sat with her in the courtyard, while Rosalie fussed and putted a rug across Hannah's lap and propped her up with cushions.

"Rosa, go home and see your girls and boy. Your husband too, they need you."

"You need me," returned Rosalie.

"I'm okay. Cassy is here. Please Rosa go home. Besides Amos will be home soon."

Rosa hesitated, but she saw Hannah wanted this time with her daughter. Things had changed since Amos moved back home. Hannah didn't ask him where he was all those months. It didn't matter. He was home now.

As Cassy sat with her mama, she looked around the courtyard. The flowers were in full bloom. The ivy glistened in the early morning light. The birds sung in the magnolia tree of their shared courtyard. Amos offered to erect a fence when they first moved in, but Hannah said she liked to see the neighbor's children play. She enjoyed seeing them chase each other around her magnolia tree.

"It's beautiful isn't it when it's in full bloom?"

"It is mama."

"I wanted to call you magnolia you know, but your papa had decided on Cassy a long time ago he said," she laughed with the memory of this.

"I didn't know that mama."

"Yes, so I got to choose Belle for you. Amos said Cassy was a strong name. You are beautiful and strong."

"I'm not mama. I'm not strong."

Hannah took her hand. The limp dampness of her palm reminded Cassy of her mama's illness.

"You will have a good long life Cassy. I know it. What is it you want to do when you're older?" Hannah giggled. "What a question to ask you."

She closed her eyes and smiled. Cassy wondered did she see her future. She opened her eyes and looked beyond the courtyard.

"Here I am teaching you to sew, but it is only to protect you Cassy. That is what I want for you. What do you want, tell me? I want to know," she said and leaned in close to her daughter.

Cassy pulled at a thread on her dress.

"I want to sing."

The words came out hoarse. She coughed.

"I want to sing Mama that's all I want to do."

Her mama sighed.

"When I look at your papa I'd worry for you Cassy. I know your papa thinks I squashed his dreams, maybe in some ways I did. It wasn't his fault, but I worry for him. I always have, especially after the accident."

She looked directly at her daughter.

"Do you remember that day?"

Cassy wanted to say to her that she would never forget it. Instead, she just nodded.

"Do you know Cassy that is the last day I listened to you singing?"

"No it wasn't mama."

"It was Cassy. You sang for me that morning. Then we got word of your papa. In those months while he lay in that hospital bed, I was hardly there for you."

"That's not true mama. You were."

Hannah continued speaking as if she didn't hear her.

"When he started drinking and going to those places to gamble, well I didn't want to know about his music no more. In addition, I shut out your voice too."

A wave of silence passed between them, each left with their own thoughts. Hannah pulled the throw across her legs up towards her chest.

"Is it wrong of me to want the best for my baby?"

Her eyes had a vacant look in them as she stood up

to leave. She swayed and Cassy jumped up quickly to steady her.

"I want you to promise me one thing Cassy. I want you to promise me you won't chase after idle dreams."

Cassy didn't know how to answer her.

"Let me explain to you Cassy, you have a gift. You can sew, not because I thought you."

A gentle wind rustled through the magnolia leaves as Cassy helped her mama into the house.

"I promise mama."

"That's my girl. I'm not saying don't ever sing, but I'm asking you to protect your future by sewing. That is all Cassy. That is all."

Cassy settled her mama on the sofa in the front room and returned outside to bring in the cushions and throw. Her papa had named her, but her mama had decided her fate a long time ago.

Chapter 5

"I have something I should tell you Cassy. Actually, I've waited until the right time to tell you. I went to school in a convent. I know I've told you that before or maybe your papa did, but there's something else," said Hannah.

Cassy listened to her mama speak. She pictured what it must have been like for her going to school at a convent.

"There was a reason I was sent there and my sister Jessie wasn't. I had a baby…"

Whether she stopped speaking then to let that sink in or whether she tried to find the words, Cassy couldn't tell.

"I had a baby before you Cassy, a little boy. My parents decided I was too young to care for a baby, so I moved to the convent. They were ashamed."

The way she spoke it was as if she told a story from someone else's life.

"While I was at the convent the nuns taught me to sew. There was one lady who wasn't a nun. I'll never forget her kindness to me. Miss Brown. She played the piano."

"Did you play mama?" Cassy asked.

"Oh no sweetheart, I left that to those with talent, like your papa."

She stroked Cassy's arm. Cassy leaned in close to her and rested back into the chair beside her.

"It was tough Cassy. They had to be tough with us, I guess. We were the fallen ones, but Miss Brown treated all us girls different. Like our lives mattered and the lives of our children."

"How did she help you mama?"

"When the time came for me to hand over my baby she was there for me. See I wasn't like the other girls; they gave their baby up to a stranger. My mama decided it best if my sister Jessie raised him. It was easy hide. Jessie was away singing at the time and she would just come home with the baby."

"You mean Eli is your son?"

"Yes Cassy, Eli is my baby, my little boy. Your brother."

"Mama, no, he can't be."

"He is baby girl."

Neither of them spoke. Cassy pieced together what her mama went through.

"Mama, does Eli know?"

"Oh no child. Again, my mama decided that. Jessie took him away for years. I don't really know where they went, upstate somewhere. By the time they returned I was just the aunt he never saw, if he even knows that."

53

"Mama he does. He knows you're sick too," said Cassy and bit her lip.

She felt wrong been in Eli's company when her mama had gone so long without knowing him.

"Let me tell you about Miss Brown. She hoped I'd have an interest in music. It wasn't for the want of trying with me. I just couldn't play. I don't have a note in my head. Instead, she introduced me to a group of ladies that came to the convent to teach the girls to sew. There was four, no five of us that went to the library on a Wednesday to learn to sew. That time away from convent life saved me. It saved me from the pain that followed.

That community of ladies united in one aim, to sew, gave me my life back, in a way gave me my voice Cassy. I had nowhere to put my grief and I know I poured many a tear in the clothes I worked on. The cruelest joke of them all was we had to sew the gowns that our babies wore when they left with other families. She sighed which went down into her core and stayed there. It was probably always something she carried within her.

"The only blessing my sister bestowed on me was she returned the gown to me. We never spoke in those days. Sure, I saw him in her arms around The Quarter, but I saw him as hers not my own. Mama adored Jessie. She was everything I wasn't. I don't mean in looks when I say that.

She had a way that filled an entire room. She was everyone's pearl."

"Jessie Pearl," said Cassy.

"Yes, how did you know that? Oh, of course from Eli."

This made Cassy uncomfortable.

"It's her stage name mama."

"Oh it's more than that my love, it's who she is, everybody's pearl. I've left out one detail Cassy, but I don't want you to hear of your mama's indiscretions."

"Mama, it's okay. You don't have to tell me."

"I'm tired. My body aches, but more than what the illness has taken from me, the secrets have taken more. You see Cassy; there was a man before your papa, a white man. I was young. He was a little older. I cannot say I ever really loved him. We were just enamored with each other. Well anyway I got pregnant."

She turned to look at Cassy then.

"I want you to know Cassy I love your papa. He just lost his way. He is a good man. Even knowing about Eli he still married me."

"Papa knows, but how can he play music with him when you don't even get to see him?"

"He's doing that for me. He hopes I'll want to see him someday."

"You don't?" asked Cassy in a whisper.

"I gave up that right a long time ago. When Jessie brought him back, too much time had passed. He was practically a grown man. Too much buried in the past and that's where it should remain, but you have a right to know. I need to rest now."

As Cassy helped her into bed she asked her, "Mama, what about the sewing ladies?"

"Well I suppose many of them moved on and had families. Some of the girls that were in the convent with me, I'd see around, but we don't speak. It's too hard. We were never friend's just young girls thrown together in a difficult time."

"What about Miss Brown?"

"Miss Brown, last I heard has a music hall in the French Quarter, over on St. Peter St. I think. Yes, I'm sure it is. Goodnight Cassy."

***

Some-time passed since that day when her mama spoke to her. Hannah spent most days in her room now, but this evening she slept on the sofa with Amos sat next to her. Cassy was busy sewing and her papa listened to the radio. Rosalie burst through the door with such exuberance Cassy thought she pulled it off its hinges.

"I've heard of a position Cassy over in The Garden

District."

Cassy put down what she worked on to listen to what her aunt had to say.

"It's in one of the grandest mansions. It's for the Le Blanc family."

"You mean Le Blanc's law firm," interrupted Amos.

Hannah awoke to all the excitement.

"Honey did you hear that? There is a position with the Le Blanc family for Cassy."

Cassy darted him a look. She didn't need his input in this, but it looks like her aunt and mama were already full of enthusiasm.

"Yes they are looking for a seamstress Cassy," said Rosalie while nearly hoping from foot to foot. "You can come and go each day."

"The way you said that you think she was free to make her own hours sis," Amos chimed in again.

Hannah laughed at this.

"No listen. Hush brother. Cassy you'd start at eight and finish at five most days."

"Most days," said Cassy.

"I've arranged for you to meet with Beth Dupree she works there."

"Beth is a friend of Cassy," said Amos and smiled at Cassy encouragingly.

"Oh she was papa. I don't see her no more."

"That's just because you are in here all day."

He took his wife's hand in his.

This pleased Cassy to watch him mind her mama, but she couldn't ignore what was arranged for her.

Beth was someone Cassy knew since she was about five. Once she started to realize there was a life outside of her family room when she played with the other kids in the neighborhood, they became firm friends. Beth was five years older than Cassy, but they were about the same height. Hannah told Cassy she was tall for her age, but really, Beth was small for hers. It had been a good year since Cassy had even seen her, maybe longer.

***

Rosalie poured tea for them and had fresh beignets. Cassy knew Beth was calling, but it wasn't long before she realized she called with a purpose. Her mama was dressed and sat with them. There was a knock on the door. Rosalie went to welcome Beth in. Cassy felt uncomfortable. She shifted her weight in her seat. She could see her papa look at her. It had been so long since she saw her friend and now she had to speak to her with an audience.

The two girls greeted each other. Beth got down to business straight away.

"So it's come to the attention of my employer

Frances Le Blanc, sorry Madame Le Blanc that you can sew and sew well. Basically all her friends are wearing your garments..."

"They are, oh Cassy isn't that something," said Rosalie as she refilled Beth's cup.

"They are Rosalie," said Beth with a hint of a smile. Cassy relaxed as Beth softened towards them.

"Do you sew Beth?" asked Hannah.

For a moment, Cassy forgot her mama was here. She was so busy taking in what Beth was saying.

"Oh no Mrs. Shaw I don't, well you know my mama would have shown me, like y'all I guess."

"Do you like it there?" asked Rosalie.

"Oh yes very much so. That's not to say the work will be easy, but if I know one thing Cassy you're a hard worker."

Cassy blushed.

"I know we haven't seen each other in a long time," offered Beth.

"I think I'm going to let you ladies talk," said Amos as he rose to his feet and went into the kitchen. Cassy watched him. He didn't look happy the way everyone else seemed to be about this position at the mansion.

"I'll get more tea for us," said her aunt and rose to her feet.

Amos came back into the room. "Rosa, sit down and quit your fussing I have something to say."

"Papa is everything alright?" Cassy asked.

"Well it's not easy you know. When you have a child of your own, you'll understand." He sighed and rubbed his head. "Of course I only want as your mama does what's best for you, but I'm unsure if this is the way. What about singing?"

Cassy wanted to tell him that he was right and she shouldn't go, but at the same time, she knew they needed the help. She sees how happy it's making her mama hearing of this job.

"How soon would I start Beth?"

"Madame asks that you be ready in a few weeks. She is overseas right now, but on her return. Don't worry I'll be there. Mr. and Mrs. Shaw, I appreciate any concerns you may have."

"Her papa knows this is the right thing for Cassy. He's just going to miss her," said Hannah.

"I don't want to stand in my girl's way," said Amos.

"Don't forget she'll be here every night, so it's not like she's leaving. Isn't that right Cassy?" said Rosalie.

Cassy knew she said this to assure them nothing was really going to change, though they knew this wasn't true.

She listened to Beth describe the grand house. Each

room had a hearth that remained unlit except for the library. Beth had described it like a furnace, so the floor to ceiling windows were always open and their lace sheers floated out onto the verandah from the huge ceiling fans. The smell of polish filled the hallways and the carpet pile that ran up the middle of the staircase was so thick your feet disappeared into it. She looked down at their threadbare rug and watched her mama nod her head each time Beth told her something new about the mansion. Cassy heard a bang at the back of the house. It was her papa. He fumbled with the screen door and tried to open the inner door while he held it.

"I'll go. I'll take the position Beth," said Cassy.

She looked at her mama as she said this and she could see her swell up with pride. For now, that was enough for Cassy. It had to be.

"I can see Madame asking you to take up board. I did. I have my own room in the house."

"And how often do you get home now Beth?" asked Amos.

No one stopped him asking. They all wanted to know the answer to this.

"Not as much as I like to, but I'm the housekeeper and respected for what I do."

"That's okay then isn't it," offered Rosalie, but not

even her mama answered this time.

"Don't worry initially you'll go home each night. It's just if the workload overtakes you, you'll have to stay. You'd be in sharing with one other girl. Therefore, you'd have company. I have to go now and bring the news back. Thank you for your kindness."

Rosalie jumped up.

"I'll see you out Beth."

When they got to the door, Rosalie asked her, "Will she be okay? She's my only niece and my sister in law, well as you saw…"

"Don't forget Rosalie, this is my neighborhood too. I haven't forgotten where I come from. What I'm trying to say is I'll be there to look after her."

"I worked as the help in one of those mansions. I know what goes on."

"She'll be okay Rosa."

"I've heard the stories about that girl Violet. Did you know her?"

"She left before I started. Cassy has an opportunity to sew exclusively for Madame Le Blanc and the other women of The Garden District. It is her way to a better life."

"When did you get so wise Beth?"

"When I had to, Rosa."

From that day on Cassy focused on her move to The Garden District. She'd be taking over from her mama as the main seamstress. Beth explained to her that there would be so much work for her amongst Madame Le Blanc's friends she wouldn't have time to sew for the neighbors anymore. Cassy knew what she was really saying was, Madame didn't want the hands that sewed for her; sew for the black folk as well.

She knew so little about The Garden District. She can barely remember the one time she was there with her mama. All she remembered was chalk white houses that soared into the sky and the tar path cut into her feet in the blistering heat. The soles of her shoes had worn out and she felt every step she took. That was the Summer Amos lost his job. Cassy cherished the days she had left here with her mama. Her papa was around all the time and even managed to get a job, but the hours were at night so it meant he was home by day. It felt like the old days when they were all together. Rosalie was there too. A gentle reminder of her much needed help with her mama. Everything leaned towards Cassy's move to the mansion. She wanted to see this world with magnolia-filled gardens and the smell of roses outside the verandah windows that led into the grand rooms filled with furniture from different parts of the world.

Emily Clarke

In those final days, there was no room for her singing. She never saw Eli, neither did her papa. She knew this because; his job took him into The French Quarter. He worked a bar at night, but didn't even get to play the piano. As for her, she closed off her voice and focused on sewing.

Chapter 6

Hannah never left her room now. Cassy busied herself with the last orders for their neighbors. The constant stream of work was enough to keep her working here, but a different path waited for her. Even in the days when she was hesitant on leaving, she couldn't tell her mama she didn't want to go. Hannah was failing fast. She spent most of the day asleep and for the few hours, when she was awake, Cassy didn't want to burden her with anything. Nobody did. Her papa was there all the time. Hannah was happy he was. Rosalie kept her distance about the house. Some days Cassy forgot she was even living here.

"I'm going to get the doctor Cassy. Your mama had a bad night."

"Rosalie I would have got up."

"Your papa and I sat with her. Actually I nodded off in the chair so your papa told me to go to bed."

"Where is he?"

"He's out in the courtyard. Leave him be for a while

65

Cassy if you don't mind me saying. I'm going to get the doctor."

"Can I go into mama?"

"Do, she'll be happy to see you."

With that, Rosalie left and closed the door behind her. Cassy stood for a moment in the empty shell the house had become since her mama's sickness, especially in these last few weeks. She could see her papa beyond the kitchen in the courtyard.

Her mama was barely recognizable to her. As she approached the bed, she saw her skin looked waxy. Beads of sweat glistened on her brow. Her hair matted to her head from sweating all night. She opened her eyes.

"Cassy," was all she managed and she forced a smile.

"Mama, don't try and speak."

"Cassy, I'm sorry."

"You have nothing to be sorry for."

Hannah looked away. Cassy could see the look of pain in her eyes. It was something else though. She leaned in closer. Tears welled up in her mama's eyes, but she drew her breath to stop them.

"Mama, you have nothing to explain." Cassy could hear herself reassuring her mama, but her voice sounded distant. She stood by her bedside silent for a long time.

Suddenly the door opened. Any conversation

between them severed as the doctor entered the bedroom. He stood next to Cassy and Amos joined him. Rosalie stayed by the door. Amos touched Cassy's arm. She took this as her leave. Once the doctor finished tending to Hannah, Cassy was able to see her. It surprised her to see her propped up in bed. Amos left mother and daughter alone.

"Your aunt is moving in Cassy."

"I know mama. I overheard y'all talking about it."

"Cassy, I know my time is short. There is so much I didn't tell you. The convent...papa sent me there."

"I know mama, rest now."

"Where is your papa?"

"He's outside. Do you want me to get him?"

Hannah managed a smile. Cassy went to the window, a shaft of light filtered through.

"Leave it baby. I want to see it."

Cassy looked to where she looked and saw her aunt pass by the window. Her shadow momentarily suspended the room in darkness. Amos met his sister outside. Cassy watched her aunt shake her head as he spoke and raise her hand to her cheek. She shielded them from her mama's view. They came back into the house.

"Mama, I'm going to let you rest now."

"Come back in a while to see me Cassy."

***

Cassy and Amos didn't speak on their way to Congo Square. Cassy felt as if she wouldn't return here for a while. She didn't say it to him. When she looked up into his face, she knew he felt the same.

"Jacques, here we are. I've brought my baby girl to sing."

"Why of course. Hey Cassy, will I accompany you?"

Both men laughed.

"That be your papa's job. I know, I know."

Cassy watched her papa sit at the piano. In this early morning light, she saw how tired he looked. Of course, everything was taking its toll on him. With her leaving to go work at the mansion, but more so her mama's illness.

"Papa, what would you like me to sing?"

"You choose."

She couldn't help but feel Eli was missing from this scene. She wondered would she see him before she left. Amos encouraged her to sing with a big smile. He looked happy as she started to sing. That day in Congo Square she vowed would be the last time she sang here. She wanted to hold onto its memory. So much of her life had changed already. She was losing her mama. Her family was about to be torn apart, just so she could escape the life her mama had. In some ways, it felt she was following the exact same path. History repeated itself with her role as seamstress in The Garden District mansion.

***

She didn't think it would be such an adjustment to her aunt moving in. She was pretty much here all the time anyway. Her daughter Ebony ran her house, so Rosalie treated Hannah's house as if it was her own. Hannah slept for hours at a time and this was when Rosalie seemed to be the busiest. She pulled the place asunder and cleaned it from top to bottom. She put everything back how she'd like it. Cassy ran the seamstress business herself. She didn't mind so much, it helped her not think about the move to the mansion. She built up an image of what life there must be like. Once she took that role, she'd see less of her mama. Amos got more hours at the club where he worked. It made a small difference to pay the medical bills. As the time wound on the doctor called less to the house. Cassy overheard a conversation between him and her aunt, that time was short. Hannah was comfortable and that was all they can hope for at this stage. Broken words came to her as she sewed. The hum of the machine dulled out the full impact of the conversation and for that, she was grateful.

"I've had word from Beth," said her mama, barely audible with the wheezing sound from her chest.

Cassy sat down on the bed and wiped her mama's face with the cloth in the bowl on the nightstand. Hannah closed her eyes as she spoke.

"She says Madame Le Blanc is ready for you."

Cassy crumpled the bed covers in her hand to steady herself. Her tongue stuck to her palette and she felt the room sway. She nodded. She didn't trust herself to speak.

"I think you should be the one to tell your papa. He's the one going to be left behind."

There it was. The one thing nobody wanted to say for months. She could seize it now or it would be gone forever, lost.

"Mama, I don't want you to go…I mean I wish you weren't ill."

"I'm dying Cassy, but its okay."

Hannah found a spot on the wall, as if the words were written there.

"I can go, happy that we have no secrets between us."

Again, she looked away.

"I want you to have everything I didn't. I know we did the best for you, but I want you to have a fighting chance at a good life."

"She knows that Han," came Amos' voice behind

them.

Cassy didn't know how long he was there. He rested his hand on her shoulder and with the other clenched his wife's hand as if he was afraid to let them go.

Hannah had days where she seemed well again. This was part of the many conversations Cassy heard her aunt have in the half-light with her papa. Cassy dreaded going on errands with the garments in case she wasn't here when her mama drew her final breath. As if Rosalie knew this, she continued to deliver them. As she sewed, she watched her mama. It was one of those days when Hannah was well enough to leave her room. Cassy took comfort from being in the same space as her. They could spend hours in the same room without speaking. Cassy settled into her role as seamstress for the ladies of The Garden District and soon enough she'd be working in the mansion. She knew this made her mama proud. For now that was enough for her to get through this.

The time came round to give her papa the news that she would leave for the mansion. It felt like a move away from him. Though he was around by day, he plays every night; so they won't see each other. It felt strange to leave the house. She realized how long it had been since she'd even walked through the neighborhood. It was that time of day when families gathered for supper. As she passed the shotgun houses, no different to her own, she could hear the sound of laughter accompanied by the sound of music. She was going to miss this place so much. Treme is all she has known her entire life. She never even thought about leaving, until Beth presented the position at the mansion to her.

The bar looked welcoming, though perhaps less so for a fourteen year old girl. It took her a moment for her eyes to adjust to the dark interior. She followed the sound of the piano. The room was relatively empty. A couple whispered to each other at the bar. He slapped his hands on the counter to ask the bar man to refill their glasses. A man swayed to the music and banged into the table beside him. There was a younger woman next to the stage and she watched Amos play. The old man called her back and he swept her into a drunken dance. A few men sat a table, but they were deep in their own conversation. Amos looked up from his playing and was surprised to see her.

"Not many in tonight Cassy," he said and sounded down beaten.

"It's very early papa."

"Not that early," he said as he glanced at his watch, which he kept in his breast pocket while he played. She knew the strap was broken, but they had no money to replace it.

"Papa, can I talk to you?"

The bar man interrupted them, "Amos, get your girl out of here. Do you want us closed down?"

"Sorry Bob. She's just leaving."

"Go on home Amos. It's quiet tonight."

The bar man cleared up the glasses around them on the empty tables and bend down to mop up the drink that spilled onto one of the chairs.

"I'm sorry papa," Cassy mumbled.

"Don't worry, you'll get paid. It'll be the end of the week though when things have picked up some."

"Thanks Bob," said Amos, but Cassy could tell he was disappointed to be sent home.

They walked towards the exit.

"I'm going this week papa. Madame Le Blanc sent word with Beth that she is ready for me."

There was the sound of a crash from inside. The young girl that was dancing fell over one of the chairs. Whoever was in the bar clapped and cheered.

"Okay Cassy. Maybe it's for the best."

That was all he said. They walked in silence.

Cassy followed her papa into 'The Sugar Club' without a word. She felt responsible for this detour on the way home. She watched him walk up to one of the tables. There was a game of cards in play. He joined in as if it was

73

the most natural thing in the world for him to be there.

"The girl, Amos. You know the rules."

"Come on cut me a break. One hand is all I need. We'll be on our way then."

One hand was all he got, he was out. Cassy could see he was upset.

"I used to be good Cassy. Not the words you want to hear from your pops I'd imagine."

"Papa, I have the opportunity to work hard and make money with this job at the mansion."

Amos stopped walking.

"It's not your job Cassy. I don't want it for you. No one around these parts can sing like you. However, I see you have decided. Not a word to your mama about back there you hear?"

"It's none of my business," said Cassy and tried to sound upbeat.

"Take a look around Cassy. The same people, the same faces. As much as I want to keep you here, and believe me I do, I know there is something bigger for you."

Cassy looked around as he pointed. She knew she'd be back here, but it felt like life, as she knew it had slipped away from her. With each passing day, she moved closer to a life away from here and she didn't know what that life would be. She turned fifteen in two days and felt like the weight of the world was on her shoulders.

When they got back to the house, Amos stopped outside the door.

"Cassy, I haven't been to "The Sugar Club" in a long time. I need you to know that."

She didn't answer him.

"I just don't deal with change so good that is all."

"Papa, this is not easy for me either, but I have to go. I need to help mama."

"I know that and I'm trying too, you know."

She softened towards him, "Papa let's go inside."

She saw one of the neighbors across the street stare in their direction.

"Rosalie keeps the drapes closed all the time. She says it stops the neighbors nosing. I don't think anything would, do you?" he said. Cassy laughed in agreement.

She was aware of her mama's fragility when she saw her. She believed him when he said he wasn't going to gamble anymore. She needed to believe him.

The next day Amos and Cassy were out in the courtyard. He decided he wanted to sow a tree for her. Cassy kicked the dirt with her feet as she watched him.

"You know my mama, your grandma drank," said Amos. "What I should say is she was an alcoholic. We lost my papa. My mama reared us, all five of us. It was hard on

75

her. She did the best she could. It was only when we were reared she began drinking. I know she died before you were born. I wish you could have met her."

"I would have liked that papa."

"Did I ever tell you she could sing? Sure you must have heard it over the years."

Cassy picked up a handful of dirt and let it slide through her fingers.

"I remember you told me."

"She never did get to sing though Cassy, not in any real sense."

He rested on the shovel as he spoke.

"I think that's the reason she drank. She put so much on hold to rear all of us. In truth, I don't know how she did it. Then when we all left, she began drinking. It's like she gave up."

Cassy could see where he was going with this. She was nothing like her grandma. She didn't sing, because right now she had to do what's best for her family. As she listened to him, she vowed when the time would come she would sing.

"Papa, can I ask you a question?"

"Of course, anything."

"Is she, was your mama the reason you drank?"

"Oh no Cassy. I'd never want you to think that. I can

never put that on her."

He poured himself a glass of lemonade and drank it down in one go.

"She was gifted Cassy, I remember that. I sometimes think I only try to chase after music to make up for her loss of it."

"Papa, don't say that."

He smiled at her.

"I know you have to take up that post as seamstress Cassy, but don't let go of your dreams. I tell you what; let's plant your dreams under this tree."

"Oh papa," she laughed and bent down to help him.

The tree was in its infancy, ready to grow; certain of its purpose. If only she knew her own. It had been a long day. The tree glistened in the evening sun. A peace washed over her. Everything was in place for her to leave.

Chapter 7

She told Rosalie she'd deliver the garments today. She needed to get out for a walk. The house had become so quiet. Everyone crept around. A whole day could pass without Cassy even seeing her mama. Eli was like a mirage. He stepped out in front of her, so she had to speak to him. On seeing him, she scolded herself for not going the other way.

"Hey, cousin."

Cassy flinched at this more than she meant to. She looked up into his brown eyes and contemplated telling him. Instead, she found herself answering him.

"Hi, Eli. I haven't seen you in so long."

It was his turn to look uncomfortable. He had a faraway look in his eyes.

"What did you hear about me Cassy?"

"Mainly you're a member of a gang."

The words sounded harsh to her ears.

"Cassy, I need to get away from here that's all."

He stepped in line with her as she continued walking.

"Where will you go?"

"New York, as soon as I've saved enough."

"Surely your mama would pay," she reddened when she said this.

"She wouldn't want her only child to leave her and go to the other end of the country. No when I go, there'll be no trumpet call. I'll just be gone."

Cassy smiled as she listened to him and found herself dreaming along with him. She wondered could New York hold a place for her. She became aware of the weight of the garments she carried.

"Here let me carry those for you," offered Eli.

She allowed him to help her. It felt good to have her arms free. Each step they took held a memory from her childhood, which now seemed a thousand years ago.

"Is everything okay with you Cassy?"

"I'm fine Eli."

She wasn't ready to tell him she's leaving all this behind.

They got to the end of St. Peter Street and Cassy took the garments from him.

"I'll come with you. Where are you bringing them?"

She looked around hesitant. Part of her didn't know

why she wanted to be on her own.

"Okay. It's just here."

She pointed to a peach colored house. It had hanging baskets over the doorway suspended from the balcony above. All the upstairs windows were open. A smell of varnish wafted down from the open windows. She could see into the room next to the front door. There was a grand piano and a bookcase and little else. Eli stood back as they approached the door. There was a shadow behind one of the open windows upstairs. It disappeared. They heard footsteps on the stairs. The door opened. An attractive woman in her perhaps late fifties smiled at her. She had dark hair, pulled loosely from all sides and pinned on top of her head. A jewel nestled in the centre of the knot sparkled in the light. She wore a green housecoat, but Cassy could see a hint of her dress underneath. It was made of silk with tiny birds as the pattern.

"Let me take that from you."

Cassy handed over the garments to their owner.

"Would you and your friend like to come in for some lemonade?"

Cassy looked back towards Eli. He came up to the door.

"Hey Miss Brown, I sure would."

Cassy looked from one to the other confused.

"Well Eli Pearl. You must have been knee high when I saw you last, but I'd never forget that smile," she laughed.

She extended her hand to Cassy.

"Lottie Brown. Never mind Miss Brown, call me Lottie. Most folks do. Young Elijah is just been polite, which I like to see. Come in, come in."

Cassy recognized her name from what her mama told her about her time at the convent.

"But it says on the garments Suzanna and there is no surname just the address."

"Cassy Shaw!"

"Yes, but how did you know that's my name?"

"I'm Suzanna. Well Suzanna is the name I gave to your aunt Rosalie when she collected the fabric from me. I met her in the market and she said she'd collect the fabric from me, when I enquired about your work. Please come in we can talk more."

Cassy was aware of the smell of alabaster and beeswax. Her nose led her to a jar on the bottom step of the staircase. That was what she had smelled from outside.

"I'm doing some refurbishment to this old place. Please let me show you."

"Now Lottie I've heard the rumors you're being modest," said Eli.

"Well young man rumors shouldn't be listened to or

spread, but yes you're right. Come this way. Y'all are the first to see."

She led them to a room under the stairway, towards the rear of the house. Like many houses in The Quarter, their exterior appearance could be deceiving in size.

"So this is it, my music hall."

She dusted her hands against her housecoat and opened the buttons to reveal the dress she wore. It was a mix of silk and chiffon. The birds looked to be hand painted onto the fabric and shimmered gold.

"Come on let me show y'all."

Cassy was speechless. She never saw so many instruments in one room. There was an elevated area at the top of the room. Miss Brown followed her gaze.

"That'll be the stage."

"Cassy, its great isn't it?" asked Eli.

"It's perfect," said Cassy.

She was in the house of the woman who helped her mama all those years ago.

"Just mind the floors. Well where we are is fine, that is dry. Near the stage is taking a little longer that's why I opened the windows before I started."

"So you weren't in the window just before we arrived?"

Miss Brown found it hard to hide her amusement.

"Ah you've met Clarabelle then. Don't worry about her; she'll pay you no mind once you leave her be."

"Clarabelle?" asked Cassy.

"Yes Clarabelle Quinn. She is my resident ghost. I supposed I am bound to have one as every second building in the quarter has one."

Her voice became distant as she left her and Eli alone in the hall and went to the front of the house. Cassy heard her call for them to come to where she was.

The floor to ceiling windows, the same as those in the music hall, were dressed in lace net. In the centre of the room was a cake trolley with every cake imaginable. She poured them a glass of lemonade each. The ice clinked in the glasses as she poured. Cassy looked around the room. It seemed smaller than the music hall, but that was only because there was so much antique furniture. It brimmed over with books. A large sofa, which looked like it had seen better days, was in front of the bookcase. The room was reflected back at them from the glass cabinet that was next to the fireplace.

"Come over here. I want to show both of you something."

Cassy hesitated. She felt unnerved from what Miss Brown told them in the other room.

"Don't worry Cassy. She stays in that other room.

Clarabelle is stuck in time and all she remembers is she came here to sing. She wasn't in her when she was alive and would have no reason to come in here now."

Every time Cassy heard her say the ghost's name, it made her uneasy. She watched Miss Brown show Eli something outside on the balcony.

"Cassy, come here. You have to see this. You'd never notice it from down below," Eli called to her.

When she looked out the window, she drew her breath.

"You see her? Well Cassy that building is going to be where I build an even better music hall someday. It isn't up for sale yet, but it will be. I heard rumors."

"Rumors come in handy sometimes then Miss Brown," said Eli.

"Cassy, step out here. Eli is going to pour himself more lemonade."

Cassy followed her out onto the balcony and looked across at the vacant building across the street. She could see right inside.

It was far grander in size than where she stood.

"Isn't it something?" shouted Eli from inside.

"Sure is," Cassy said almost in a whisper, but Miss Brown heard her.

"I'm going to build the finest music hall in New

Orleans someday Cassy, in that very building."

"What about here?"

"Oh I'll never give up the ghost of this house, Cassy Shaw. Do you sing any?"

"I sing," Cassy heard herself answer.

"Maybe you'll sing over there with me someday."

Eli shouted with delight on discovering a double bass in the corner of the room.

They both laughed.

"I sure would love to play there someday Miss Brown...Lottie."

Before they went back inside, she took Cassy by the arm gently.

"How is your mama?"

"She's sick," Cassy, answered.

"I'm sorry to hear that. Your mama was a student of mine, Hannah Pearl. Shaw now of course."

"She told me," said Cassy warming to her.

"Come on let's go back inside."

She offered Cassy a seat on the sofa. Cassy sank into its softness. Eli was still busy, lost in the instruments.

"When you mama was sent to us..." Miss Brown looked over at Eli as she spoke.

"It's okay Miss Brown mama told me what happened."

It was her turn to look at Eli now, cautious that he wouldn't hear.

A change came over Miss Brown then, "Thank you for bringing my dresses sweetie."

Cassy followed her lead and in a way was relieved with the subject change.

"You have such beautiful clothes. I don't mean the ones I made, but how do you have so many for a..."

"You can say it sweetie, for a woman of color. I did good. You will too Cassy, I can feel it."

The conversation drew to a natural close and Eli was ready to leave.

They said their goodbyes to Miss Brown. When they were back out on the street, Eli commented, "She is some lady."

"Do you think you'll play in her music hall Eli?"

"Never mind me playing, Lottie don't want the likes of me in her hall. Besides cousin, you're the one with the voice. Will you sing there?"

"Maybe," Cassy answered, but wondered what he meant by the likes of me. She didn't want to ask him. She felt she couldn't handle any more secrets.

Chapter 8

Cassy rode the streetcar to The Garden District. Some months had passed since that day in Miss Brown's house. The time had come for her to begin work at the mansion. Carondelet Street was her stop. She was to walk from there to Second and Prytania Street, to the Le Blanc mansion. Rosalie wrote directions for her. Some of the ink smudged from her palms sweating. She saw where Rosalie put a red 'X' for the Le Blanc residence. She focused on where the streetcar stop was. She didn't want to miss her stop. It was only 7.30 and she wasn't to start work until 8.30, but she wanted to give herself enough time to get there.

The streetcar rolled past the oak trees, which lined the street on both sides and covered it in shade. Like a grand reveal, she saw the first of the mansions. They were the most beautiful houses she had ever seen; each one majestic and all individual. Some had vines that crept up along the walls and led to magnificent windows with balconies. Others were pristine white, with columns to the front. All had perfectly manicured gardens, surrounded by trees or exotic plants encased by intricately woven ironwork fences. The streetcar stopped and a woman got out at the front. Cassy stepped off at the rear exit.

The pavement was smooth under her feet and not a weed in sight. The streetcar rolled past her and for a moment, she wanted to run after it. Nothing prepared her for the walk she found herself on today. She knew her life had changed and she wasn't sure she was ready. She came to the end of the oak trees and looked down at the crumpled up piece of paper, to the 'X.' Each step brought her closer to the Le Blanc mansion.

She was overcome by the heady smell of blooms, which hung out over the elaborate ironwork fences. Her bag felt heavy. Rosalie helped her pack it. Some nights she would have to stay, if her work kept her late on into the night. She planned to go home every night to see her mama. She set the bag down to give her arm a break. Her attention was drawn to a figure at a window in the house opposite. At least it looked like someone stood watching her. Whoever it was closed the drapes. She wondered about the lives that went on behind all these houses.

Suddenly she was conscious of her blue pinafore. The lace hat, which was pinned into the knot in her hair, itched. As did the black pantyhose, which she was sure had lost their elastic. They were an old pair she got from her aunt until she could buy some of her own. She looked down at her scuffed shoes and cursed herself for not polishing them. She quickened her step. She glanced down at the pocket watch her papa allowed her borrow. It was 8.15. She must have looked so out of place, a colored girl, laden down with a bag, which held all her worldly belongings.

As she turned onto the corner of Second Street, she didn't need to look at the paper anymore. She knew she arrived, because in front of her stood the most opulent mansion in The Garden District. For all of Rosalie's description and praise, it did nothing to justify what lay before her. Large columns surrounded the entire house. It had sweeping lawns and a row of magnolia trees perfectly in line with the ironwork fence. As she walked towards the fence, she saw the detail engraved into it of vines laden with grapes. She stood at the first gate. It had a plaque of a woman who held a vessel next to a well. Cassy followed the pavement onto the next gate. It had a man embossed into it begging for alms with his hand outstretched.

She looked up at the house itself, which only came into view. From a distance, the willow trees on each side of the porch shaded it. The porch was the full length of the front of the house and it dipped on both sides with a flight of steps. Large planters filled with exotic plants stood at the base of these steps. At the side of the house was a corridor of vines, which created a passage all the way around the back. She walked on another while. It was an entire block to reach the end of the house. She came to the final gate and this was the staff entrance. There was no engraving that she could see at first, until she looked at the doorknob, it had an engraving of Jesus knocking on a door. The door was heavy as she turned the knob and pushed it back. It dragged along the gravel and she had to push it back to close it. She was startled to see a fallen angel engraved into the door, wings clipped, face distorted, falling from the sky.

"Unusual picture", said a voice from behind a tree.

An elderly black man appeared. He had a few grey hairs across the top of his head. He was digging an area around a tree. He left the shovel in the soil and approached her. She saw that his shoulders were hunched. His eyes were piercing blue. He shook her hand.

"I'm Jacob. I look after the gardens and grounds around here. You must be Miss Shaw; they're expecting you up at the house."

His hand was covered in welts, from all the years of working the soil. He pointed in the direction of the house.

"Miss Dupree said you were to start today."

Cassy had to think who Miss Dupree was, until she realized it was Beth. She had never been called Miss Shaw in her life.

"Come on I'll show you in," said Jacob.

He reached out for her bag and she allowed him to take it. She swayed suddenly, free from the weight of it heavy on her arm.

"Steady," he said and offered her his free arm. She took it and walked with him towards the house.

"She can be a lot to take in the first time you see her."

"Who?" asked Cassy and looked at the door ahead of them with its narrow stone steps that led up to the rear entrance.

Jacob followed her eyes.

"The house child," he said with a smile.

Cassy let go of his arm and stared up at the chalk ceiling of the balcony above her. She saw a figure at the window above it and then it disappeared again.

"You best look away. That is the Master of the house, Monsieur Le Blanc. They all call him Master. I make sure not to see him," he said.

He walked ahead and leaned to one side with the weight of her bag.

"Ah there's Grace," he called back to Cassy.

A kind looking woman waved at them from the door of the kitchen, who wore what looked like a baker's hat. It barely covered her mop of hair. She went to take the bag from Jacob, but he shooed her away and he disappeared into the house. She ran to greet Cassy and a few wisps of hair blew across her face. She had flour on her cheeks.

"Oh look at you. Are you ready for your first day? Wouldn't it have been something if you were in the kitchen with the others and me? That would have been fine, wouldn't it?"

Cassy was caught up in the whirlwind of questions and the energy of this woman.

"Let me shake your hand," she gushed and offered Cassy a flour covered hand.

"I'm sorry," she said and wiped it in her apron. "What did you say your name was again? I'm Grace, Grace Ellis. I'm married to William. He runs the dining room, while I run the kitchen as you can tell."

Cassy figured she better shake her hand.

"I'm Cassy."

"Come on let's get you inside and settled, Cassy."

They climbed the flight of steps that led into the kitchen. Cassy saw another entrance, with a wider flight of steps similar to those at the front of the house. It had planters on both sides and stone statues that she couldn't tell what they were from this distance. She felt watched from above as she entered the belly of the house. Grace ran down the step that led into the kitchen and Cassy followed.

"Everyone this is Cassy and she..."

"Miss Shaw," Jacob corrected her. "It's Miss Shaw."

"Well come in Miss Shaw and let's be seeing you," said someone from the corner.

"William, give the girl a chance," said Grace.

"I'm just saying its mighty warm out, though it isn't no better in here with them ovens on with my wife's baking."

"Oh hush now William."

"She'll be in the cool part of the house," said Jacob.

This silenced them all and Cassy felt uncomfortable.

"Grace haven't you dinner to be preparing?"

Cassy recognized the voice of her friend Beth and saw the way everyone scattered when she came in.

"And Grace it'll be Miss Shaw from now on do I make myself clear?"

"Yes Miss. Dupree," said Grace and turned her back to them, not without giving Cassy a side wards glance.

Cassy looked for Jacob, but he was gone with her bag.

"Jacob is bringing your bag up ahead to your room Miss Shaw."

The wave of relief Cassy felt when she saw her friend was short lived, when Beth introduced her to everyone as Miss Shaw. She couldn't help but notice how some of the staff looked at her.

"Come with me Miss Shaw," said Beth with an air of authority.

Cassy followed her out into the main hall.

"I only have time to show you around quickly as Master Le Blanc has returned unexpectedly. Work must begin immediately in preparation for tonight's dinner. You've arrived on a very important night. Mr. Le Blanc is throwing a dinner party for his law associates and I have to organize it all."

Cassy couldn't help but notice Beth's pride when she said this.

"I'll show you to your room. You'll share with one of the others. I'm not sure who yet."

"I didn't think I'd need a room as I go home each evening."

Beth didn't answer for a moment, but Cassy was sure she saw her smirk.

"Trust me you will need a room. The third floor is less opulent than the rest of the house. I started up there and finally got a room on the second floor. So consider yourself upgraded on arrival," said Beth laughing at her own wit.

Cassy felt her palms sweat onto her dress. She was filled with the enormity of this new life that lay before her. Her father's words had gotten her as far as here, but now his voice was silent to her.

They walked in silence as Beth showed her to her room. Cassy looked into each room as they passed it. Beth walked ahead of her. She turned a corner suddenly and called back to Cassy.

"Through here," she called.

Cassy turned the corner in time to see which room Beth went into. She disappeared through a door. It led into a small room, a little smaller than her own bedroom at home. The two beds practically took up the whole room. Over by the window was the sewing table, presumably her workspace. The footstool didn't even look the right height for the table. She could see the drapes were pushed in behind the table.

"As you can see, there is little room in here, so work hard and you will be moved quickly as I was."

Cassy tried to smile and must have succeeded, because Beth smiled.

"It's fine Beth thank you."

"Miss Dupree if you don't mind. I'll return the honor to you Miss Shaw."

Cassy felt her cheeks blush and all she could do was look out the window to hide her embarrassment. She saw the street she walked on to get here, behind the line of magnolia trees and it felt like an eternity had passed since she was back in Treme.

"Be downstairs in the main hall in ten minutes."

Cassy nodded. She was sure she saw Beth give her pocket watch a disapproving look, but maybe she imagined it. When she was alone, the enormity of it all hit her. It took every bit of strength she had not to break down and cry. She looked at the bed next to hers and wondered who would she have to share a room with. Already she started to feel like she might have no choice but to stay here.

As she left to go downstairs, she saw the grand staircase for the first time. She had taken the staff stairs to get up here with Beth. Her feet sunk down into the thick red piled carpet. She put one foot on the top step. The carpet ran up the middle of the stairs and was a rich contrast to the dark wood of the steps and banisters.

"Cassy, this way," said a voice from one of the rooms.

She didn't recognize who it was. A girl about her age with bob length hair pinned behind her ears approached her.

"Hi I'm Jo Lynn. I was sent to find you. We have to come to the hall for a meeting."

"Hi I'm Cassy. It's your first day too right?"

"Yes. We're you about to go down that way?"

"The main staircase. Oh no, I was just looking that is

all."

"We're not supposed to use it."

Cassy watched this girl Jo Lynn who was a bubble of energy and looked to be excited about working here.

"What is your role here?"

"I don't know. I suspect cleaning or maybe the kitchen. Oh, I would love to work in the kitchen. My mama says I am a bad cook. What part of the house do you think you'll be in?"

She skipped on ahead. Her voice sounded bubbly and light as she skipped down the narrow staircase ahead of Cassy. She sounded like she didn't have a care in the world. The staircase for the staff was behind a door in the hall, behind the grand staircase. Jo Lynn's words echoed back to her. Cassy wondered how she ended up in this mausoleum of a house.

"I found out our room is above Madame's," she called back.

"Is it close to Mr. Le Blanc's?" Cassy called.

Jo Lynn waited for her on the final step.

They were in darkness, until she opened the door that led to the grand hall.

"He's on our floor. His room is down the hall from ours. Apparently he is hardly ever here, ever since Violet worked here."

She opened the door before Cassy could ask her anything else. She wondered how someone so whimsical could know more than she did about the place.

"Come on ladies, Miss Dupree awaits us."

It was William from the dining room.

"Finally," said Beth, loud enough for all the staff who had gathered in the hall to hear.

Cassy wasn't sure what she was meant to do, whether to stand with Beth or join the others. She looked at them all in their black uniforms. The kitchen staff wore full-length aprons over theirs. With moist fingers Cassy tied the apron she was handed by Grace, sucked in her breath and relaxed her clenched jaw. She tried to act as if she knew what she was doing.

"William, will you show Patty where the fresh linen is and see to it that the dining room is perfect. Jimmy tends to the drinks when a function is on and is the only one permitted access to the drinks cabinet."

"Jacob, are you finished those flowerbeds?"

"Miss Dupree, I had to fix the fence at the bottom of the lawn and paint over the rust."

"Fine, just make sure you get them finished before evening."

"Yes ma'am."

"Anna, you can work in the kitchen with Grace?"

98

"So that just leaves Jo Lynn."

Beth looked at her a moment as if trying to decide there and then her capabilities.

"You can help Miss Shaw. She is going to be very busy. Everybody I forgot to introduce Miss Shaw. She is now the staff seamstress. So any of you need uniforms mending you bring them to her. Her room is on the second floor."

Cassy felt embarrassed that she got an introduction when none of the others did.

"One last thing to remember, only use the staff staircase. Y'all know where it is. Anyone unsure come with me now," said Beth.

The new members of staff followed Beth to the staircase, except Jo Lynn and Cassy. Everyone else scattered to his or her designated corners of the mansion. William remained with them. Grace gave him a withering look and headed in the direction of the kitchen.

"Don't mind my Gracie. She just don't want me putting me neck out for anyone that is all. However, I want to tell you girls if y'all need anything at all, y'all come to me. I be seeing to it y'all okay. Take no mind of Miss Dupree. She is not all bad. She just have a big job here as the housekeeper and well Madame…she's not the easiest."

He winked at them. Someone called for him from the

dining room and he disappeared behind its French doors. Cassy felt more at ease, but was getting a clear picture of who Beth was here.

They walked to their room in silence. Cassy couldn't tell was it because Jo Lynn had to help her; or was there something else? She was tired and part of her didn't want to know. She thought about Beth and how different she was here than when they lived in Treme. She realized that she wasn't her friend here. The distance between them was obvious. They had a title here, but that's where Cassy felt the similarity ended. She needed to get on with the rest of the staff if she was going to survive here. She wondered was that possible if she was already set apart by her title?

***

Beth summoned Cassy to the library. The door to the library was open and it looked like Cassy had arrived before Beth. She didn't know what to do. There was a sofa by the window and two high backed chairs next to the fireplace. Instead, she chose to stand in the centre of this magnificent room. She saw some embers glowed in the hearth, as if a fire was lighting earlier.

"This will be the first and last time you'll be in here," said Beth as she entered the room.

"Make sure of it for your sake Cassy."

Cassy was surprised to hear her call her by her first

name.

"It's fine for me to call you Cassy in here. None of the other staff ever come here, except Violet…but she is gone now. So it's only us."

"Okay," said Cassy.

She was unsure whether to welcome this change or not.

"Tonight after dinner is served; Master Le Blanc will take his drinks back here, alone. Be sure you are nowhere near here as he likes to "meet" the new staff."

"I don't understand," said Cassy.

"Just do as I advise and you'll be fine."

"But I would have no reason to come here," said Cassy flatly.

"You do now. Madame Le Blanc has requested to meet you."

Beth left her and went out onto the verandah.

"Will I follow you?" she called to Beth.

"No Madame will come through those doors. Just be ready for her. See over there," she said and pointed. "Well that is my room, quarters really. I'm going to leave you now. I can't be seen talking to you in here. I still have so much to get ready for tonight."

Before Cassy could ask her what she meant, she disappeared down a flight of steps. She watched her as she walked across the lawns and disappeared back into the house. Cassy waited patiently for her employer to arrive. The gentle swish of the fans overhead combined with the heat from the fire lulled her into a dreamlike state. She'd heard ghost stories all her life, about the old antique shop on Royal Street, or the building on the corner of Dumaine Street, haunted by a mother and her children, but she was sure this mansion held its share of ghosts.

The door opened and pulled her back to where she stood. A woman walked towards her. Her dress swooshed as she walked and her heels clipped against the wooden floors, till she stood beside her on the rug in the centre of the room. The rug was big enough to cover her entire front room at home. She brushed past Cassy without even looking in her direction and threw herself down on one of the armchairs next to the hearth. Her perfume hit Cassy, a mixture of orange blossom and something stronger. She couldn't tell what it was at first, until she was called to come closer. Cassy obeyed. Again, she didn't know whether to take the chair opposite her employer. Madame waved her hand and pointed towards the chair. Only she pointed to somewhere beyond the chair. Cassy realized the other smell was bourbon.

"Jimmy, Jimmy," called Madame.

She reached out to ring a bell on the bookcase beside

her. No sooner had she rung it than Jimmy entered the room. Cassy remembered him from earlier. A whippet of a boy with his hair greased to his head. His bowtie looked comical. It bobbed up and down as he rushed around the room.

"Jimmy, I haven't got all day. Miss Shaw here will have a glass of…"

"Water," Cassy answered.

Jimmy looked like he tried to hide a smirk. He handed the water to Cassy without even looking up. Madame reached out for her glass of bourbon, drank it down and raised her glass for more. Cassy thought she saw his hand quiver, till she saw it was Madame whose hand shook. Jimmy took his position in the corner of the room next to the drinks cabinet. A trickle of sweat ran down Cassy's spine. She looked up at the golden nest on top of Madame's head.

"So you're the seamstress for the house," said Madame Le Blanc.

"Yes," replied Cassy.

"No, I know you are. And you share a room with the other girl…"

"Jo Lynn," Cassy offered.

"Yes. Your mama was quite the seamstress. For a woman of color she was known among the ladies around

103

here. What happened again?"

Cassy felt herself get angry. She looked into the hearth.

"My mama is sick and she can no longer sew, so I have taken over from her. Beth...sorry Miss Dupree told me about the position here."

"Stop right there...Jimmy," she called.

Jimmy was beside them instantly and filled her glass.

"Beth? Is Beth a friend of yours? She must be. Y'all live over in Treme. Y'all probably related."

Her eyes didn't even land on Cassy and looked glazed over. When she spoke her spit landed on Cassy. Madame rose to her feet. She swayed as she moved to the far side of the room.

"Well don't just stand there. Come over here I want to show you something."

"Yes Madame."

Cassy took in all the books that surrounded her and wondered how someone could own so many books. She was relieved to get away from the fire. Madame waved her arm wildly bidding her to join her on the chaise lounge that lined the back wall. It was between the bookcases. Cassy ¬dn't noticed it when she first came in here. The seat was ¬er than she anticipated and she reached it with a ¬adame didn't seem to notice. Cassy heard someone poke the fire. It was Anna from the kitchen. She didn't see her come in.

"I want to see you sew," she said matter of factly. Cassy was confused. Beth had taken some of her work to the mansion weeks ago and she was chosen for the position as the staff seamstress.

"Don't keep me waiting," said Madame raising her voice.

Cassy was aware that Anna and Jimmy were still in the room. Anna scurried past them and left as quickly as she entered.

"Who was that?" demanded Madame Le Blanc.

Cassy didn't know whether to answer her, so instead she took the cover off the sewing machine next to the chaise lounge and fed the thread through the needle. She held her breath to steady her nerves and stop her hand from visibly shaking. It wouldn't have mattered. Madame was too busy summoning Jimmy to refill her drink. He poured Cassy a new glass of water. She silently thanked him for that. It was strange to her to sew under inspection. Whenever she sewed at home, her mama always looked happy to see her at work and her aunt was so busy running the house she didn't even take no notice. She figured she should have known that Madame would want to see her work.

"That will do. You can stop now. Close the door on your way out," said Madame with a wave of her hand.

Cassy rose to her feet and left the room, relieved to be back out in the coolness of the hall. She exhaled and took the stairs to her room. She welcomed the darkness of the staircase as she processed what had just happened.

Chapter 9

The house was a hive of activity that night. Cassy remained in her room. She told Jo Lynn there was no need for her to miss going home to her family that she would be fine on her own. Jo Lynn argued that if she stayed and helped that maybe they would get the workload done quicker and Cassy could go home and see her mama too. Cassy didn't have the heart to tell her that she was slowing the work down and that she would be quicker on her own. Instead, she thanked her for her help and told her to take advantage of getting home. Cassy reassured her that she wouldn't be missed. No one was expecting them to be downstairs when the dinner party was on. Jo Lynn left her alone in the room. Cassy could hear her steps retreat down the stairs and the door close behind her. She felt completely alone.

Just then, she thought she saw a shadow out in the hall, but her eyes were sore from sewing for the last few hours non-stop. She decided to take a rest, seen as she was here for the night anyway. The uniforms were simple repairs, a stitch here or button there. She didn't realize how boring the work could be. It was dark now. The house looked different at night. What seemed like a bountiful of beautifully decorated rooms now were voids that she knew nothing about, empty shells with no life in them. It was as if this part of the house was unlived in.

She heard the sound of cars roll onto the gravel drive outside. The lights from them flooded across her room. She turned off the lamp by her sewing machine and leaned across the table to look. Ladies in fine clothes stepped out of cars with doors held open by the men that accompanied them. She watched as the staff lined up outside. Then she saw a rear door of a car open. A tall man got out with a shock of black hair. He wore a dark suit. The staff made a fuss as he approached them. Cassy leaned further into the window, but she couldn't see anything else. They all went into the house. She wondered if that was him, her employer; Anton Le Blanc. She knew nothing about him, except that he ran the most successful law firm in New Orleans and was the owner of the finest mansion in The Garden District. Jo Lynn told her he also owned the family plantation on the River Road, but none of the staff had seen it except Beth and Jacob. It had been a long day and as much as she wanted to be home right now with her mama, she needed sleep. She lay down on the bed and drifted off.

She slept in fits. She felt like she was aware of the room the entire night, but she was sure she must of got some sleep. When she strained in the moonlight to look at her papa's pocket watch she saw only a few hours had passed. It was not even midnight. She decided to go for a walk.

The grounds of the house were so different to the house itself. She took the staircase down to the main hall and passed through the kitchen unnoticed. She could see light come from the room next to the dining room. She tried to remember what room Beth had told them that was. It was the main family room. Mr. Le Blanc must have brought his guests in there after dinner. The sound of laughter came from the room and the air reeked of cigar smoke. She hurried past. Once outside she felt she could breathe. The house cast shadows on the lawn in the moonlight. She followed the path to the end of the lawn. The trees to the rear of the house were mainly willow, unlike the unison of the magnolia trees that lined the front. Cassy found shelter walking amongst them. The further she walked the more at ease she felt.

"Great night isn't it?" said a voice from behind one of them.

She gasped. She didn't expect to meet anyone out here. It was a younger man's voice than that of Jacob, the gardener. Then he appeared from behind a low-lying branch. He was handsome she could tell even in this light. He had wavy fair hair and as he approached, she couldn't help but notice his terrific blue eyes. He had a kind face.

"Don't be startled. My name is Louis."

"I'm Cassy," she heard herself say.

"Well Cassy what brings you out here?"

"I just felt like a walk."

"The lawns have their limits you know. Would you like to come with me?"

She felt a rush of excitement course through her. She wasn't sure was it the proposition of getting out of here or him.

"I can't."

"Yes you can. Come on. I'll have you back before my father's party is over."

She took a step back when he said this. She knew she should tell him she was one of the help, but her heart wouldn't allow her too. Instead, she took the hand he offered and followed him into the night.

He took her hand again as they climbed over the iron wrought fence.

"I don't know if you've noticed but the gates here are noisy. Someone will hear the gravel."

As she allowed him to help her over, she realized she was wearing one of the dresses her mama made for her at home. It was green chiffon. She had mistaken it for a nightgown in her tiredness earlier. She didn't look like she was one of the staff. She wasn't going to ruin this moment.

He didn't let go of her hand as they walked.

"Here, take my jacket."

Cassy blushed. The only boy her own age she'd ever really been around was Eli and he was her cousin. Now tonight as she walked past all the chalk mansions and the shadows they created in the dark, she felt a million years had passed since she had seen Eli. Sadness came over her. Louis placed his jacket around her. She could smell his cologne. She felt a pang of longing she was sure she shouldn't feel. He was older she could tell. He had a confidence about him that none of the boys in her neighborhood had.

"So who did you come to my father's party with?"

She couldn't keep up the pretence any longer, but before she could answer, he interrupted her.

"I didn't go you know. Truth is I don't like my father. Sure, he's my father, but we're so different. Actually we couldn't be anymore different."

It was his turn to blush now.

"My father doesn't like…well my father hates people of color. If he knew I was walking here with you."

He spun around to face her and forced her to stop

walking so she looked up into his eyes.

"I don't know how you came to be at a party thrown by my father."

"I thought it was a business meeting for his law firm," said Cassy and hoped to change the subject.

"His law firm," he said upset. "Which he wants me to take over one day, as soon as I finish law school I'll be working with him."

"Is that what you want to do?" asked Cassy.

"I don't know for sure what I want to do, but I know it isn't law. In this family, you have no choice though; law is what I will do. I come from a long line of lawyers, my father and his father before him. My great grandfather owned the family plantation. He worked the land. It is hard to believe no one has since him. The plantation is still there of course."

"Maison Belle," said Cassy.

"Ah you've heard of it. Come on let's go. I'm tired talking about my family."

He offered her his hand, which she gladly accepted. They turned onto Second Street. Cassy looked at the same oak trees she had passed only yesterday and wondered where he was going to bring her.

"Sorry I'm talking about me all the time. What about you? What would you like to do after you finish school?"

She couldn't keep it hidden any longer.

"I'm the seamstress at the mansion, at your house. I wasn't at the party. I work for your family. And I come from Treme."

She hoped that was explanation enough for the fact she wouldn't be going to college.

He said nothing for a moment.

"I can go back now if you like. I know the way," she said hoping to break the silence.

"No it's not that. I'm trying to see where I'll take you. I know how about we go to Café du Monde?"

Cassy beamed. "I'd love to."

The further they walked, the mansions disappeared behind them and she felt they were equal even just for tonight.

The place was full. This surprised Cassy, but then again she never came here. He pulled out a chair for her. He ordered some beignets for them and a pot of coffee. When the girl brought them to the table, Louis started to eat them straight away. Cassy hesitated when she saw the powder that covered them. Not exactly first date food. She felt foolish for thinking of this as a date. They only shared a walk. She tried not to laugh at the powder on his lips from the beignets. She caught a glance of herself in the mirror behind him and saw her own face was the same. He leaned

113

forward and wiped a smudge on her cheek. She warmed to the soft touch of his hand as it lingered on her face. She really liked it here. The taste of the beignets, their powdered loveliness passed her lips like delicate kisses and just melted on her tongue. She drank down some coffee. It was strong, but it was good.

"There is somewhere I'd like to show you after here. Do you have to get back just yet?"

"It's okay for another while," she smiled.

When they finished eating, he left some cash on the table. She was sure it more than covered the bill and took her hand.

They crossed over the street to Jackson Square. It looked so beautiful this time of night. She had only ever seen it by day. Carriages passed them with couples laughing as the horses clipped past them. Some artists had their paintings hung on the ironwork fence. Louis lingered to look at them. She wondered did he do that to impress her. They walked through Jackson Square and there it was, St Louis Cathedral. She had seen it only a few times as a child and never as an adult. She was never at this side of the city.

"Come on let's go in and take a look," he said and offered her his hand.

She took it and he pushed open the doors. She looked up to the front of the church at the altar and a strange looking piano.

"Will I play the organ?" he asked her and smiled mischievously.

"Who taught you to play," she asked intrigued.

"Oh my mother used to play, before she started drinking. She drinks all the time now."

Cassy said nothing and sat in one of the pews. She watched him sit down behind the organ. He began to play. She recognized the hymn and started to sing. The sound of her voice echoed around the empty church.

"Where did you learn to sing like that? Forget about it, a voice like yours is a gift. You have a natural gift Cassy."

The way he said her name sent a thrill down her spine.

She stopped singing. He was up off his chair and sat next to her.

"You have the most beautiful voice I have ever heard. I can't believe you work for…What I mean is…I can't believe you don't sing instead of sew."

He blushed.

"It's okay. I know what you're saying, but well for someone like me it's best I have a trade, like being a seamstress. If I have any hope of a future…"

She broke down crying. She sounded like her mama, her aunt and any other woman from Treme who believed

115

their destiny was planned for them with no chance of a future. He put his arm around her.

"My mama is sick. She is dying."

She stopped speaking, that was the first time she said it aloud.

"I'm sorry," he said.

She turned to face him.

"I wanted to be; well I hoped to be a singer. My papa plays the piano."

She nodded towards the organ.

"I bet he could play that too. He has loved music all his life. I can remember as a little girl, him playing the harmonica to me and my mama."

She looked up at the stained glass window.

"Mama doesn't like music so much. She's just scared that is all. That I, well that I'll end up like him, a dreamer."

"Does your papa make money from it? I don't mean it like how that must have sounded. What I mean is does he do it as his job?"

"Papa had a job, but he lost it. He worked on a housing project in Treme, but the building collapsed on him."

"I actually read about that in the paper. Wow, that was your papa. Is he alright now?"

"Well, let's just say music saved him, but so did

116

mama. Mama saved us all. If it weren't for her working every hour under the sun, we'd be out on the street. I am sure of it."

She looked away when she said this. How could she expect him to understand coming from where he is from. He reached out for her hand.

"Now mama is sick. I took over from her as seamstress for all our neighbors. There is a huge workload in that, but my aunt found a job for me at the mansion and here I am."

She pulled away from him and rested her hands on the wooden pew in front of her. She felt exhausted.

"Who else knows about your singing?"

"No one at the mansion if that's what you mean."

She knew she sounded defensive, but the reality of it all just hit her.

He persisted.

"Have you anyway of your voice being heard? Maybe your papa has contacts."

"My cousin Eli has heard me sing and well he said I'm not half bad," she laughed.

"Where is he?"

"Oh he's probably at the club now. Although last I heard he got himself into some kind of trouble."

"Which club?"

117

"It's over in Treme."

"Come on," he said and sprung to his feet. "I'm going to bring you home. To your family I mean."

"What? No I can't."

"You can and you will. We'll go hear your cousin play. If we're quick I can take you to see your mama."

"She'd be asleep," said Cassy all in a flurry. "Besides I'll get home tomorrow."

"She would, but you would know you saw her. I know one thing for sure, my mother knows how to work her staff and you may not get home tomorrow."

They left the cathedral and as they walked Cassy felt the familiarity of streets she knew all her life. She breathed in the warm night air as they made their way through Congo Square.

It was more than yesterday since she had seen Eli. When he finished his set, he ran over to her and swept her up in the air.

"Well my little cousin has come to hear me play. It's so good to see you. I should explain to you where I've been at…sorry hi I'm Eli," he said and turned his attention to Louis.

"I'm Louis. I'm a friend of Cassy's."

"Eli, where have you been? I wasn't sure if you were playing again."

"I'll get us some drinks. I have so much to tell you. Lemonade for Cassy. What's your poison Louis?"

"I'll have bourbon if it's going. Here I'll come with you and give you a hand."

Eli threw back his head and laughed.

"You're lucky it's dark and they can't see you none. Why you want and show yourself up at the bar. I'll go."

Louis sank down into his seat. It was Cassy's turn to reach for his hand.

They all chatted together for what seemed like hours, but Cassy kept a close eye on her papa's pocket watch.

"Cassy, how about a song for your cousin?"

"Oh I don't know Eli."

Eli wouldn't take no for an answer as he led her to the stage. He accompanied her on the double bass. She looked down at Louis as she belted out one of her own songs. Louis clapped and cheered louder than anyone in the room. He was up off his feet.

Cassy went back to her seat and whispered to him, "Can we go now? I want to see my mama."

Eli joined them and told Louis a funny story he heard backstage. The two of them laughed uncontrollably.

"Will you have another drink with me Louis?"

Louis squeezed Cassy's hand reassuringly.

119

"We have to go buddy. I promised Cassy I'd bring her to see her mama."

"I heard about my aunt. Cassy before you go, I want you to know I'm doing alright. I'm doing my best. Once I keep the music with me, I'll be fine. Tell your papa I'm doing okay too."

"Will you see him Eli?"

"Doubtful. I just play the odd gig. I like to keep it that way. Can't get mixed up in nothing then."

Cassy smiled. She looked back at him as they left. He was gone back up to the bar and sharing a laugh with someone else.

They walked to her house in silence. Cassy was deep in thought and Louis seemed to know that. She felt comfortable not to have to speak around him.

When they got to her house he said, "I'll wait here."

She didn't argue with him. Her aunt was asleep on the sofa. She stirred when she saw Cassy.

"What time is it?"

"Oh it's late aunt. I have just come here to see mama."

"You not finished yet?"

"It looks like you were right aunt to tell me to pack a bag."

"Who is that with you?"

Cassy jumped. She looked to where her aunt looked and sure enough, Louis was visible through the window. He paced the porch.

"That is Louis."

"It may be late Cassy Shaw and I may be tired, but don't try and tell me he works at the mansion too. Look at him, he's white."

Cassy sighed. She didn't come here to argue with her aunt. She left her with her questions and went into her mama's room. The air was cool. The air con was beside her bed. It made a clicking sound as it blew out the cool air.

"Cassy?"

"Yes mama. It's me. Rest. I have just come to see are you alright."

"I'm fine child," she coughed. She closed her eyes and was asleep again.

Cassy sat with her a while and wiped her brow with the cloth on the nightstand. She thought of Louis stuck out on the porch with her aunt. She had better go rescue him.

To her surprise, they were sitting on the bench and her aunt had poured him some tea. He smiled when he saw her. Her aunt managed to burst any elation she felt on seeing him so comfortable in her home.

"Louis tells me he leaves for law school in a few weeks."

121

She went back into the house and left them. A few weeks. For some reason Cassy thought surely they would have longer than that.

"I'm sorry," Louis said.

"I best be getting back to the mansion," she said.

He nodded and set down his cup. She felt sorry for him how awkward he looked.

"Cassy...I really like you. I know we've only met tonight, but I know how I feel."

"Don't say anything, neither us can promise anything. I'm the help at your family's mansion and that is all."

"I don't believe that," he said.

He stood in front of her as she stepped down off the porch. She thought he was going to stand in her way. Instead, he swept her up into his arms and planted a kiss on her lips.

Chapter 10

She was on her way home to see her mama and papa after another busy day at the mansion. Rosalie's eldest son, Leroy Jr., ran past her as she walked through Congo Square. By the time, she noticed it was him, he'd outrun her. She thought it strange he should be in that much of a hurry to run in the direction of her house at this late hour. She could have had to stay overnight at the mansion, but she twisted and turned last night so much that she got up to sew. As a result, she was way ahead of her schedule.

She was close to the house when she was stopped in her tracks by a piercing scream. It was her aunt. Something must have happened to Leroy Sr. or one of the kids. Before she knew what was going on, Rosalie ran out of the house with her son directly behind her. She was shaking and grabbed onto her son to support her, as if she didn't trust her own legs to keep her upright.

"Rosalie, what is it? What's happened?" Cassy called to her.

She could see her aunt struggled to even walk let

alone speak. She clutched her chest when she saw her niece. Cassy knew them something terrible had happened. She looked to Leroy for an answer. He looked at his mama and knew he'd have to be the one to tell her.

"I don't know how to tell you this Cassy, but Eli, your cousin has been stabbed."

"Wait what? No, no, no," she cried out.

Rosalie found her voice, "Your papa was with him."

"No, no, no." Cassy cried.

Sounds came from her that weren't even words. She shook all over unable to control the wave of emotion that coursed through her.

"Mama, where's mama?" she asked.

"Ebony is with her."

Before she turned to go into the house she asked, "Is Eli injured badly?"

Rosalie broke down again. This time she bent over and wailed.

Her son bent down to help her to her feet and answered for her, "I'm sorry Cassy. He's dead."

There was nothing to reach out for. The ground sunk into a bottomless pit. The clouds swam in front of her eyes. Buildings disappeared into a spin.

"Eli," she cried as she collapsed.

***

When she awoke, she was on the sofa in the family room. She knew this house her entire life, but it looked different, like everything had changed. Her head still spun. She'd a dull ache by her temple. There was a bowl at her feet, filled with what could barely be called vomit. The last dregs of her stomach. As the room came into focus, she saw she wasn't alone. She saw some familiar faces from the neighborhood gathered in the kitchen. More filed in through the porch door from the courtyard.

"What happened?" she asked Rosalie.

Rosalie looked up from where she sat with the doctor next to her. Leroy came in from the kitchen. Ebony appeared from Hannah's room.

"My uncle was with him," said Leroy.

Rosalie shot him a look to silence him.

"I was there when he lay on the ground Cassy," began Leroy.

"I think that can wait till later," said Rosalie.

Leroy wouldn't be silenced.

"Myself and papa, along with the younger ones passed by on our way home and we saw him."

He went back into the kitchen to greet the neighbors.

"Your papa is fine, Cassy. Doctor, can you give her anything to steady her breathing?" asked Rosalie the panic rose in her own voice.

125

He handed her a pill he took from his case. Ebony raised a glass of water to Cassy's lips. She took the pill from the doctor and handed it to Cassy. She watched him write up a prescription.

"See that someone gets this from the drug store. I'll leave y'all now."

Cassy took the prescription from him and thanked him.

"Where's mama?" Cassy asked.

"She is asleep," answered Ebony.

"Does she know?" asked Cassy.

With that, Ebony left them and went into Hannah's room. Cassy tried to stand up to follow her.

"Cassy, you've had a shock. It's better if you rest," suggested the doctor.

Cassy spun around. Immediately the room swam. She could hear the doctor tell her to be careful, but her mind raced with questions.

Rosalie stood next to her son and whispered something into his ear.

"Leroy, take your sister with you. Ebony, go with your brother."

Cassy watched the two of them leave without so much a look in her direction. The doctor excused himself and left the house.

Amos came into the room from outside.

"I tried to save him," he said breathless from running to get here.

He went directly to Cassy and put his arms around her. He brought his sister into the embrace. There was blood on his shirt.

"Papa, what happened?" Cassy asked.

Amos looked to his sister before he answered, "Eli was stabbed by two men who jumped him. I finished up in the club and I heard a racket out on the street. It was too late when I got to him."

Rosalie went over and pulled one of the armchairs closer for him to sit down. He slumped down into the chair and buried his head in his hands. Cassy noticed his shirt then. She wanted to comfort him, but she needed to know what happened.

"Papa, but why would they kill him? It makes no sense."

"Hush now child, your papa has been through enough tonight," said her aunt.

"No she's right. It doesn't make any sense."

Rosalie stood up.

"Well not unless he owed them money."

Amos shot her a look.

"He didn't gamble if that's what you mean sis."

127

"Look Amos this has been a hard night on us all, don't go turn on me."

"You're right. I'm sorry. They have no way of getting in contact with Jessie. She's out at sea. They have to wait for the ship to dock before they can tell her that her son…her son is dead."

Those last words lingered on the air, as each of them were left with their own thoughts. Amos broke down and held his daughter. She felt the weight of his broken body against her. She felt nauseous.

"I need to go see mama, is she awake?"

"Please Cassy, do as the doctor says, isn't that right Amos, your girl needs to rest," said Rosalie.

Cassy did as she was told. Her aunt put a blanket over her. She pulled it up around her. She closed her eyes, soothed by her aunt as she stroked her head like her mama did when she was young. Her papa stood in the doorway of the kitchen; he hugged a cup with both his hands.

***

When she awoke the morning sun streamed through the window. She could smell grits cooking. It smelled good. The nausea had passed and she was hungry. She stood up. Her legs though weak, supported her. She folded up the blanket.

"Cassy, you're awake. Your papa is making grits."

It's as if the night's terrors had vanished. She looked over at her mama's sewing table. The cloth covered the machine. She saw the outline of the three little birds her papa painted. Their wings fluttered for a moment in the ray of sunlight that danced across the table.

"We'll get through this together child," said Rosalie. Cassy followed her through to the kitchen and a fresh pot of coffee waited for her. Her papa looked tired. He was wearing the pants from his good suit and a clean shirt.

When she'd eaten breakfast her aunt said, "Your mama is awake and is asking for you."

Cassy jumped up.

"Finish eating Cassy. We'll have to tell her together," said her papa.

The memory of the night before hit her with a thud. Eli was dead. Her brother.

Hannah looked rosy cheeked, well even. The multitude of pills on her nightstand reminded Cassy how unwell she was.

"Come sit by me Cassy. Till I see my baby girl," she sounded hoarse.

Amos approached the bed the same time as her.

"There was an accident my love."

Hannah looked as if to check they were all present in

the room. Rosalie stood behind the door.

Cassy remained sat next to her mama while her papa tried to find the words to tell her about Eli. He took his wife's hand in his.

"Elijah," he said.

Hannah shook her head. Cassy reached for her other hand.

"I tried to save him, but I couldn't."

Amos explained as much as he could to his wife. How he finished work and came across Eli on the ground. He left out the part about the two guys that ran away after beating him.

"It was a random attack that could have happened to anyone."

Amos stopped speaking. Rosalie reached out for Hannah as she wailed. Amos stood back to let his sister help his wife. She just held her while she cried.

"My boy, my boy," Hannah cried.

It was like a light in the darkness. Something was brought forth that had lay buried for a long time, the pain of losing her son for a second time.

Cassy left her mama in the care of her papa and aunt. She looked at the prescription on the table in the kitchen. She read her name on the small white piece of paper, with the name of some pill she didn't know. It was something to take all her pain away, to help her through. She looked out into the courtyard at the tree where he papa helped her plant her dreams. She promised Eli she'd find her voice and sing. Right now, that seemed far away. She had to look after herself and if that meant taking a little medicine to feel better.

Her papa left her mama's room and asked her to join him on the front porch.

"Cassy, please listen," begged Amos.

"Papa I don't understand."

She looked out at the street she knew all her life. Her papa told her about the day they moved in here, so proud to own their own home. They started out living with his parents along with his brother and his family. Amos sat down beside her on the bench and took her hand.

"Your mama was very young when she had Eli. She was forced to give him away."

Cassy turned to look at him and saw how much this hurt him.

"Your mama loves you Cassy. She never wanted you to know how much she failed her first born. That's how she sees it. And now he is gone."

Rosalie interrupted them.

"She's asking for you Amos," she whispered.

Amos went inside. Rosalie took his seat. She hugged

Cassy, who welcomed her embrace. None of them knew how close she was to Eli. All the times he heard her sing, when she met him in secret. He believed in her. No one knew, except Louis.

"Come on let's go back inside," said Rosalie.

"I'll follow you in," returned Cassy.

She looked up at the sky. A dusting of stars had burst out into the darkness and cascaded across Treme like a blanket of hope. She promised Eli she would find her voice and sing.

***

Rosalie poured some coffee. Cassy breathed in the aroma. Her stomach settled. Somehow, the change of scene, a different room brought a sense of calm to her. There was always something about the morning light, when an upset from the night before vanishes. The brightness can make you feel foolish and whatever caused, the upset is thrown into the shadows. However, this is different no amount of comfort from anyone could change the fact Eli lay dead in the morgue. The neighbors filed into the house again this morning. Some brought food or a simple nod of the head. Others offered words, which seemed harsh, too fresh, too raw. Words spoken from a different place;not knowing the impact of what they said. Everyone tried to give some solace.

Hannah slept through this. At least no one was allowed to see her. Cassy excused herself and retreated outside. She looked back into the house; every inch was filled with people. They came in through the courtyard, shuffled quietly from the kitchen to the front room. Amos waited for them in the family room, accepted their condolences on behalf of the family. They left through the front door. Cassy remained out of sight behind the magnolia tree on the seat her papa had built for her mama. The tree was in full bloom. She wondered did they all know Eli was her brother.

Hours passed before the house was empty again. At some point Cassy had fallen asleep. She stepped out from in under the shade of the silky leaves. The air was thick with humidity and the sun was hidden behind dark clouds. Rosalie met her at the door. She had her bag and her eyes were hidden under a sun brimmed hat. Cassy could tell by her voice she'd been crying.

"Your papa is gone to the funeral home to make arrangements. I said I'd go home to the kids for a while. I need to see them."

Her tears flowed as she said this. Cassy had nothing to offer her aunt to comfort her. Rosalie reached out for her, but Cassy passed her in the door.

"I have to go see mama."

"I'm glad she slept through the night," said Rosalie.

Cassy knew what her aunt meant by that.

"I couldn't believe how many came and there will be more at the funeral..." she broke of then and left.

She heard the hum of the fan as she entered the room. The window was closed to keep out the humidity. The drapes were partially open. Cassy glanced at life outside. She recognized faces, busy about their day. She was sure she saw them cast a sideward glance at the house.

"Cassy is that you?"

"Yes Mama."

"Would you pass me that glass of water? My throat is so dry."

Cassy busied herself in pouring the water.

"I never wanted to give him up you know. I had no choice. Mama said it was for the best."

Cassy handed her the glass of water.

"You look so pretty Cassy. Is that your uniform?"

Cassy touched her clothes absently. It felt like she'd only arrived. The hours of last night evaporated like water on the pavement scorched by the sun.

"Yes mama."

"Do you like it? At the mansion, I mean Cassy."

"Mama I work for the Le Blancs. You used to..." She bit her lip, she was sure she was going to cry.

"I do mama. It's a good job. I'm happy."

She took her mama's hand in hers. It was Hannah's turn to look away.

"My papa never spoke of him Cassy. He never spoke of my boy."

"Mama you don't have to talk about that."

Hannah sat up a little. She hadn't seen strength in her mama in a long time. Her eyes searched her daughters, as if trying to determine how much she could tell her.

"I love your papa Cassy and you must know that. I was young and charmed by him, Eli's father. He never saw him Cassy. He never wanted to neither."

Cassy tried to piece together the life her mama lived, a story she knew nothing about.

"I didn't love him. We were young. I'm ashamed to tell you that Cassy."

She looked away again and spoke as if she could see it all mapped out in front of her. Each vision a step back to the past.

"I saw him with a woman of his own color. He was white. He married her and they moved to New York. I never heard from him again. I left the convent. I told you before, the nuns taught me to sew, so I started work as a seamstress. Mama met me in secret, but eventually stopped. I never saw papa again."

Cassy jumped when she heard a door slam shut.

"That is your papa. He went to see about the funeral arrangements."

Amos came into the room. He stood silent for a moment.

"There was a free…he will be buried tomorrow. It's all arranged."

He sighed somewhere from the depths of his being.

"Can I get you anything my love?" he asked Hannah.

"I just want to rest a while," she said. "Cassy, will you stay with me?"

Hannah closed her eyes and fell asleep. Cassy lay down next to her.

Her papa whispered to her, "I don't know how we'll get through tomorrow?"

Cassy wanted to ask him is her mama able to go instead she closed her eyes.

"Before I leave you be Cassy, you okay in that mansion?"

She kept her eyes closed and pretended she was already asleep. She couldn't lie to him. The noise of the fan helped her drift off to sleep.

Chapter 11

Nobody knew how close she was to Elijah. He listened to her sing and believed that she would make it. Her papa stood in the doorway of the funeral home on Canal Street with the minister. Cassy recognized him from her church, but it was a while since she'd been back. It was decided that it better they have the service here as Eli wasn't religious. If Cassy thought about it, he didn't like church. He'd no problem with "the big guy", his reference to God. He just didn't like where He inhabited. He said he'd like Him a whole lot better if he played at the music halls. She told him that God was everywhere, which always made Eli laugh. He'd tell her that he had no doubt her voice was heavenly. This made her smile as she remembered.

Eli was always full of laughter. He was tall and physically strong. Maybe even a little clumsy in how he carried himself, but once he sat behind his double bass his confidence shone. He was so talented. She dreamed of one day joining him not just as a guest, but permanently with him on the stage as resident singer. All of those dreams dashed as she looked at his casket. Dark brown with chrome handles. There was a knot in the wood. It formed a shape, an outline of sorts. Someone touched her shoulder. She looked around to see her mama take her seat in one of the pews to her right. The division in the group of mourners was evident, well perhaps only to anyone who knew. Eli's mama, the woman who reared him sat nearest the head of the casket. Her seat was only a fraction away from where he lay. She pulled it forward away from the crowd and nobody stopped her.

Cassy saw Rosalie help her mama to her seat and placed her bag in the pocket that stows a copy of the bible. She placed the bible on her knee, though Cassy knew she wouldn't turn its pages. Rosalie took a fan from her bag and batted it in front of Hannah's face, whose hair gently fluttered. Cassy watched her wipe the worn leather cover on the book in her lap as her tears fell onto it. She looked around for her papa. Everyone was in their seats. She would create a fuss if she went to her mama now. Rosalie put the shawl back around Hannah's shoulders. Hannah allowed to her help her and used the back of her palm to dry her cheeks just as the minister began to speak.

It was an awkward introduction for Cassy as she passed this woman, her aunt Jessie Pearl, on the way to the altar. Cassy had never seen such a glamorous woman in all

138

her life. She had seen pictures of her in her house, but none did her justice. Her long dress looked to be made of silk or was it crushed velvet, she couldn't tell without staring at it. It glinted as she moved. She too wore a shawl, but unlike her mama's which was sewed remnants of fabric. Her aunt's shawl looked like it was made from the finest fabric. She must stop in so many ports; see so many places, the availability of fabrics to her endless. Her hair tumbled down her back in loose waves, clearly forced into submission with hair lacquer. She wore a string of pearls around her neck, as she did in every picture in her house. However, in those photos she held them in jest, waved in the air with a twirl of her dress. Here they are stationery around her neck. They hung low and met the top of her dress, which did little to disguise her ample chest. Cassy felt herself redden at forcing Jessie Pearl to stoop down to pick up her large hold all bag and she felt she deliberately stalled to give the minister a glance. So this was Eli's mama whom he spoke so fondly about. Though at times she could hear a tinge of resentment in his voice when Cassy asked if he minded her been away. She stopped asking him that. She was fascinated by her life, her singing career at sea, but now she understood what she had seen, as an opportunity was her chance to get away, to sing. Jessie settled back into her seat, as did the entire room as if each had moved a little to strain to see the reaction of the dead boy's mother, to see her meet her sister's daughter, or maybe they didn't.

Cassy looked down at the blinking faces, waiting for her to speak. She had two choices, either look at this woman in all her glamour or down at her brother's body. Her eyes rested nowhere near him. Out of the corner of her eye, she saw one of the chrome handles caught in the sunlight. It blurred her vision, if she leaned her head slightly she saw the start of the lining of the casket. A volume of white surrounded him. That was all. She wasn't going to look in. Instead, her eyes rested somewhere else. She could see her mama in the foreground being quietly comforted by her aunt Rosalie. Just beyond then she saw her papa lean forward, head bowed in the seat with one arm placed on the pew between his wife and his sister. Anything more and it would be obvious to the crowd he was trying to offer comfort. Surely, the grieving family was to her right now, her aunt Jessie Pearl to anyone that watched.

Cassy's eyes landed on nothing of significance, a crack that ran from one window ledge up to the height of the next window. A bunch of plastic flowers that stood on a pedestal between the two windows did a good job of hiding that hairline crack, but she saw it. As far as services go it was short, but she suspected that's how Eli would have wanted it. The air was stifling, as everyone moved towards the exit. Only the family remained. Cassy, Hannah, Rosalie; and across from them Jessie. Before them were a couple of faces, young and old. Cassy recognized them from the neighborhood. She suddenly thought of Eli's father, but a quick scan of the room showed he wasn't there. Cassy looked around again, she didn't see her papa. She was aware of the ceiling fan overhead. She felt a thickness gather in her ears. She panicked. The minister approached them. Cassy couldn't hear him speak. There was a buzzing sound. She tried to swallow to create saliva to aid the dryness of her throat. One of her little cousins put a bottle of lemonade in her hand. She felt like she'd been given manna from Heaven, the closest spiritual connection she'd had here. She drank it down in one go. The minister lost his calm demeanor and looked at her horrified. Her aunt was too busy clipping her small boy's ear for bringing the bottle to church she called it. Cassy looked around again for her papa. She saw him come back in from outside. There was something surrounding him, a beacon of light. He used his two hands to close the double doors behind him. The room bathed in a warm glow. For the first time she noticed the stain glass window behind the altar. Her focus was on getting past Jessie before, but she was already stood by Eli's casket.

Cassy looked at her.

"Will you sing on last song for him?" asked the woman with the pearl necklace. Cassy looked to her mama who seemed to be transfixed by the light coming in the stain glass window, but Cassy knew better. Her mama was trying to deal with this. Cassy looked into Eli's casket. The sight of him dead shook her to the core. The air felt tight. She held onto the pew in front of her to steady herself. Her eyes landed first on the satin pillow under his head. It filled the entire base of the coffin, and raised his head up slightly. There was something sewn into it. She strained to see what it was. The initials, H.S. It was her mama's signature. She signed this on special pieces, such as embroidered quilts or frames of fabric for a customer's wall for one of the mansions in The Garden District. For people that fabric could be used as an addition to the furnishings and not just a staple to wear. Next to her initials was an "S" sewn in brown thread. On closer inspection she saw the 'S' was actually a treble clef. The minister was still waiting to say the closing words.

Cassy looked around at each of them. Tears flowed as she took to the pulpit to sing. Some of the younger relatives were crying, most of them too young to realize why they were here. Amos took the pew next to her mama. Cassy thought she saw Jessie give him a look of indifference. Maybe she imagined it. Rosalie nodded at her to begin.

"Cassy, its okay you can stay next to the casket." Jessie's voice broke the sound of crying. She didn't want to stand where she asked. She didn't trust herself not to collapse against the casket. She obeyed and took her place next to Eli and sung for him one last time. During it, she was sure her tears fell, an outpouring of grief for him; her brother. But her eyes remained closed the whole time and no tears came. They would come later. She sang the words, which escaped her mouth with such ease where speech failed her today. It was one of her brother's favorites, from a little known singer. She was sure no one in the crowd knew it except her. Out of the corner of her eye, she saw her mama's lips move echoing the words she sung. On her right Jessie's lips moved and Cassy could hear the low tone of her voice.

As Cassy stepped down from the altar, she deliberately went to her right to avoid her brother's casket. The minister blocked her way. He took her arm and led her back to her seat. She was sure the entire room bore holes into her back as she stood with them to sing the closing hymn She buried the song inside her. A tidal wave of emotion tried to surface. The minister said a final prayer. One by one, each member of the family came up to the

143

casket to say their final goodbyes.

There was a disturbance at the back of the room. She saw the start of the front line marching band come in. It was time to let Eli go. There was an order to these things. Everything happened in a pattern, that everyone knew when it was time to leave. Over the years, she had been at wakes in people's homes. She shuffled towards the door easily with her papa or mama depending on who had died in the neighborhood. She was never shielded from death. Today was different. How could she just file out of her like someone who came to pay their respects, removed from it all.

Each member of the family walked up through the middle of the room and left down the other side. As they passed her, Cassy listened to her relative's quiet muffled cries. She saw a few of Eli's musician friends among them. They must have come in near the end of the service. She wondered were any of them with him that night, but her papa told her he was alone when he found him. She looked up at her papa. He took her hand without saying a word.

Hannah stood up and Amos let her pass. Rosalie went to go with her, but Amos stopped her. She went over to Jessie who made for a lonely figure on her own. Cassy and Amos watched as the two women embraced. Two sisters united in shared grief for the boy they both loved.

"Cassy, go say your goodbyes," said Amos.

"Are you coming up papa?"

She knew he wouldn't, but she had to try.

"I want to remember him as he was, baby. I'll wait outside."

He got up to leave. She wanted to grab him, keep him there, and force him to accompany her on this final goodbye. She watched him leave. The light from outside flooded in as he opened the door. Two figures stood in the doorway. It was the undertakers.

When Cassy reached the top, her mama joined her. Jessie stood back. At least Cassy no longer saw her. It was just her and her mama ready to say goodbye to Eli. The minister left the altar and went to the back of the room. He whispered something to Jessie as her passed her. Whatever it was it made Cassy bite her lip; a final word of condolence perhaps. He shook her hand.

Eli's clothes went up in under his chin. Cassy knew this was to hide the wound in his neck. There was the faint outline of a bruise by his temple. The undertakers concealed it with makeup. His eyelashes looked so long and tipped off the start of his cheeks. It looked as if he could open his eyes at any moment. She looked at his hands with a Bible placed under them. He used to mock her for her church going. He told her she didn't need to go

145

to church to sing, that she could find her voice somewhere in the world. Hannah leaned in and touched his hands, cupped hers over them. Her sudden movement made Cassy flinch. She didn't want to touch him, to feel the cold pallor of his skin. She looked at his nostrils. Air passed all around him, but he couldn't breathe. Hannah leaned in over his body and blocked it from Cassy's view. She ran her finger across the initials on his pillow. Cassy had seen enough. She had to walk away. Every time she blinked the image of him, lying there played over and over.

She was relieved to step outside and join the crowd gathered there. Someone handed her a candle. Night had found its way and the sky was caught in its twilight. An elderly man led the band. He carried a black parasol. Its fringe moved as he walked. Behind him was a drummer. All gathered here played a part in Eli's life. She stepped in line with the vigil to Congo Square.

Then she saw him, Louis. He held a candle. She was relieved to see him. The crowd parted slightly with his presence. Some of the women from the neighborhood glanced as he stood next to her. No one said anything and the line kept moving.

"I'm so sorry Cassy. He was a good person. Sorry I hope its okay I'm here."

"We're going to Congo Square."

It was all she could think of to say. She wanted to tell him how much it meant to see him here. How she hasn't stopped thinking about him.

"I'm with you Cassy," he said.

Hannah was helped from the funeral home by Rosalie. She looked tired. Her papa was behind them with some of the other men. He went to help his wife down the steps. Cassy watched as her mama and aunt were escorted to a car by the minister. She gathered he offered to drive them. Everyone continued on the walk. As Hannah bent to get into the car, she caught Cassy's eye and smiled. Even in the midst of her pain, Cassy felt in that moment that her mama approved of Louis.

"Is she okay?" asked Louis.

"Will you hold my hand?" she asked in return.

He took her hand in his.

Her aunt Jessie approached her.

"Cassy, I'm sorry to have met you like this."

She leaned in to hug her, but it happened so unexpectedly Cassy hesitated. Instead, Jessie offered her hand to Louis. He let go of Cassy's hand to shake her aunts.

"He was a good boy. I was blessed to have him."

She quickly corrected herself.

"I was blessed to rear him as my own."

147

This open admission was too much for Cassy to bear.

"Louis, will you bring me up to where papa is?"

Cassy couldn't even see her papa; such was the amount of people that joined the line on route to Congo Square.

"Cassy, it was never my intention to hurt your mama. She is my sister. I love her. I don't blame her for hating me."

Cassy couldn't listen to anymore.

"She is sick."

Jessie looked confused. Louis looked uncomfortable and fidgeted with the candle he held. The wax ran onto his finger. He yelled. Both Cassy and Jessie stopped talking and looked at him.

"Ladies this is nothing to do with me and you can tell me to mind my own, but aren't we all here for Eli?"

He didn't expect them to agree with him and hoped he hadn't overstepped his place. They all walked in silence as the band played in honor of Eli.

When they got to Congo Square, the line dispersed a little. Most gathered over by where Eli used to play music with Amos. Some stayed back a little, perhaps not feeling right about been so close to the family. Cassy walked through them, as they separated, a sea of mourners around her.

"Cassy wait. I don't want to fight with you. I want to ask you something."

Jessie Pearl took Cassy's hands in hers, in front of everyone. The band changed to a more upbeat tempo in honor of Eli's life. Cassy looked straight into her dark brown eyes. Jessie Pearl was beautiful. Cassy noticed it and so did every man that was gathered here.

"Eli told me you sing. Not only sing, but you have a real gift."

The mention of his name and hearing he spoke of her with pride warmed her to this woman, who under different circumstances would have been her aunt.

"Please Cassy hear me out. I'll return to the cruise ship in two days. It's quick, but please don't judge me for that. With Eli gone, there is nothing here for me."

"I understand," Cassy said.

"Your mama is gone direct to St. Louis Cemetery isn't she? I thought she would have come here too."

"My mama? Oh no. Not cause of Eli though."

"She loved music as a young girl you know, when we were growing up."

"Oh I used to hear her hum at the sewing machine," said Cassy.

"It's not your papa she's annoyed with, you know."

"Oh I know," answered Cassy.

She wanted to defend him, but surely Jessie knew the choices Eli made; and her papa was there for many of them.

"But the past is the past. Eli is gone and all his dreams died with him. Cassy that is the cold truth, but you're still here. I want to give you the opportunity to sing."

"If you mean, come away with you on the ships. That life isn't for me."

"For me neither baby girl I can assure you. Never mind that. You've met Lottie Brown with Eli over on St. Peter St. She owns a music hall there."

"How did you know?"

"I was away a lot, but my boy did speak to me. Well anyway I want to give you a chance to audition for her."

Cassy loosened herself free from her.

"That's foolish talk. I will be back at the mansion tomorrow. Madame Le Blanc will be expecting me."

"That's her boy, isn't it?"

She nodded in Louis's direction.

Cassy felt her cheeks flush. "Yes but no one knows about us."

"Sweetie they do now. Look around everyone sees and everyone talks."

"What are you saying?"

"I'm saying a time may come where you'll have to make a choice. I had to."

"You walked out on your child."

"I'll allow you that one. I had no choice, in taking Elijah I mean. My papa decided and my mama agreed that Hannah was too young to care for a baby. I gave up my dream till Eli was old enough to fend for himself."

Cassy thought the irony of that, considering he died at the hands of a gang. Louis returned to them.

"They're leaving for the cemetery now. Should I leave?" he asked.

Cassy shook her head and took his hand.

"I want you with me."

"Louis, can I just say goodbye to my niece for a moment?"

"Of course, you can."

"You're not coming to bury your own son?" Cassy asked defiantly.

"I believe that last journey belongs to my sister; and to you Cassy."

She leaned in and embraced her. She held her close as she whispered, "Miss Lottie Brown will visit you at the mansion. I can't tell you when, but it will be arranged. She'll help you with the rest." She stood back and looked at her.

151

"I wish I knew you Cassy Shaw, but someday I think the world will."

When they got to the cemetery, the music stopped. In the distance, Cassy saw her mama. She was seated next to Rosalie. Eli was to be buried in Jessie's family tomb. Cassy didn't really think about where he'd be buried. The last few days had passed in a haze.

"Cassy, I'll wait here for you. I don't think its right I stay for his burial," said Louis.

"I'm Amos. Cassy's papa," said Amos from behind them.

Cassy didn't know where he appeared from.

"Louis, Louis Le Blanc,Sir."

"Don't be calling me sir, you hear. Amos will do fine, but don't let her mama see you hanging around. Its best you wait by that tree. Stay out of sight. Cassy will see you later."

"No I won't. Sure I'll be going home with you and mama."

"I'm not going directly home Cassy, but you're right you best accompany your mama home with Rosalie."

She didn't want to know where he was going and she didn't want to talk about it in front of Louis.

The service by the tomb was short. It was really only a prayer by the minister. One of the men stood with Amos as he placed his hand on the casket. They were all musicians from the club. Cassy had met each of them and knew them all by name. They all filed away. Rosalie followed the minister to his car. It gave Cassy a few moments alone with her parents. Here they were gathered together, all of them as a family.

Amos explained to Hannah that some of the men are going to the club to toast Eli with a few drinks and he won't be late home. It didn't seem to matter to Hannah. Usually she'd kick up a fuss with the mere mention of him going to "The Sugar Club", but it didn't seem to matter to her now. Louis appeared just as Amos was leaving. Amos didn't try to stop him from approaching Cassy or her mama. He got his leave and he was going to take it. Drown his sorrows with drink. Cassy resented his ability to leave. Not that she wanted to leave her mama.

"I'm sorry for you loss," said Louis.

Hannah looked at him and didn't speak for a long time. Rosalie interrupted to tell them the minister is ready when they are to take them home. Hannah went to get up, but struggled. Louis reached out to help her the same time as Cassy.

"Thank you," said Hannah. "You know my daughter?"

"Yes I do. I care for her a lot."

He blushed as he said this.

She smiled and allowed him to help her to the car. Cassy was sure her mama would have something else to say, but she didn't. Just as Rosalie reached across to close the door, her mama said to Louis, "Take care of her for me."

"I'm not angry with my papa you know," said Cassy as Louis walked her home. "None of this is his fault." She laughed then. "I'm sorry Louis; you don't even know what I'm talking about. I found out that Eli was my mama's boy." She allowed herself to cry.

Chapter 12

Cassy didn't hold out any hope for her fifteenth year being any better than fourteenth. Her mama was dying. Rosalie took over the care of Hannah after Eli's funeral. Cassy found it hard to accept that she had to continue working at the mansion. She couldn't be there for her mama. Hannah had been sick for over a year now. She went to her bedroom to see was she asleep. Rosalie was fast asleep on her fold out bed. The drapes were closed, which bathed the room in darkness. The only light filtered in from the smoked glass window of the washroom, next to her mama's bedroom. She looked around at her mama's belongings. All the little things she collected over the years. Her closet door was open. It was easy to see each item of clothing she owned so little. She touched the edge of her bed and leaned in close to kiss her and Rosalie stirred.

"Papa is here," said Cassy.

"I know child. I let him in last night, a pitiful sight he was stood out on the porch in the rain…"

Cassy didn't want to hear anymore, so she went to

where he was in the kitchen.

He stood by the open door and looked out onto the courtyard. The charred remains of whatever it was he cooked were on the stove. Smoke rose from the cigarette he smoked. Every so often, he reached back inside to tip the ash into the sink. She hadn't seen him since Eli's funeral. His pants were frayed at the ends and his shirt hung out over his trousers.

"How are you, Cassy?" he asked without turning around.

She coughed partly, because of the smoke from his cooking and the cigarette.

"I cooked us some grits and bacon."

Cassy looked around to where he pointed. Sure enough, breakfast was set at the table.

"I bought some fresh juice down the market. It was busy this morning whatever was on."

She couldn't help but smile at this.

"They're always busy. Thanks papa. It smells good."

"I said it would be grand to have breakfast with my baby girl; seen as it's your last day being fourteen."

She sat down where he set a plate for her. She looked at the empty place where her mama always sat, next to the door. When he sat down to join her, she busied herself with eating.

"How is she this morning Cassy? I haven't seen her yet."

"Were you working all night papa?"

"I can't turn down the gigs when they come up. The bars they all seem to be staying open later and later, so it keeps me longer. Ah there she is. Rosa will you join us?"

Cassy looked at her aunt. She pulled out a seat and sat down.

"I'll have some if it's going," she said.

"Why sister, I thought you've already had yours," Amos chuckled.

Rosalie looked too tired to respond to him.

"A joke sis, a joke," he said as he plated her up a serving.

"I've to bring Hannah some water first," said Rosalie and went to stand up again. Amos gently touched her on the shoulder.

"I'll go."

"Cassy, sorry don't mind me," said her aunt.

"It's okay. It's hard to see her…"

Cassy found her words trail away. They all knew the time was close and she didn't feel like hearing it again.

They ate in silence. Amos returned to the kitchen.

"Go home when you're finished up Rosa and get

157

some rest. Cassy Belle and I are here. We'll see to her.

Isn't that right Cassy?"

Cassy nodded. He hadn't called her that in a long time. It brought back so many memories for her, of when she was a little girl and planned to be on stage one day and all the people would chant her name. She looked around the kitchen her papa built years before with some of the men in the neighborhood when he and Hannah first moved here. It was really only three walls, a tiny space for a window and a screen door. The roof was galvanized metal. Most days it was like a hot house and this morning was no exception. He leaned in to kiss her as she set about to wash the dishes. She looked out onto the courtyard. The tree he planted for her next to the magnolia tree was in full bloom. The neighbor's cat groomed herself under its shade. Outside it was another balmy New Orleans day.

Rosalie returned that evening. Cassy watched her aunt take the glass of water from her mama's clenched hands and prop her legs onto a pillow to keep the circulation going while she slept. The doctor had advised this. Amos sat opposite them. The drapes were partially open to let in some light from the street rather than the glare from a light in the room. Rosalie got up, touched her brother's arm, and went to bed in Cassy's room. Amos looked around their bedroom, where his wife lay dying in front of him. It had been a long time since he slept in here. Ever since the illness, it was Rosalie who stayed in with her on a fold out bed set up each night. Rosalie insisted there was no point in him disturbing Hannah when he came in at night, so it became the norm that he slept in Cassy's empty bed.

The cloth was still draped over the machine from the last time her mama sat here, which is months ago now. Cassy lifted it off and set up the needle to begin to sew. As she sewed, she smelled the cream she rubbed onto her mama's arms to help with the pain and tears welled up and blurred her vision. She sewed on into the night. As she sewed, she tried to remember a time when her mama wasn't sick. She thought of when it started here at this machine, her mama wiped her eyes and complained of tiredness. Cassy thought it was from working too hard. Then one evening when she was on her way back from the grocery store, she dropped her bags and all her groceries were on the street. Her arms had no strength in them. Her eyes were sunken into her head. It was only with Cassy's insistence that the doctor visited. She listened now as she sewed to the raspy sound of her mama's breathing while she slept. She wondered was her papa awake or asleep. Tomorrow she turned fifteen and the only thing she could think of was if her mama would see the morning.

Her whole body ached as she got up from the sofa. At some point during the night, she must have stopped sewing and fell asleep. A new day shone in through the windows. It was her fifteenth birthday. Her aunt was busy in the kitchen. She tip toed past the French doors and went directly to her mama's room. She wanted hers to be the first face she saw. There was an overturned glass of water on the nightstand, but she pretended not to notice. Cassy looked at her mama, her plump frame long gone replaced with the skeleton of the woman she once was. Her hair was thin and matted into her head. Her eyes were sunken. She sat up in bed and wore a little rouge Rosalie put on her, but it made her look like a fragile doll.

"Happy birthday baby," she whispered.

Rosalie came into the room and opened the drapes fully. Amos woke up and smiled on seeing her.

"Happy birthday Cassy," he said.

"Amos, Rosa will y'all help me to the front room. I want to enjoy my daughter's big day."

"Mama you don't have to."

"I want to, Cassy. Your papa agreed its fine. You don't mind Rosa?"

"I think it's a great idea," chimed in Rosalie.

When she was settled on the sofa, Hannah gave Cassy a card she had tucked away in her robe.

"Rosa helped me write it," she whezzed.

Then she handed Cassy a parcel from underneath her blanket.

"I wrapped this one myself. I've had it a long time. I was going to give it to you when you're older."

Everyone tried to ignore what this meant. Cassy took the parcel from her mama. Amos came back into the room. He looked shaven and more awake. She noticed his trousers and shirt looked new and his shoes shone.

"Open ours first Cassy. I think your mama's is special," said Amos. "First of all…"

He swept Cassy off her feet.

"Happy Birthday Cassy. Fifteen you aren't my baby no more. That's a song. How about we have a song?"

He looked around at Hannah seeking her approval. She was smiling watching the two of them. Rosalie sat down beside her.

"How about it Hannah? Let's hear the birthday girl sing," said Amos.

Cassy looked to her mama for approval. Her mama nodded. Cassy sang and her papa accompanied her on the harmonica.

When the song ended Amos said, "Come on into the kitchen. You can help me serve up breakfast for the ladies of the house."

161

He bowed and pretended to tip an imaginary hat to them.

They prepared the food together. Cassy watched him as he worked his way around the kitchen. They carried the food into the parlor.

"We'll eat as we give you your presents," said Rosalie. She was like an excited child. Rosalie handed her a small box tied with a bow. Cassy pulled open the bow to find a bottle of perfume inside. She sprayed some on and offered some to her Aunt and mama. Next was her papa's gift. He gave her a beautiful shawl. It was decorated with a print of a vine of flowers. Cassy wrapped it around her shoulders and pictured wearing it around The Quarter with Louis. Then Rosalie handed her her mama's gift. It was wrapped in shiny paper. As Cassy opened it she pictured her aunt wrapping it for her mama. Inside was a sheet of tissue paper tied with a blue bow. She smiled at her mama as she opened it.

"Come on," said her papa and hopped from foot to foot with excitement.

Cassy lifted out the most beautiful little dress she ever saw. It was a baby size, pure white with a tiny ribbon on the bodice.

"It was yours and Eli's," her mama whispered. "I

want you to have it to pass onto your baby and to remember me by."

Cassy knew her mama wouldn't see the birth of her firstborn, but when she clarified this, it upset her. Amos put his arm around his daughter.

"Let me see Cassy. I can remember the day your mama put you into that dress. You were so tiny and you cried and cried. We didn't know what to do with you. Isn't that right Han?"

Her mama nodded and smiled with the memory.

"I know it's not a gift for today, but I said you'll be meeting the girls in the neighborhood later; there'll be loads of presents bought for you. I wanted you to have..."

Her voice trailed off as a fit of coughing overtook her.

"Mama I wasn't planning on leaving you to go meet them," said Cassy.

"Go meet your friend's sweetie," answered Rosalie seeing how weak Hannah had become.

Rosalie reached for the array of medicines that sat on the shelf above the sewing machine. It was time for Hannah to take more pain relief and she would be asleep for the afternoon.

Rosalie went to help Hannah to her room, but Amos signaled to her that he would. Cassy watched her papa tenderly brush her mama's hair back off her face and carried her to her room. She remembered how he used to take her in his arms and the two of them would dance and Cassy as a young girl tried to join in and held onto her mama's dress. Amos closed the bedroom door and Cassy looked down at the cake. They never lit the candles. Hannah passed away that night surrounded by her family.

***

Some months had passed since Hannah's death. Rosalie was busy in the kitchen, but Cassy knew she could hear every word from where she stood behind the door. She had a towel in her hand for drying the glasses and was ready to run back to the sink should either of them come in.

"Please stop sewing," said Amos. "I can see the pressure you're under working here and for them. Do you think it's time you moved into the mansion?"

The way he said it, made Cassy stop what she was working on and look at him.

"It's different for me and Rosa, our chance is over."

There was a clatter in the kitchen as if Rosalie had walked into the table on her way back to the sink. Instead, she came into the room where they both were. Cassy felt her cheeks redden for her aunt.

"Your papa is right about one thing Cassy you don't

164

belong here."

"So do you think I should move into the mansion Rosalie?"

Her aunt looked to her papa, for permission to answer.

"Yes I do."

Her papa stood up and went to the window.

"I don't want you to send any money home. Rosalie tells me the rate is quite good, but I want you to save Cassy and use it to work towards your dreams."

Cassy stood up and found she spoke louder than she meant.

"Papa no, I will send money home."

"You don't need to Cassy. I'm making good money now over at the bar. I'm going to prove myself to them. Who knows maybe they will hear you sing one day. You and me, on the same stage together."

She dreamed along with him. Her papa's name was lost so many times from been found in doorways drunk and kicked out of places for gambling. At his lowest point, he was found stealing from one of the bars after a gambling night went wrong. She knew she would have to move into the mansion because, that is where she can gain more customers.

"You know your mama knew you had a voice Cassy.

She was just scared for you, that is all."

Rosalie rubbed her hands in her apron and knotted the ends of it anxiously, unsure of how Cassy would absorb what her papa just said.

"I'm not going to reach for the bottle to solve things again and I want you to know that when you move away that we'll be okay. All right that I will be okay. My sister is fine; you're always doing okay Rosalie."

Rosalie relaxed her hands.

"Yea sure, oh always," she said and winked at Cassy.

"Your mama saw sewing as a safe option for you. No, I am telling it wrong. She saw it as a way to give you a life."

"I know papa," said Cassy.

"She loved you, as did your brother."

Cassy didn't answer him. She wasn't sure if she could find her voice to speak. He shook his head, annoyed at his inability to convey all he wanted to say to his daughter.

"I wish she could know that I've turned it around now."

He looked from his daughter to his sister searching for an answer.

"Come on I've prepared dinner, your favorite; gumbo and grits. And for dessert it's pecan pie," said Rosalie.

Amos put his arm around his daughter's shoulder as

they went into the kitchen.

"I must have been good to deserve pecan pie."

"Sure must pops."

"Rosalie, do you still go to that church over on Governor Nicholls Street?"

Rosalie was mid a mouthful of gumbo. She set her fork back down on the plate.

"I do," she said.

"Well I do, we do now too. We're going to join you Sunday. How about it Cassy? You up for a little church?"

"I already go there papa," Cassy laughed.

"Right settled then, we'll all go tomorrow. I need a little God in my life, just a little now mind."

They continued eating in silence and enjoyed the meal. The radio played in the background. A jazz tune belted out by some singer.

"I sing in the choir in church papa," said Cassy.

She reached for more grits and busied herself with plating up more food waiting for his answer.

"Not the big stage I have in mind for you, baby."

"Oh hush now Amos, the child got to start somewhere, ain't that right Cassy?"

This was the last time for a while she would sit down to have a meal with them. It felt real, leaving everything she has known her entire life; to move into the mansion.

Chapter 13

Cassy's workload had expanded throughout The Garden District. Her papa telling her it was okay she moved, helped her to leave home. The last time she saw Louis, was at her mama's funeral, before he left for law school. She decided to go to Congo Square one last time. Her papa offered to come with her, but she needed to go alone. It was at the square she had her last conversation with Eli. There was part of her wanted to stay here with her papa, but she couldn't refuse the work at the Le Blanc's mansion. Cassy felt a responsibility towards the women she sewed for and for now, this replaced her need to sing.

It wasn't long before life in the mansion took over. With each passing day, she felt her dream of becoming a singer slip away. She told no one about it. Her room was tiny, which she shared with Jo Lynn. Cassy rarely saw her ,because she was called a lot to work in other parts of the house. Her only reprieve from her solitary existence was to take the back stairs from her bedroom and go to the kitchen. Grace was always cooking and baking and was always happy to chat. Another girl named Anna who started the same time as Cassy was there too, but she wouldn't even look in Cassy's direction never mind speak to her. Patty on the other hand, when she came in from the dining room was always giddy and ready for the chat. Grace kept her busy when she wasn't in the dining room under William's watchful eye. Grace and William were a comfort to Cassy; they had an easy way about them. Jimmy on the other hand always gave Cassy a look when he saw her. He probably saw her as Beth's accomplice. She knew it was easy for anyone to make that mistake, that her and Beth were friends. Beth never came to the kitchen to eat with the other staff. In truth, Cassy's only confidante here was Jacob. She often took a break from being hunched over the sewing machine and went out to the garden to speak to him. It gave her comfort to see him busy at work and she envied him, outside away from the atmosphere of the house. He seemed free. She didn't feel free. She felt trapped in this new life.

One time when she went outside to see Jacob, she sensed someone watch her. Jacob went to one of the outhouses to retrieve something. At first, she thought she saw a dark shadow from behind the cypress tree, but a filter of light blocked her vision when Jacob came towards her with a pane of glass.

"What is that for Jacob?" she asked.

"Oh Miss Shaw you startled me," said Jacob.

Cassy rushed to help him with the glass. Together they carried it across the lawn.

"See, someone smashed a pane of glass in the library last night."

Cassy saw something move out of the corner of her eye. A shadow from behind the outhouse closest to them.

"That be Master Le Blanc."

"I haven't met him yet," said Cassy as she looked towards the outhouse again.

"If you don't mind me saying Miss..."

"Cassy, please Jacob."

"Okay Cassy. That ain't a bad thing."

For some reason unknown to herself, she didn't feel to ask him what he meant by that. A chill ran up her spine when she saw Mr. Le Blanc stare in her direction as he crossed the lawn, headed in the direction of the house. She felt the coldness travel up her spine and land on her shoulder, in a cold damp clasp.

***

The second floor was as long as the eye could see. There were rooms beyond the periphery of her vision that she had no reason to go to, but she wondered about them. Sometimes she heard a whimpering sound. It sounded like a child. One night she was sure she heard the cry of a newborn, but she'd wake up to silence and the light changed under her doorframe as if someone stood there and then walked away. She was no longer able to sleep until Jo Lynn returned to the room for the night, which was often late. She and Beth were the last to finish up for the night. They checked on the fires in both the library and the dining room. The stove in the kitchen was lit all night, because Grace would be up at five to bake the bread for the day. It was the hours between midnight and morning light that the mansion seemed to come to life in a strange way. Cassy often sewed on into the night in order to keep on top of her orders for customers. The hum of her sewing machine drowned out whatever was going on in the house. Her papa gave her a little radio to take with her when she left home. She listened to the one channel she could tune in on that played jazz. She kept the window and door closed when she listened to it.

Later that night as she went to sleep she was overcome by homesickness. She lay there thinking of her papa and Rosalie. Memories of her mama came to her as she drifted off to sleep. Some would be jealous of her back home in Treme and believed her to be living a life most of them longed for, but all Cassy wanted to do was sing. She was disturbed by a noise. Her papa told her never to let a fear grow so big in your head without knowing what it is you're afraid of, always go investigate it. She pulled a gap in her drapes to look out. One of the lights on the front porch wasn't lit. Jacob meticulously lit them each evening, so it struck her unusual that one of them wasn't. There it was again a scratching sound. She leaned over and looked down to the lawn below. The house cat ran across the lawn, but that wasn't it. There was someone stood underneath the broken lantern. Cassy jumped back quickly from the window.

Just then, Jo Lynn burst into the room.

"They're sending some of us to the plantation tomorrow. I just heard Patty talking with William on the stairs."

"Are you sure that's what they said?"

"They stopped me and Patty, said it could be any of us."

"To "Maison Belle", are you sure Jo?"

"And another thing I heard that girl Violet, you know the one who worked here before any of us? Well they say she was raped by the master; and hasn't worked here since."

Cassy stood a step back towards the bed.

"That can't be true, Jo. You must have heard wrong."

"Well if it is true I pray I'm sent to the plantation than stay here."

"Come on now hush and let's see what tomorrow brings. We've only just started here. I can't see them sending any of us away."

Cassy wasn't sure she convinced Jo Lynn, because she knew she didn't believe it herself.

Jo Lynn settled down into bed and fell asleep straight away. Cassy lay awake for ages and decided she wouldn't be getting to sleep tonight so she got up to sew.

The lights of cars flashed across the ceiling. Cassy looked out to see a row of cars drive up the driveway. There was the sound of voices, then silence. She continued sewing. She leaned across and looked out the window. She switched off the light on her machine and took her foot off the pedal. Nothing could have prepared her for what she saw. Cloaked shapes got out of their parked cars, walked up the gravel drive, and crossed the lawn. They were headed towards the rear of the house, but instead of walking around by the staff entrance, they walked past the library windows. Cassy's bedroom was above the library as were many of the rooms on this floor, such was the length of the room. She pulled back a little, even though the lace sheers kept her from view. Jo Lynn woke up.

"What are you looking at?" she hissed.

"Nothing go back to sleep. I thought I saw something that is all. It's nothing."

There was no way she was going to tell Jo Lynn what she saw. She knew about The Klan, but this was different they all wore black robes and she could see their faces. She couldn't see them now, because her view was blocked by one of the columns of the house. She looked at the rail filled with clothes ready to be delivered to some of the women in the morning. She looked away again, down at the doorframe, and could see the light grow dark outside and then become bright again.

The next morning as Jo Lynn had said they were summoned to the library. When they got there, they saw all the new members of staff gathered also. The door closed behind them. One of the sheers moved and settled again as someone came in from the verandah. Cassy drew her breath when she saw him. Jo Lynn saw Cassy's reaction and looked in the direction of the window. He stood and faced the fire. He turned around. His eyes pierced Cassy as if he could see her very soul. Madame Le Blanc was sat in the chair next to the fire. He sat down in the one opposite her. He had a small smile on his face, as if amused by his wife's state. She was drunk again. The door opened and another man walked towards them. He was a younger version of their employer. He spoke first.

"Well thank you for gathering here. I know y'all must be busy with your duties, but I wanted to introduce myself.

I'm Robert Le Blanc, the youngest son and this is my soon to be wife Olivia. Olivia darling please come forward."

There was a separation in the staff as they made room for his fiancé to come to where he stood. She had long flowing curls, which tumbled down her back. She wore a green dress, which fitted her perfectly. Cassy could tell it was cut from the finest fabric. Around her neck, she wore a choker made from a string of pearls, but at its centre was the most elaborate jewel.

"Olivia and I reside in "Maison Belle", that is the family plantation for any of you not aware."

Cassy heard Jimmy mutter, "Family palace more like."

"The reason I am here today is we're looking for some staff to join us. My father has kindly said I could choose from y'all first."

Cassy stood back a little so she was now behind Grace and Jo Lynn.

"So let's see mother, who do we have?"

All the staff waited for Madame Le Blanc's response. She stood up. Mr. Le Blanc looked away when she struggled to her feet.

"You can take all of them for all I care," she slurred.

Cassy couldn't comprehend being so far away on the family plantation. It was over on the River Road. She would never get to see her papa she knew it.

"But you cannot take my cook or my seamstress."

"And which ones are they?"

Grace stepped forward. "I'm the cook sir and Cassy here she be the seamstress. Madame and all the ladies of the district be lost without her work."

Cassy felt relieved.

"If she is so good maybe Olivia would have some use for her."

"The girl stays here," said Madame.

"So, how about you then? William isn't it?"

"Yes sir."

"You'd be a fine farmhand."

"That is no farmhand son. He runs the dining room and I won't be without him."

"Now, now mother. You still have Jeffery is it?"

"Jimmy," said Jimmy all pleased with himself.

"Yes you have Jimmy here. William will leave with Olivia and me today, along with you and you."

He pointed out two other members of staff that Cassy had seen on that first day, but not since.

"Olivia you need a maid, a personal maid for yourself."

"Is she pregnant?" asked his mother.

Cassy saw the look on Olivia's face. Robert touched

his fiance's arm.

"Now my dear take your pick, though I'll admit there is not much left."

Olivia didn't even speak as she pointed in the direction of Jo Lynn. Jo Lynn surprised Cassy by taking her hand behind her back.

Mr. Le Blanc stood up. He towered over his son. Beth was busy helping Madame from the room. Robert thanked them and left with his wife.

"I think that is settled then. Y'all can leave," said Mr. Le Blanc. Cassy felt every inch of her body being taken in by him, as he looked her over. She was marked by him, chosen and she knew this mansion had only so many places to hide, only some much staff to fill it. She was in a room of her own now and he would find it.

Cassy was moved to a room in the same part of the house as Beth. She hadn't seen this area of the house up to now. It was a separate corridor from the main hall, hidden behind a white paneled door. The door looked like it was part of the wall. Cassy watched Beth pull it back. She hesitated on following her inside.

"Come on Cassy. Don't look so shocked, it's only a door."

This part of the house even smelled different. It was very distinct, but she couldn't place what it was.

177

"That's all Madame's orchids, you see lining the windows."

Sure enough, there was a long corridor in front of Cassy with many rooms and dividing each room from the next was a long paneled window. On each window ledge was an orchid. Cassy could see the steps at the main entrance to the front of the house from here. She stopped and stared at it.

"That's probably you're first time seeing that," said Beth.

"Yeah," said Cassy as she took it in. She hadn't noticed the statues on either side of the porch on her way here that first day, which seems like such a long time ago. They looked like wingless angels. Their stone stillness was haunting. In front of them were the two planters. The double door into the house gleamed in the early morning light. It looked like it was made of marble. She counted seven pillars that she could see at the front of the house. They were the thickness of some of the magnolia trees that lined the drive. She could see her former bedroom hidden behind one of them.

"This is my room Cassy," said Beth as she opened the door.

Cassy followed her inside. It was painted a pale blue and was simply furnished. There was a desk by the window and against the wall opposite a single bed with a desk. There was a stand next to the bed with some books. Cassy couldn't imagine Beth ever having the time to read them. As if Beth could read her thoughts she said, "It's simple, but then again I only sleep here and some nights I don't even do that. No rest for the wicked, eh?"

Cassy looked around the room. Behind the door, she could see another door that led into a small toilet area with a bath tub. Next to the bathroom door and hiding part of the second window was a closet.

"It's practically empty except for my uniforms. I keep everything at home. It helps not to feel like you've moved your whole life here."

This made Cassy turn around and look at her in the face. Beth didn't acknowledge her reaction at all.

"Come on; let's go to your room."

A breeze of air brushed past Cassy as she walked to the door. She shivered.

"Did you…" She stopped herself.

She had been told the house was haunted. Beth opened the door and waited out in the hall for her. She walked towards another door further down on the left. When Beth opened the door, Cassy saw the narrow bed next to the window. The drapes had a heavy floral pattern on them. Even her Aunt Rosalie would find them dated.

There was a trunk at the end of the bed. Beth followed her gaze around the room.

"That trunk contains all your fabrics. I had them moved in here for you."

She talked fast as if she didn't want Cassy to interrupt her.

"Here's your closet. I know it's small, but you could always use this as well," she said and pointed to a clothes rail.

Beth walked into the room, which adjoined the bedroom and beckoned Cassy to come in. It had a workstation with Cassy's sewing machine all set up.

"Jimmy moved it down from your room. I wanted it ready for you to move in. You had no space up in that shoebox upstairs. Look at the light you have with that window."

Cassy considered Jimmy in here going through her things. She looked behind the door and saw a mannequin.

"I wanted to make the room more homely for you. I found this up on the third floor."

Cassy never had one of these to work with. Her mama certainly never had one either.

"The ladies you'll be working for will want their pieces perfectly tailored. Not saying they all fit this dress size. Look at her waist it's tiny."

The two of them burst out laughing.

"Couldn't see many of us girls back home fitting the size you'll be making. Not if your mama's gumbo and rice had anything to do with it."

Cassy looked at the ground. The mention of her mama here stung her more than she thought it would, but she warmed to this rare glimpse of the Beth she knew.

"You'll spend so much time here. I figured it was a good room," continued Beth.

If she noticed Cassy's discomfort, she chose to ignore it. Cassy nodded and looked around the small workroom. There was ample light, more than upstairs that was true. Beth went back into the bedroom. Cassy followed her.

"They like to be like the French ladies," said Beth in her familiar superior tone.

She pulled back the drapes, which revealed a door out to the garden. Cassy allowed herself to be carried along with this new life.

"When you go to the kitchen at meal times, take the garden, past the outhouses. It will lead you to a path; follow it to the porch which will bring you to the kitchen."

"Can I not walk through the house?"

"What, walk through the main hall each time?"

Cassy felt her cheeks redden.

181

Beth noticed her discomfort and corrected herself, "If it's any consolation every time I pass through the main hall I get summoned by Madame. Well not every time, but you know what I mean. Be thankful."

Those last words stayed with Cassy, as she was left alone.

A sound came from the room next door. She never asked Beth if anyone occupied the other rooms, although she thought Beth said they were the only ones in this part of the house. She looked outside and saw a figure stood by the cypress tree. Whoever it was walked towards the nearest outhouse. They wore a long coat, but she couldn't see their face. She drew the drapes even though a net covered the window. She looked at her reflection in the free standing mirror behind the door to her sewing room. She looked tired and went over to lie down on the bed. There was a screen to dress behind, tucked behind the closet. She decided she'd move that into the other room tomorrow for the women when they were here for fittings. She stared at the oriental pattern on the screen, so out of place to everything else in the room. There was a gap in the drapes. She mumbled to herself that she should close it, but she drifted off to sleep.

Cassy awoke with a start. Her breath came low and shallow and she held it to try to stop it being so loud. Part of her wanted to hide underneath the bedclothes, but she needed to know where that crying was coming from. Her nightdress clung to her with the sweat. When she got

out of bed, she could feel the damp sheets under her. The room was unfamiliar to her as she made her way in the dark. She stood by the door and watched the handle turn slowly.

"Who is it?" she called out.

"It's me. It's me."

She recognized Beth's voice.

"Are you alone?"

"Yes let me in," demanded Beth.

Cassy could hear the desperation in her voice, while her own breathing settled a little. She waited for Beth to open the door.

"Cassy, where are you?"

"I'm right here," said Cassy as she closed the door behind Beth.

Beth held a torch down by her side, its light lit up both their feet. She raised it towards the windows.

"It's coming from out there," she pointed.

Cassy looked at Beth's long nightgown, head to foot in white with her usually tied up hair in a plait over her shoulder. She shone the torch again at the window.

"I hope you locked that door earlier?"

She didn't wait for Cassy to answer and ran across the room, a blur of white, the torch danced as she ran the short distance. Cassy felt her heart thump in her chest.

"What is it?" she demanded.

The porch lights across the lawn came on and whatever way Beth stood in the doorway she looked more ghost like than human, illuminated in the half-light.

"I thought I saw someone," said Beth and shook her head in confusion.

She walked over and sat down on the trunk at the end of the bed. Her breathing was shallow. Cassy looked out across the lawn at a part of the house she hadn't seen until now. This area overlooked the neighbor's backyard though it was some distance away. The trees kept their house hidden. Beyond the cypress tree, she could see the roof of one of the outhouses. There was a light on.

"What are they used for?"

Beth didn't answer her.

Cassy looked around to see was she still there.

"The outhouses. What are they used for?"

"They were the old servants quarters Cassy."

"You mean the old slave dwellings surely," said Cassy, but Beth didn't lift her head when she said this. Her entire body was hunched over as if in pain.

Cassy lifted back one of the nets to get a closer

184

look.

"It's Jacob."

"What?" asked Beth and looked up. This surprised Cassy to see her come back to herself so quickly.

"Yes, he was on the porch. He lit the gas lanterns. He's gone back around to the kitchen now."

"Are you sure?"

"Yes why?"

But before Beth could answer, there was an unmerciful scream. It came from the direction of the outhouses. The one closest to them was in darkness, but in the distance light lanced across the lawn.

"It's happening again," said Beth, buried her hands in her face, and cried.

Cassy couldn't tell which horrified her more the scream that pierced the night air or to see Beth break down and cry. Beth dropped the torch to the floor. Cassy watched it snuff out from the fall. She dropped the drapes, not sure, she wanted to know what Beth meant. She knew this house had history and some of its ghosts had never left.

"Philip finished with me tonight."

Cassy had to think who Philip was.

"You don't know him. He doesn't work here. He works for…well it doesn't matter where he works. We

185

were going to be married."

"I'm sorry. What happened if you don't mind me asking?"

"He met someone else. I don't know why I'm telling you that. I don't even know why I'm here."

Cassy wanted to reassure for, but she was at a loss as to what to say. Instead, she confided in her about Louis.

"There is something I want to tell you too," whispered Cassy.

Beth stopped crying and stared at her, briefly distracted from her own problems.

"I'm in love,with Louis. We love each other. We used to meet in secret, at St. Louis Cathedral while I was still living at home. It was the only place we could meet without been seen."

Beth looked horrified and Cassy wondered had she made a mistake in trusting her.

"You mean to say you were with Louis Le Blanc."

"We love each other."

Beth said nothing for a long time.

"Cassy, what you just told me you mustn't tell anyone else."

"I know that," said Cassy trying to hide how hurt she felt.

"I shouldn't have come here tonight. And you shouldn't have told me what you did.

 You might never see him again."

Beth walked towards the window.

"Beth, would you get a letter to him?"

"Cassy, I can't have any part in this. You know I can't. Besides who knows when he'll be home. Madame would…well I don't know what Madame would do if she knew about this. And as for Master Le Blanc, well that's just another story. They would never condone a relationship between their son and a black girl."

With that, she went to the door.

"I'm sorry I should never have come in here. Forget you saw me Cassy and don't mention this night to anyone. And for goodness sake lock your door."

"I didn't know I had a key," said Cassy sullenly.

Beth handed her the key from a hook and left the room.

Chapter 14

The events of the night before remained with Cassy as she left her room. The outhouses looked less ominous in the early morning light. This route meant she had to walk past his study every day. The lace sheers were so full she couldn't see in, but as she passed the first of the full-length windows, she saw a shadow.

As she walked the length of the house, she felt the shadow follow her. She quickened her step and stepped off the cobble path onto the lawn.

She stopped when she saw Beth approach her. Cassy wondered why she was out here at this hour.

"Cassy I was looking for you."

"I was in my room Beth. It's only eight."

Beth ignored her.

"Madame has asked to see you in the library."

She acted like nothing had happened the night before.

"Now?" asked Cassy. She was hungry and wasn't sure could she withstand an encounter with Madame on an empty stomach.

"Of course not. She won't be up yet. Be sure you're there for nine. I meant to tell you yesterday."

Beth didn't wait for her to answer. She turned the corner at the rear of the house and headed in the direction of the kitchen.

"Good morning Miss Shaw," said a voice from behind her.

"Jacob, Good morning."

He appeared from behind one of the rose bushes.

Once she moved to the same part of the house as Beth many of the staff, practically all of them changed towards her, except Jacob. He was a welcome sight with the morning sun behind him. The grey coat he always wore over a shirt was soaked through with sweat.

"How goes it?" he asked.

"I've to meet Madame in the library."

He nodded and looked in the direction of the house. She was sure his face clouded over.

"What they want with you Miss Shaw?"

"I don't know."

"Will you join me for some lemonade before you go Cassy?"

She looked at him with that big smile on his face.They walked past the rose bushes and in the direction of the glass house. The lawn dipped as they walked and put the house in even more of an elevated position.

"Here you might as well earn your lemonade," he said as he pointed to a rose bush in the wheelbarrow.

She picked up the bag filled with soil and carried it for him. She set it down where he showed her on the counter.

"It's a rare one Miss Shaw. Look at its buds. I don't know if you can see, but it's going to be orange and yellow, a beautiful mix of colors. Cassy looked around at all the plants. She recognized some from the courtyard at home; though there were varieties here, she had never seen.

"That's Camellia, Miss Shaw and that be Jasmine," he said as he poured her a glass of lemonade.

He concentrated hard as he poured and she pretended not to notice when his hand shook.

"Why is that rose bush not outside like the others?"

"It's in here till it gets strong enough to withstand outside."

He stopped what he was doing, wiped his hands in a towel, and poured himself some lemonade. Cassy looked down into her glass.

"You be like me Miss Shaw, you don't mind me saying."

"Jacob, call me Cassy," she said.

He continued to plant the rose bush.

"You say you fine, but your eyes tell a whole other

190

story."

She didn't know how to tell him that she missed her mama and that she wanted to be a singer like those jazz singers she listens to on the radio while she sews. She didn't mean to tear up in front of him, but the tears flowed. He set down his glass and placed his arm around her shoulder. Grace had told her there had been an accident and his wife was killed along with their daughter. She stopped talking when some of the other staff came into the kitchen and Cassy never asked her about it again.

"You'll get to see your family soon Cassy," he said.

She wondered when that time would come.

"It's just my papa and my aunt lives with him. I lost my mama."

"I understand," he said.

She stepped away and apologized for the outburst.

"Cassy, no one can ever take our memories."

"You best get on Cassy. You don't need any trouble from them."

"Jacob can a place change you?"

She waited for him to answer. He looked like he chewed over his words before he spoke them.

"This be a strange place, Cassy. I see things, strange things, but I tell no one and that is how I survive. You be careful and trust none of them."

191

He sighed. She couldn't tell if she had upset him.

"Can I tell you something Jacob?"

"Of course child."

"Louis and I we're a couple. Not in the traditional sense. We used to meet in secret."

Jacob set his glass of lemonade down on the counter.

"Did any of them know this do you think?"

"I'm certain no one did."

"It's best you tell no one else this. Louis, he nothing like any of them. I've known that boy since he was a baby. You get on now. It's quarter to nine."

She left him pottering around the glass house and made her way back up the embankment. A million things ran through her mind all unanswered. As she looked up at the mansion in front of her, she could never picture getting used to its grandeur.

"Cassy, will you try some of my bread, it's a new recipe?" asked Grace as she came into the kitchen.

"Good morning Grace. I have to go see Madame."

Grace turned around and busied herself at the stove, as if the mere mention of Madame was enough to send her into submission. Cassy caught sight of Beth as she crossed the hall. She was talking to one of the housekeeping staff who was busy cleaning the portraits that lined the hall. Cassy stood back and waited for her to leave. As she waited she saw a picture of Louis, but it didn't hang with the others. It was under the stairs. It seemed hidden away from the rest of the family portraits that went back generations.

"That is Louis, the eldest of the master's son," said the girl as she cleaned the banisters. "He went to law school."

"I know," answered Cassy, distracted by his smile in the frame.

"I heard," she corrected herself.

"I'm Mary."

She was one of the older members of staff. Cassy couldn't help but notice, she seemed frail as she bent down to clean the lower part of the banisters. Her grey hair was hidden under her hat and she was swamped by the large apron around her waist.

"I'm Cassy."

"I know you be the mistress' seamstress."

"I am for the rest of the house too, if you need any sewing."

She just smiled in response. She looked at the picture again and a dark expression came over her.

"He was the only good 'un that came out of this house, this family."

"He was?" Cassy tried not to show her interest.

"Well Cassy I can't see him coming back to this

house. I have it on good authority he wanted to drop out of law school. He loves books you see. I think he wants to do something with books."

"And his brother?" asked Cassy. She had to get the subject off Louis.

"Well he is like his father; a ruthless man. Mr. Le Blanc, and Robert learn to be like him."

"Doesn't Violet normally work with you?"

"I am capable on my own you know," she said and looked around her as if to be sure no one listened. "Did you not hear?"

Cassy shook her head and felt her palms sweat.

"Violet is gone. She was sent away."

"You mean to the plantation like the others?"

"Oh no Cassy. You had better go. She's stood in the door for you."

Cassy looked around to see who she was talking about. Sure enough, Beth stood at the French doors to the library.

When she entered the library, Beth stood over by the window next to Jimmy at the drinks cabinet. Cassy dared not look at him with that constant amused look on his face. It was enough to face Madame without an audience. He fixed a drink and brought it to where Madame sat in her usual seat beside the hearth. The embers from last night's fire still lingered. Cassy was relieved it wasn't lit. The humidity was high today. Jimmy returned to the drinks cabinet and stood like a statue. Beth left the room and went out onto the verandah. Something stirred at the drapes. Cassy thought it was Beth had changed her mind and came in again. There was a purring sound. It was that scrawny cat she had sighted a few times out on the grounds. She lay down at Cassy's feet and cleaned her coat.

"Sit down girl," said Madame. She was clearly drunk.

Jimmy refilled her now empty glass. Madame sat back down in her chair with a drunken smile, satisfied they were all here to help her.

"You will be my personal seamstress from now on. No more sewing for your own kind."

Jimmy's hands shook a little as he poured a glass of water for Cassy from the jug of water on the table in front of her. Cassy reached out to help him before the glass smashed to the floor. He lost that constant amused look on his face and held her gaze as if to silently thank her.

"You will sew for me and the ladies from the other mansions and nobody else. Is that understood?"

With that, Madame stood up, walked close to the fire, and leaned against the mantelpiece. Cassy looked at her dress; it was a dark blue with lace detail around the cuffs. This matched the lace at her collar, which covered her neck in a billow of lace. The same style of buttons on the cuffs was on the front of the dress. She wore white gloves, which stopped at her wrists. They were black at the tips from smoking. Beth told Cassy Madame smoked in here on her own at night as she waited for Mister Le Blanc to return. Most evenings he never showed.

Beth returned from outside. She stood at Madame's chair.

"Madame, the ladies are outside now. I had tea brought from the kitchen and Grace has prepared enough pastries for a feast."

Madame turned around and considered what Beth had said.

"Let's go to the verandah then," she said with a great sweep of her hand.

Cassy stood up as she passed her. The smell of liquor from her was palpable. She could see the women as Beth held back the drapes for Madame. Their chatter silenced as they greeted her. Cassy took in the pastel weakness of their dresses with their hair combed up high into fancy styles. The smell of coffee and the sight of Grace's pastries struck her all piled up high on the cake stand in the center of the table. The pastel tablecloth matched what they wore, just blending them all together; except for one woman that stood out from amongst them. She wore a brown dress, with her hair partially up. It was shorter than the others. When Cassy stepped outside, she saw it was Miss Brown. She remembered the day she met her with Eli. If she recognized Cassy, she didn't show it.

"Ladies, there is someone I'd like y'all to meet, Miss Cassy Shaw. Cassy is my seamstress and has been solely my seamstress for some time. The poor girl must be bored with the amount of dresses I need made up."

To this, all the ladies laughed.

"So Cassy I'd like you to meet Mrs. Whim, Mrs. Sly, Miss La Beouf and Miss Brown."

They all looked in her direction from over the rim of their teacups. The powder from the pastries dusted across their painted faces. One of them Mrs. Whim even shook her hand, but it was like a slippery fish, gone before she could catch it. Miss Brown reached out to shake her hand, firm and reassuring and she had recognition in her eye.

"Miss Shaw wanted to be a singer, but her mother; a hard working woman had the common sense to direct her in her own path. She didn't want her daughter to get above her station as a person of color if you know my meaning ladies."

Cassy felt she mocked her by calling her Miss Shaw and talking about her singing.

"She has yet to meet my husband," she laughed.

Cassy noticed the reaction amongst the women at this.

"But I know Anton will approve of her," she said again with a laugh.

Cassy wanted to remind her that she had met him that day in the library when some of the staff were moved to the plantation. She decided against it and remained silent. Cassy saw her employer's eyes glaze over when she spoke of her husband, but it could be the drink either.

Beth pulled out a chair for Madame to sit down.

"Frances, can we see a sample of the work she has done for you?" asked the woman introduced as Mrs. Sly.

"Of course, actually I suggest y'all go to her with your orders and she'll get to work immediately."

"Are you taking orders today?" asked the youngest of the women, Miss La Beouf. "I have a ball coming up and I need to look my best."

"We're going to that too aren't we Mrs. Whim?" asked Mrs. Sly.

"We sure are. Yes I think we'll come over today."

"It's settled then, no better time than the present. How about you Miss Brown?"

"I'm not going to the ball, y'all are going to," said Miss Brown.

"Miss Brown, I honestly think that is why you have

no husband. You need to come to these events with us ladies," said Madame Le Blanc.

"Will Mr. Le Blanc be home to go?" asked Miss La Beouf; to which she got a swift kick under the table from Mrs. Whim.

"What she means is, y'all very busy," said Mrs. Sly.

"Cassy, I do have something I need a dress for, I forgot. If y'all don't mind it's a special request, so I will go first," said Miss Brown.

A silence fell upon the women, except Madame who rose to her feet.

"That is fantastic Lottie."

One of the staff came out and whispered something into Beth's ear; she leaned across and relayed whatever it was to her employer.

"Ladies, let's move into the dining room."

One by one, they followed her through the door adjacent to the library and into the dining room, except Miss Brown.

"You're probably surprised to see me," said Miss Brown as she followed Cassy to her room.

Cassy didn't speak until they were at her room. She opened her bedroom door and went into her sewing room.

"I met you that day when I delivered to your house on St. Peter Street," said Cassy.

"My father left that house for me. I moved in when I left the convent."

"The convent?" asked Cassy.

"I suppose if this is going to work I have to be honest with you. My papa is from here, but my mama was black. She was sent to "Madonna House" to have me, but she died. The nuns kept me."

"You were in "Madonna House"? I thought you just taught there."

"See I stayed on, as I had nowhere else to go and taught the girls. It's not as if I was sent there to have an unwanted child. I was the unwanted child. My father could afford to keep the nuns silent."

Cassy sat down.

"Do you mind if I sit down?" asked Miss Brown. "The heat in here. This room is like a glass house."

"How was it for my mama back then?"

"She had her baby, Eli and was forced to hand him over to your aunt like all the rest."

Cassy was thrown on hearing his name. She'd managed to busy herself with her work and put thoughts of him aside.

"Did he know about you when we came to see you?"

"If you don't mind me saying Cassy, Eli had enough going on without worrying about the past. I knew him through music. He told me about the gang that...well ultimately killed him."

"How are you accepted here? I mean, you're an equal with those other ladies."

"I taught piano to their children. Well any of them that could play."

"I don't want to seem rude," said Cassy as she fidgeted with some fabric. "You look black."

This made Miss Brown burst out laughing. She became serious then.

"You're right I do, but my papa was Mr. Quinn. After your employers they were a very affluent family in New Orleans."

"He owned practically everywhere," replied Cassy.

"Well not quite, but yes he had a lot of businesses in the city. Anyway come on we didn't come here to discuss me."

"Sorry, yes of course. Have you a color in mind for the dress you want to wear?"

"Sweetie, I didn't come here to talk about fabric with you. As I told you, I don't do "ladies who lunch". I'm here for a very specific purpose and that is you."

"I don't understand."

"I want you for my music hall Cassy Shaw. I want to make you a singer. Well not me, but I know a man who

201

can. Mr. Godfrey. He's a music executive from New York. He's coming to New Orleans and he's going to hear you sing."

"But you haven't even heard me sing," spluttered Cassy.

Miss Brown stood up then.

"That's not exactly true. I came to Eli's funeral. I heard you sing. I knew then you had talent and your aunt knew it too. Only Jessie ended up on the cruise ships. I don't want to lose you to those. I want you to sing right here in New Orleans."

"You were at Eli's funeral?"

Miss Brown nodded.

"I was also at your mama's. I was sorry to hear about her. Hannah was the best seamstress at "Madonna House." Heck she was the best seamstress this town had. However, Cassy, that's not where your destiny lies. You were born to sing and I'm going to help you."

"My aunt said you would come."

" Jessie and I used to practice together. That was long before she left for the ships. Long before, she got all above herself. Don't let that happen you Cassy, that is ugly. Even so she sees something in you."

"So you would have known Eli then as a boy."

"Sorry Cassy I didn't mean to talk about this."

"No it's okay. I know she had no choice but to take him, as my mama had no choice but to hand him over to her. It's done now."

She didn't mean to make Miss Brown feel awkward so she changed the subject.

"When did you leave the convent Miss Brown?"

"I never really left. I still go back. Once you've grown up somewhere, well its home. However, I couldn't continue teaching, because music is my soul's home. Now please call me Lottie."

"Lottie, how come your name is Brown, if your father was Henry Quinn?"

"That's a fair question. When I moved to the convent, I took my mama's name. The nuns never objected, but when speaking to my father they referred to me as Quinn. It was funny sometimes I forgot who they were talking about. Not that he ever visited. He'd ring to check up on me, but that stopped eventually. So I became Miss Brown, but Lottie to you."

Cassy listened to her as she told her the plan she had for the music hall. How the other ladies judged her for having no husband, but included her, because she was a Quinn.

"How will I be able to come to the audition? I barely know when I'll be able to get home again, never mind get

203

to the audition."

"You sure ask a lot of questions. Don't worry I have it all arranged. You need to deliver garments to your customer's right?"

"They mostly have their staff come to collect them."

"Okay let me think…fabric. You'll need to buy fabric."

"The trunk at the end of my bed is full of fabric."

"I've got it. Thread, needles. Only a seamstress would know her tools. They're not going to contradict you about what you need. Supplies! You'll need supplies," she said with a rush of enthusiasm.

"When is the audition?" asked Cassy.

She felt the optimism that she had some time ago return to her.

"Next week, February 10. An easy date to remember it's the start of Mardi Gras."

"What if I impress them?" said Cassy.

She clasped her hand over her mouth, a bit embarrassed by her confidence.

"I know you will. I'll be there to accompany you on the piano. Now let's pick out a dress for me."

"I thought you didn't need one."

"I don't, but I'd like to see your sewing skills for myself," she laughed.

"Lottie, can I tell you something?" asked Cassy though she didn't wait for an answer.

"I was seeing Louis."

"You mean Louis, their son," said Miss Brown barely able to hide her shock.

"Yes, before he left for law school. It was before I moved in here. We used to meet at St. Louis Cathedral and we'd go to Café du Monde for coffee and beignets."

"Girl, you talking like a fool."

Cassy blushed.

Miss Brown held Cassy's arms as she spoke, "Do you know what would happen to you if they ever found out?"

"They won't," said Cassy and freed herself her from her grip.

"I'm sorry Cassy. I shouldn't have grabbed you like that. Who else knows this?"

"No one. I ain't telling anybody."

"Good, keep it that way."

"I know he loves me Lottie. He told me."

"That not for me to say, but I'd be wrong if I didn't warn you.

I want you to promise me you'll make the audition."

"I will Miss Brown. I'm sorry."

"No child, don't ever be sorry for love. But you have to think of yourself for now. Remember February 10 is your first meeting with Mr. Godfrey. Just think of Mardi Gras."

Miss Brown gathered up her bag and left the room. The only sound Cassy heard was the hum of the sewing machine as she worked and dreamed.

Chapter 15

Everything changed for Cassy from that day on. She felt she was working towards something, that the chance to meet Mr. Davis and Mr. Godfrey could change her life. She spent most of her time in her room sewing. Word spread quickly amongst the ladies of The Garden District of her work. They treated her with respect, but most rarely spoke to her beyond their choice of fabric. Some told her about their lives in The Garden District and they always wanted to look their best. She listened and pictured them in the clothes she made, socializing at all these functions. Within the community of ladies, there was a degree of importance based on money, but it was based on name too. The Le Blanc's ranked the highest.

Cassy was asked to collect fabric from Madame's room. It was beyond her former bedroom. A part of the house she was never in. She held her breath. She felt like an intruder into a world that she knew nothing about. There was a vanity table by the grandest window display she'd ever seen, swags and tails they called it. Sunlight streamed in through the floor to ceiling windows. Beside the four-poster bed was a trunk. It wasn't at the side of the bed. She opened the trunk. It was filled with an array of fabrics, bold exotic prints like nothing she'd ever seen before. She dug down deep until she found the gold fabric she was asked to find. As she stood up, she was sure she saw a reflection of someone in the vanity mirror by the window. Cassy dug down deep until she found the blue ribbon to accompany the gold fabric and the fur pale blue in color. She touched something cold and jumped back. Curiosity wouldn't allow her to go until she knew what it was. She reached in again and pulled out a bottle of bourbon. She walked towards the door and noticed a ball of fur asleep on the bed. It was that scrawny cat again. She had been warned she would only let Madame stroke her. Her beaded eyes like glass eyes in a teddy bear followed her around the four-poster bed. Cassy's eyes rested on the wine bottle beside the nightstand by the bed. She noticed the two glasses and like she'd seen someone naked, she looked away and tried to forget. She looked at the vanity table with its array of glass perfume bottles and strings of necklaces hanging from jars and powder puffs strewn about and some rouge.

She walked down the stairs and opened the door, which led into the grand hall. Mary was cleaning the grand staircase, but she didn't look up from her work. Surely, she must have heard the door close. There was a silence about the staff, but it wasn't just because of Cassy's change in role. Grace told her Violet had been taken ill and left the mansion unexpectedly. Cassy never actually met her. She asked Grace could she be gone to work at the plantation. Grace shook her head and said that she was sent home and not to speak of it again. Jacob was the only one who would talk about her. He told her that the staff didn't know what happened to Violet, but they say something don't feel right. He changed the subject then to talk about the plantation. He described "Maison belle" as she. He had worked there years before on the land for Mr. Le Blanc's grandfather. Jacob described him as a generous man, though the same would be said about his son, even though they all knew this wasn't true.

When she passed the dining room, the door was open. She looked in. She remembered the night of the function when all the dining room staff were running from here to the kitchen and she left for the evening. That was the night she met Louis. She never saw inside this room. She hadn't seen the entire house yet.

"Cassy I was trying to find you," said Beth behind her breathless. "Get yourself to the library. Mr. Le Blanc is going to meet you there."

"On my own!"

"I'll try and come in for some reason."

She reached out and touched Cassy's arm. Cassy wasn't expecting this reaction from her.

"Don't ask me anything else. We can't be seen to be talking like this," she said and with that she walked in the direction of Mary who was looking at them. She got back to her cleaning as if she hadn't seen them. Cassy hadn't seen Mr. Le Blanc since the day in the library when some of the staff was sent to the plantation. He was at the firm since she moved in here, staying in his apartment in town, above his firm on Canal Street. There was so much fuss about the house on his return. Nobody saluted anybody. Each busy with their own work.

Cassy took in the wall to wall of books as she waited alone. Something she couldn't do the day she was here with Beth and Madame. The hearth was lit as usual and made the room unbearably hot considering the humidity of the day. All the French doors were closed and the four fans it took to cool the expanse of this room whirled over her head. She lowered her eyes, feeling dizzy from the motion of them. She heard the doors close behind her. She used the mirror over the drinks cabinet to see who it was. It was Beth. As Beth took her usual spot near the doors Cassy saw him behind her. Jimmy appeared beside the drinks cabinet to fix Mr. Le Blanc a drink. Cassy wondered was he there all along. She hadn't seen him come in. Surely, he would have spoken to her. He looked small next to this giant of a man. It was as if he stooped in his presence, bowed nearly; as he took his position again next to the drinks cabinet.

"Miss Dupree, you can leave us now."

Cassy was surprised to see Beth use a door between the French doors that led outside and the double doors back into the hall. She didn't notice it before, but realized it led into the hall to where her and Beth slept. Beth looked at Cassy as she past her, with a look of distaste. But no wait it wasn't directed at her. It was for Mr. Le Blanc who was too busy taking in every inch of Cassy. She felt dizzy and her tongue stuck to the roof of her mouth. A taste rose in her throat. She opened her mouth to speak, but she couldn't breathe. When Jimmy closed the doors behind him, she felt sealed in with him.

"I want you as my personal seamstress…," he said and paused. Whether that was to unnerve her, she couldn't tell.

"As much as my wife thinks you'll be busy with the ladies from around here, you won't. Besides, you'll have the added bonus of sewing for us men folk too. I'm out of town until February 10. I leave today. You will ride the streetcar and be at my office for 6pm that day."

Cassy felt herself slip, falling fast, but the ground was

211

still beneath her feet. All she could think of was how was she going to honor her meeting with the music executives. The more he spoke, the more she became aware of her place here and felt foolish for thinking she could rise above it.

He stooped over the fire to pick up something, cursing his wife for having it lit. The bell. He rang the bell that Madame kept next to the fire. Nobody dared move it. Even in her drunken state, she always managed to find it. He stood up his full height and looked at the painting above the mantelpiece. Cassy followed his eyes. It was a painting of the house. It looked different. Maybe it was painted before the new part of the house was added on.

She realized it was where the rest of the staff were sent, the plantation "Maisonbelle". She looked at it again. She could see what looked like the outhouses here, but there was a group of them all clustered together.

"That was my father's house and his father before him. And someday it will be Louis's..."

Again, a pause. Cassy felt she would collapse at any moment.

"I never wanted to live there. I'm too busy with the firm. My sons will follow me into law."

He turned around then. Jimmy came back into the room.

"Robert is the more academic, but Louis always had his head stuck in a book. He spent days in here as a young boy. Oh I'm sorry," he said with a snort and then laughed, "Why am I telling any of this to the help, to the Negro staff? Jimmy my glass."

Jimmy rushed past them with a glass of bourbon.

"Spillage boy, spillage!"

"Sorry Sir."

The fire crackled and spat out sparks onto the rug and the embers dissolved on the marble hearth. So it was arranged that Cassy would make the trip to the Master's Canal Street office. She couldn't shake off the look in Mr. Le Blanc's eyes. She was back in her room thinking about her meeting with the music executives. There was part of her felt foolish that it could become a reality.

Chapter 16

Saturday, August 27, 2005.

As Cassy left Treme, the hurricane winds had increased and it was harder to walk. She knew she needed to get to the bookstore. She crossed over at North Rampart Street. It was from this same street she used to ride the streetcar to The Garden District. She was now back in the Quarter. The buildings on Bourbon Street sheltered her and made it easier to walk in the high winds. She noticed how they were all boarded up in preparation for the storm. Warnings had been issued and only those who couldn't leave remained. For some there was no chance to leave without a car. She saw the occasional candlelight from inside some of the bars, where people were tucked away. She could hear laughter, which comforted her amidst the otherwise deserted Quarter. It brought back memories of a time she had forgotten about, when her papa used to play here. He came to her again.

"Cassy," he called.

She kept moving, ignoring the sound of his voice.

"Cassy, leave. You don't have to stay," he said. "They can't harm you now."

"Papa," she called out, but nobody answered.

She looked around the empty streets and the balconies overhead were all abandoned.

Some party bunting blew wildly and hung down onto the street from the second floor. Someone else spoke to her now.

"You don't have to play in Congo Square like your papa," he said. "They want you Cassy Shaw."

The music rose until it was ringing in her ears. She walked into the room in a long blue dress and took to the stage. They cheered, clapped and asked for more.

They called out her name, "Cassy, Cassy". She looked over at Miss Brown who was seated at the piano and beamed up at her. Her papa stood at the back of the room. She left the stage and walked through the crowd. They separated and made room for her. She led her papa over to the piano. Miss Brown moved aside to let him play. The cheers and the shouts of joy. The room moved to the sound of the music. New Orleans was stuck between the late night drinkers and the early morning risers, as her and her papa made their way home. All the party revelers gone home and the room filled with people that overflowed onto the balcony all gone. The streets were empty now. The music stopped. His voice silenced to her once again; as she wandered alone through The Quarter.

As Cassy passed the music hall tonight on St. Peter Street, she looked in through the windows; they were covered in a layer of dirt. The room was bathed in a yellow hue from the tinted glass. It was here she met Mr. Godfrey and Mr. Davis on February 10, 1960, during Mardi Gras. She thought back to when the streetcar stopped on Carondelet Street; she felt a sense of peace she had not known since she stepped foot inside the Le Blanc's mansion. She was going home. This Mardi Gras was her papa's first year working on the floats since she was a child. It was different he would be playing with the band. Cassy pictured him, very high on one of those floats playing the piano. She felt so proud.

Mardi Gras held special memories for her. Her papa used to carry her up high on his shoulders; so she had a bird's eye view of his art work on the floats. Her mama used to wave up at her and looked so happy. She remembers them always smiling and happy. That was before his accident on the building sites. Even at a young age Cassy can remember that job was the big one. They all spoke about it, the men in Treme. There was jealousy amongst them. When he landed the job on the new development, her mama was so excited. Cassy remembered she danced around the kitchen. He promised her a new tub would be the first thing they bought.

The 'accident' made the papers. Only it wasn't an accident. One of the men drove the cement truck into the scaffolding where her papa worked. All the other men saw it happen; some even kept working until their supervisor sounded the whistle. There was an article in the paper. A different story entirely, but one her papa had to go along with. He was afraid he'd lose his job otherwise, but the truth was his job was lost already. He turned to drinking at "The Sugar Club" and was welcomed back into the circle. Only this time he spends day and night there.

The part the papers left out that her papa was stuck underneath the scaffolding. "Lucky to be alive" was what the article said. Cassy remembered her mama on that day. She couldn't see her papa. He was brought quickly to hospital. Her mama screeched at the door when they came to tell her. One of them held his hat in his hand. Her mama grabbed Cassy and they ran through Congo Square to the development, to find him under all that rubble. Arms around her mama then, words spoken, but no one leaned down and told her, her papa was okay. Cassy looked that day at the rubble and saw her papa lying there with the cement truck half covered the scaffolding and her papa lay underneath all that rubble. She could see his head, his neck, part of his shirt, but everything else was covered. A hand, she could see his hand reach out for her and tell her it was okay.

It was months before her papa was able to walk unaided. He used two canes. It never stopped him leaving them and going out. Everything had changed. Mardi Gras passed that year without a mention. When he finished with the canes he was left with a limp that even when he was sober made him look drunk. She wished her mama could be here today to see him play on top of one of the floats. She remembered the walk back to their house after the parade and she'd run on ahead singing. Her papa laughed and cheered. Her mama would shake her head and tell her papa stop filling his daughter's head with his foolish dreams. As time passed Cassy noticed things more, her mama's pained expression. Cassy wondered was it her papa's drinking, was it the lack of money, or was it her singing. What she didn't know was her mama was sick and didn't tell them until the sickness was all any of them could see.

She turned onto her street and could see her home in the distance. For a moment, she pictured her mama standing there, but as she got closer, she could see it was her aunt at the door. When she walked up the little path to their house, she could see her papa stood in the hall. She dropped her bag and ran to them. Rosalie beamed and let her pass to go to her papa first. Cassy turned around and took her into the embrace. It felt so good to be home. When she stepped back from her papa's embrace, she looked at him. Gone was the tired eyes and unshaven face. There was a glint to his eyes that she could barely remember seeing before.

"My baby is home," he said.

"Papa it's only for one night," she laughed.

"One night is enough for you to see me play at Mardi Gras."

"Rosalie has moved back home, haven't you Rosa?"

Rosalie was gone into the kitchen to prepare dinner. Cassy followed the smell of her cooking.

"I have Cassy," said her aunt as she plated up a generous helping for her.

"I figured it's about time I start looking after myself," said Amos.

The walk to Mardi Gras that night was so exciting. Congo Square was a hive of activity. All the musicians that usually gathered here on a Sunday were here to play for all the city's visitors. As they made their way to The French Quarter people spilled out of bars to hear the music. Cassy and her family went into one of the bars to see Amos' crew play. Old man Bob was playing the double bass and he waved at Amos. She also recognized Moses on the trombone and Jim on the harmonica.

Through the crowd, she saw Jessie Pearl. She waved at them.

"Oh great is she going to be with us for the night now?" said Rosalie with a sigh.

Amos ignored her, went, and threw his arms around his sister in law.

"My, look at you Cassy, you've grown," she said.

"Oh it's only being a few months aunt," laughed Cassy.

"Never mind a few months can change a lot."

An uncomfortable silence fell on them. Each of them left with their own thoughts of Elijah and her mama.

"Eli would of loved this, wouldn't he Cassy?" said Jessie.

Her papa answered for her, "I know he would."

"We best be going," said Rosalie.

"I'll join if y'all don't mind," said Jessie.

"Of course," answered Rosalie. One thing about her aunt Rosalie she wasn't a party pooper and the party had just started.

The crowds lined the streets. The energy in The Quarter was electric. Cassy smiled thinking of her papa on top of one of those big floats. She could see them in the distance, above the heads of the crowd ready to fill the streets with their glory. Amos walked on ahead and cleared the way for them to walk through. Rosalie said hello to people that she knew and it delayed them from getting through quickly. Cassy was introduced to each one.

"I'm going to have to go over there and get set up Cassy with the others. Now don't go running back to that job of yours till I come back do you hear?" said Amos.

The reminder of the mansion changed the mood for Cassy. She'd had the best night with her family last night and it felt so good to wake up in her own bed this morning. She didn't want to show him she was upset.

"No papa I surely won't."

" Papa wait, there's something I want to tell you."

She called after him, but he was gone into the crowd. Rosalie was still busy chatting.

"What did you want to tell him Cassy?" asked Jessie.

Cassy studied her for a moment, with her hair rolled up high on her head and kept in place with a sparkly brooch. She looked radiant in her purple dress. As usual, she had a string of pearls around her neck, which went down to her tiny waist.

"Oh nothing aunt, it can wait."

Jessie watched her for a moment, before she turned to answer something Rosalie asked her. She was nothing like her mama she decided then. With her head constantly

221

held high and her big hair and all her glamour. Cassy can't even remember her mama wearing any jewelry besides her wedding band. It would probably have gotten in the way of the sewing machine. She wondered how Jessie got all the luck. She got her big singing career and she got her mama's baby to rear as her own son. A loud cheer went up from the crowd. The parade was ready to start. A host of beads were tossed in the air and the floats moved through the Quarter.

She hadn't told them about her meeting tonight with Mr. Godfrey. Time passed quickly. Rosalie kept saying how she had found them the best position to watch the parade, when really Amos had. They all waited in eager expectation for his float to pass. Cassy stood on her toes to try to see him before he approached. She didn't need to; she could hear the piano above the cheers of the crowd. It was his solo piece. Her papa had changed into a black suit with tails. His hair was slicked back and he looked like a movie star. That's what Rosalie kept shouting with Jessie laughing in agreement. Cassy didn't notice what he wore as much as the look on his face. She hadn't seen him that happy, well as long as she could remember. Just as he passed, she shouted out to him and he smiled. The other musicians joined him playing, for the rest of the way. Cassy felt so proud.

"Did you ask me to tell you when its quarter to five Cassy?" asked Jessie Pearl.

"Yes why?" asked Cassy remembering where she had to be.

"Well it's just leaving it now sorry sweetie. I got so wrapped up in the music."

Cassy gasped.

"I have to go."

"You have to go already," asked Rosalie.

Cassy looked at her papa's float in the distance and knew it would be a while before he was back this way. She had promised him she would see him before she left, but she couldn't miss her meeting with Mr. Godfrey. She knew an opportunity like this might never happen again. She had to make it to Miss Brown's place.

"I can't explain and I should have told y'all earlier, but I'm meeting someone for my singing," she gushed. "I promised papa I'd see him, but I have to meet Mr. Godfrey. He's come all the way from New York to hear me sing, well not just me. Probably others..." she stopped speaking. She was out of breath.

"Wait Cassy we've only just seen you," said Rosalie with tears in her eyes.

"Rosalie, she can't stay. She has to go. She will be

home soon again," said Jessie in a bid to comfort her.

Rosalie nodded. Jessie took Cassy by the hand.

"Cassy, I know who it is your meeting. This is a big deal. I've never crossed paths with him, but I've heard the name. Where have you to be?"

"It's only around the corner on Peter Street. It's at Miss Browns."

"You met her," beamed Jessie. "Cassy go, go. I'll explain to your...we'll explain, won't we Rosalie. We'll explain to your papa," she reassured her.

Cassy hugged them both.

"I didn't want it to be about me Aunt," she said addressing them both.

She made her way through the crowds to Miss Browns' house. The crowd dispersed a little with the parade over. The ground was covered in beads and looms. She felt a pang of guilt for not telling her papa in person what she was about to do. All those years he encouraged her to sing. Here she was on the threshold of not only the first opportunity to come her way, but probably the greatest. She was on her way, just a few short steps from meeting Mr. Godfrey, who could change her life.

Chapter 17

The quietness struck her in contrast to the crowds outside as she entered the hallway of Miss Brown's house. She climbed the steep stairs to where the receptionist sat at her desk. She looked up when she saw Cassy.

"Go ahead in Miss Shaw. Mr. Godfrey and Mr. Davis are up there waiting for you."

"Will Miss Brown not be there? I mean I thought…"

"She's over at the school, but she will be here shortly. She said to tell you she'll be here for your audition."

"Of course, I forgot about that. Even with Mardi Gras on?"

"Oh they don't leave, the girls. She like their mother Miss Shaw; if you understand my meaning."

Cassy smiled and walked into the room. She did understand her meaning. Her mama was one of those girls one time. She pictured her mama and knew she would be proud. She knew she would breathe a sigh of relief and somehow find it was all worthwhile. All the worry, all the hoping that her life could be different, led to this moment and Cassy was going to seize it.

"Miss Shaw, how are you?"

She didn't need to turn around to know Mr. Davis had come into the room. With him was a distinguished looking man, older with black hair and olive skin. He walked towards her, not waiting for Mr. Davis to introduce him.

"Al tells me I'm going to hear quite a talent. You don't mind if I sit Miss Shaw, it was a long day. Had a bit too much fun in Mardi Gras. It's quite a show y'all put on. I'm Mr. Godfrey, but they call me Charlie."

He was a tall man in a dark suit with a comb over of grey hair. He reached out for the chair in front of him and almost instinctively, a girl appeared with a glass of bourbon for him.

"You don't mind Miss Shaw. I have a little, to help me concentrate."

Mr. Davis joined him at the table. When he was offered a glass, he politely refused.

Cassy took to the stage. She had thought about it all week what song she would sing, because she had been told to have material prepared.

"Miss Shaw give me your best rendition of 'I'm Walking'. You know it, I'm sure."

"Yes Mr. Godfrey. I used to sing it with my papa all the time."

"Does your papa sing too?" he asked.

"He plays the piano Mr. Godfrey."

"I see. Cassy, start in your own time."

Cassy found a place on the wall. A crack that ran up to the ceiling. She followed it with her eyes and it was here she fixed her gaze and sang. She felt the words leave her body in waves. She was relaxed, composed and never felt so confident in all her life. In that, moment she knew this is what she wanted to do. She thought of her mama as she sang and could see her by the sewing machine, hands poised waiting for her to finish. She had a smile on her face, which she always quickly pulled away. She didn't want her to suffer for her dreams. All she ever wanted for her was to have a life far better than what she had now. Cassy wished she was here in this room, listening to the words Mr. Godfrey said. She had barely finished singing when Mr. Davis, stamped out his cigarette on the floor and came running towards the stage. He nearly lifted her off the ground.

"Miss Shaw, you have what we're looking for. Your

voice is so rich, mature way beyond your years," he said and turned to Mr. Godfrey who didn't change his expression at all. Cassy could tell this was who she needed to impress.

"Miss Shaw, take a seat beside me. I'd like to show you something," said Mr. Godfrey.

As she walked to the table, she could see the look on the faces of the two girls who waited to sing. She was reassured when she looked over at Miss Brown. She must have come in during her song. She winked at Cassy and waved the next girl to come on and take her position. Cassy sat in the seat across from him, so her back was to the stage. He waved his hand towards Miss Brown to signal for her to start to play. The girl on stage started to sing. He watched her closely, but about half way through the song, he turned his attention back to Cassy.

He pushed a book across the table to her.

"Take a look."

Cassy opened the book. As she turned the pages, singers and musicians looked up at her. They were a lot older than she was. The women looked so glamorous; they reminded her of Jessie Pearl. All the black and white photos had one thing in common they were of people of color. He put his finger to his lips when she went to speak. This made her blush.

He called up to the girl on the stage, "Thanks for your time. Next."

Cassy dared not turn around and look at the girl's face. The next girl was called on stage and Miss Brown played. When the song ended the same thing, again, he thanked the girl and she left the stage. Cassy watched them leave the room without even looking in her direction.

Miss Brown set a glass of water down in front of Cassy. She gladly drank it.

"Cassy Shaw, you can sing and I've found a place for your voice right here in New Orleans. There is so much happening in the music business right now, you couldn't imagine. Talent is being discovered every day. Many of these singers are taking this talent out of the city, which I think is a shame. Did Mr. Davis tell you about our music hall?"

"No I didn't know whether to, till you heard her sing," said Mr. Davis.

"True, Al. Well I can share with you that we plan to build a music hall right here on this street. Actually if Miss Brown doesn't mind me saying so, it will be here."

Miss Brown joined them.

"I don't mind at all. I'm very excited for it."

"All I know it's going to be big. Miss Brown has kindly offered this to be the starting off point and who

229

knows from there."

Cassy was swept along with every word he said.

"I tell you, they will never see me over at the school," laughed Miss Brown.

"Now Lottie I believe the work you do is exceptional, they'll be still needing you surely."

"I'm sure they can find someone else. There are so many of us over there, unlike before," replied Lottie.

"Okay Lottie you make a good argument. Well Mr. Davis is moving here and he can help you run it. I've big plans for this place, so it will take a lot of input. That's where you come in Cassy. I want you as our main act. I want to put you in place as our sell out show."

Cassy didn't know what to say.

"I can see this is a lot to take in Miss Shaw and I know you have commitments to your job as a seamstress, but I really see you here working for me."

His words whirled around above Cassy and she was afraid to reach out and touch them in case they disappeared. She wondered could her life really change. Of course, she had to go back to the mansion this evening and continue her work as a seamstress, but this opportunity was her dream. He explained to her that there was a lot of work needed to be done on their end, a lot of planning and refurbishment. They told her should anything change on her end, be sure to tell Lottie as they would need to plan another act. This upset Cassy a little that they should think she would change her mind, but she knew she was also a business for them. She understood this. There was no way she was going to let anything ruin this chance for her.

"Miss Shaw I know this can change your life," he said.

She listened to them talk about plans and watched Mr. Davis point out to Miss Brown where everything would be as they walked around the room.

"I don't think it will be this room Lottie, I've my eye on that great big hall downstairs," said Mr. Godfrey.

"Oh I don't own that part of the building Charles."

"That can be easily solved," he said and winked at her.

She smiled. Mr. Davis led the way downstairs. He was eager to see the hall. Cassy followed them. The girl at the desk looked up at her and gave her a great big smile. Cassy smiled back and felt the warm glow of something new on the horizon.

"I think it's going to be locked," said Miss Brown peering into the room.

Mr. Godfrey took a set of keys from his pocket.

"I wasn't sure about this place till I came back here today and now I'm certain."

231

Cassy couldn't help but notice that he looked at her when he said this. One by one, they walked through the narrow door into the room. It was suspended in darkness.

"Hit the lights, Mr. Davis."

He turned on the lights to reveal the room. The peach walls held the evening sun and created a warm glow. The floors were wooden as was one of the walls. On the other three, the paint hung in peels. Cassy looked towards the stage. It was the width of the room, but was only two raised steps high. To the left of the stage was a large window looking out onto a courtyard. It was belong to the neighboring building. It was draped in branches laden down with magnolia blooms. There were three other windows, floor to ceiling encased behind wooden shutters.

"Open those shutters Al, till we get a better look at her," said Mr. Godfrey.

The light from outside spilled across the floor and they all stood in silence. They could all see them, the band set up in the corner over by the window that faced the courtyard and the singers on stage. The room was filled with noise, the chink of glasses, the whispers of praise from the audience and the sound of singing.

The time had come for Cassy to return to the mansion. She had to leave straight away or she would miss the next streetcar. It was a bit of a walk to Carondelet

Street. Mr. Godfrey told her that if it weren't for Mardi Gras, Mr. Davis could drive her back. She thanked him, but what they didn't know was now she had to make her way to Canal Street to meet Mr. Le Blanc. This was a journey she had to take on her own. Miss Brown followed her out into the hall.

"Cassy Shaw, this is really going to happen for you and I'm so glad to be a part of it all," gushed Lottie.

"Miss Brown, the way I see it, if it wasn't for you this wouldn't be happening."

Miss Brown hugged her, which took Cassy by surprise, but she welcomed it. She knew once she got to the mansion she would be devoid of human contact.

"Cassy, they could have easily offered you a position on one of the cruise ships. Mr. Godfrey has investments in one of them, but I overheard him talking to Mr. Davis saying it wouldn't be enough of an opportunity for you. And please call me Lottie."

Cassy thought of her Aunt Jessie and wondered what she would think of this. Her given an opportunity she never had. She knew she would be happy for her and proud. Her thoughts turned to Eli then.

"You okay?"

"I'm fine. Do you think you'll leave the school?" Cassy asked. "I'm sorry I shouldn't have asked you that."

"I think I will. Who would have thought this building would become a music hall. I mean I dreamed of it. Anyway Cassy I better not keep you or you'll miss your ride."

Cassy stepped out into the street. The crowds had dispersed and people were either gone home with their young families or they filled the bars. She looked at all the beads and looms on the street. It was a path of color.

Chapter 18

She felt sick to her stomach as she looked at the building that loomed in front of her.

"Le Blanc's Firm, Attorneys at Law".

There was no mistaking which building, it was the sign was visible from down the street. It was 5.45 pm. She was to meet him at 6pm, but she figured it looked good to arrive before the appointed time. All the staff had finished up for the day. The light remained on in the porch downstairs. She was met directly by a steep staircase. There was nowhere else to go, so she went up. She didn't expect to see a receptionist still at her desk, but Cassy saw she was gathering up her things to go home. When she saw Cassy, she gave her a disgusted look, as if she was going to be delayed by her.

"We're closed. You're going to have to come back tomorrow. Here take this actually and ring ahead for an appointment."

Cassy watched her fuss around her desk to find a card and left it on the counter in front of her.

"I have an appointment. I'm supposed to meet Mr.

235

Le Blanc here."

"Are you now? Can I ask what the nature of your business is? Oh don't tell me, I'd rather not know. I'm gone home."

She brushed past Cassy. Her scarf trailed behind her on the ground, but she swept it up in a grand gesture as she went to go down the stairs and threw it over her shoulder. She hesitated on the top step as if she was going to say something, but decided against it and ran down the stairs. Cassy heard the door to the street close. Suddenly she realized she was completely alone. The only light was from the banker's lamp on the receptionist's desk and the exit sign up over the door to presumably Mr. Le Blanc's office. The building was old and musty. She could smell the years of history that lined the walls. She expected a bigger building for the most affluent lawyer in New Orleans.

Just then, the door opened and a man passed her without even looking at her. A few seconds later, another man passed her.

"Anton will see you now. He said to go ahead to his office. Don't get lost in there, it's a maze."

With that, he was gone too. He let the door fall behind him. Cassy quickly grabbed it before she was left in darkness again. He was right; it was a maze of doors. She didn't know which one was his office. She could only hope it was the one in front of her at the end of the hall with a large oak door partially open. Smoke wafted out to greet her and then she heard him call her. Every part of her being was afraid to be alone with him. She remembers how she felt as she approached the looming building in front of her she didn't want to return. She looked down at the crumpled up pass in her handbag. The room was empty, but she could see through it to a connecting room. She heard voices and laughter. As she got closer, she saw it was a boardroom and nearly every seat was full.

"Come in Miss Shaw," a voice called her.

She recognized it as Mr. Le Blanc. How he saw her she didn't know. Each of the men with him looked up from what they were doing.

"Gentlemen, this is our seamstress. She'll take our measurements this evening."

The men looked at each other. She knew exactly what they were thinking. What was a colored girl doing here?

"Well, Miss Shaw have you any questions for us?"

Cassy didn't answer. She wasn't sure what he wanted her to say.

"Sorry now Anton but what is this for? I mean I get my suits tailor made here on Canal Street," asked one of the men.

"I know where you're talking about. My wife brings

mine for me," said another.

"I buy mine. So what's the deal Anton?" asked another.

"Well gentleman Cassy is our personal seamstress, but it's not suits she's going to be sewing for us."

"Surely you haven't brought her here for our entertainment," said another.

"She'll be making our robes," replied Anton.

With that, the room exploded into laughter.

"I like your style Anton."

Cassy didn't know what they were talking about.

"Come on gents whose first? Stand up and let her measure you. I'll be last," said Anton.

So one by one, they stood up where they sat and raised their arms. Cassy wasn't even sure what it was she was sewing and she didn't want to ask. She didn't plan to speak at all, if she could help it.

"Just take the chest width and sleeve length that should suffice. That's it for the day then gents. Our first meeting will take place over at mine."

"When you thinking?" asked the man she was measuring.

Anton didn't answer him straight away for effect.

"Well I know my wife leaves tonight. She's going out of state to visit her sister. I tell you men I forgot she even had a sister."

Again, they all exploded in laughter.

"So we say tomorrow."

"Around this time, Anton?"

"No later. Nine pm. Come in the staff entrance. I'll meet y'all by the side door. Not by the kitchen."

Cassy couldn't understand why he was saying all this in front of her.

"She knows now," said one.

Cassy felt the sweat gather in a pool at the base of her spine, sending a chill back up it.

"Leave that to me. Right if you're done men. I'll see you tomorrow."

As much as Cassy felt uncomfortable around them all; she dreaded when it was just going to be her on her own with him. If anything happened, no one would hear her scream. She noticed the room had no windows and she became acutely aware of the sound of the ceiling fans. One by one he turned off the banker's lamps on the boardroom table until the last one was on. He reached out and grabbed her in one swoop. The cabinets rattled as he pushed her against them. Her face pressed into the glass and she felt the full weight of him against her.

He was disturbed by a knock on the door. A well-dressed woman walked into the room. Cassy wondered what room she came from. He released his grip on her and stood so far back, it was arguable anything happened. Mr. Le Blanc was completely composed. Cassy shook and saw the fog her breath created on the glass disappear, like any proof of what just happened.

"Sorry for interrupting?" said the woman surveying Cassy as she spoke.

Cassy settled her dress and prayed to be saved by this woman. She knew she made a judgment of what she saw, but nevertheless didn't act on it.

"Not at all Susanna. Miss Shaw was just leaving. You have everything you need, Miss Shaw?"

Cassy couldn't speak.

"Straight back to the house now. You know yourself Susanna. They take liberties colored folk, if you don't keep an eye on them."

Cassy didn't wait to hear the reaction from this woman. She gathered up her sewing apparel and made her way through the corridor of doors, out through the reception area where she waited only a short while ago and down the flight of stairs.

She welcomed the humidity that greeted her outside. It was in sharp contrast to the suffocating interior of where she came from. On the ride back to The Garden District, she played today's events over in her mind. She looked down at the crumpled pass in her hand, wet from her sweating palm. She clung to it in the hopes of getting back into her prison. She was late. It read 6.30. Sure, there was no way for her to get back within this timeframe, considering he requested to see her at 6pm. Why did she not factor that into it, but who would she tell and who cared. She can't remember the journey back to the mansion, but suddenly she was in The Garden District.

The house was bathed in that time of evening where the staff had returned to their quarters for the night. She never returned to the house at this late hour. Anytime she delivered garments to her customers she was always back before dark. She walked along the path that led to the staff entrance and opened the same door she entered that first day with the Savior's image on the doorknob. A light shone from one of the outhouses. Even Jacob had finished up for the day. She turned the corner. All she had to do was walk past the library, which was in total darkness. She looked back towards the kitchen and could see shadows at the window. Grace was probably still in there. She became aware of her breathing. She thought of what Jacob said about the outhouses, how strange things happened there. As she passed the first one, it was in total darkness and the one after it. However, the one nearest her room had light coming from it. She heard voices and laughter. She kept walking. She saw her room, just a few steps across the lawn. She stayed off the path, so the sound of the gravel under her feet wouldn't give away her presence.

Her pass expired two hours ago. She wondered did Beth know. She heard laughter again, this time it came from the outhouse behind her as she moved. It sounded like Beth. Cassy looked through the open door and saw Beth with her head thrown back laughing. She couldn't tell who else was with her. Cassy ran the rest of the way to her room, but she found it hard to breathe. She barely felt her feet touch the lawn as she crossed it. There was her room suspended in darkness just ahead of her. All she had to do was reach the door and she'd be safe inside. The trees looked menacing as she reached her room.

Wait. Someone was there. She felt someone watch her from behind the cypress tree as she ran past. A light came on inside her workroom. It was the one she worked by; she never left it on. She wasn't going to draw attention to the room when she needed to leave that evening. Her head spun. There was no time to feel sick. Lottie, Mr. Godfrey, her papa, Jessie Pearl, her aunt Rosalie all of them slipped away as she was thrown into the only existence she could know tonight; that of a colored girl at the mercy of her employer. She needed to have an answer for Madame. No time to run. She can't run. Pass expired hours ago. She must go inside. Wait it's not her. She saw a shadow. It's a man. He saw her. He left without saying a word. He didn't even look in her direction. He crossed the lawn and walked towards the outhouse. It wasn't the master. He was small in stature and bowed his head as he walked. When she reached her door; she looked back to see he had disappeared. This house contained secrets she didn't want to know. She closed her door and revisited the events of the day. No matter what she had to find a way out of here; and that would be her voice.

Chapter 19

Fate was to delve a different hand for Cassy. It had been decided. Days rolled around of sewing for the women. Then by night when everyone was asleep, she began the sewing of the cloaks for Mr. Le Blanc. These cloaks looked no different than the cloaks worn by lawyers in court of law, except the emblem on the lapel. To her it may as well have been emblazoned across them in blood. Each cloak had a fiery cross. He told her to sew the initials for each member on the reverse. No stitching was to show through so as not to affect the emblem.

As Cassy sewed, she thought of her mama sewing her signature seal on every item she worked on. She thought of the treble clef sewn onto the pillow in Eli's casket. The tears came now and fell onto the midnight darkness of the fabric she worked on.

***

One evening Beth was sent to tell her that there would be no more excursions from the mansion. It was an order from Madame Le Blanc. Cassy hoped Beth would drop her guard with her a little, but that never happened.

"You mean to Canal Street, to his office?" Cassy asked her.

"To the master's office; but also no more outings to buy fabric or anything. It will all be sent to you here at the house."

Cassy felt herself panic.

"But what if I run out of something or what if...?"

"Cassy, you're not listening to me. Furthermore Madame has curtailed anyone going home for a while."

"But she can't," wailed Cassy, unable to conceal how she felt.

"You're only back from seeing your family. Do you think I get to go home whenever I want? No, I don't. Besides, it's not open to negotiation. Now if you don't mind I have so much to do. Who is that for?" Beth turned back towards the machine.

Cassy felt the blood drain from her face. She looked down at the fabric she'd fed through the machine only moments earlier.

"Miss Brown," she answered.

Beth held her gaze. "And what about these? You've a

pile building up."

Again, Cassy looked to where she pointed. Sure enough, it did look like a pile of clothes, but the layers of fabric disguised what really filled her basket, the order for Mr. Le Blanc.

"Oh and another thing you've to go to Mr. Le Blanc's office tonight."

"But I thought you said I wasn't to leave."

"None of us are to leave Cassy. His office is here in the mansion. Surely, you've seen it. It's next to the library."

Cassy shook her head too overcome with fear to think.

"Okay so when you leave our corridor, turn right after Madame's parlor. She doesn't spend her life in the library you know."

She laughed at this, but Cassy didn't join her. Nothing could relax the anxiety that had taken over her.

"Well it's the room next to this."

"Just me!"

"Why would he ask just for you? The others will be there."

With that, she left her alone.

Cassy sat on her bed for a long time afterwards and contemplated what could it be about. She'd lived here long enough to know when there was a staff meeting they were all summoned to the library or the grand hall. A shadow passed her window. It seemed, but when she stood up to look, she could see it was Jacob further away. The sun had set and he was bathed in the afterglow as he worked. She looked beyond where he was. There was a light on in one of the outhouses. She knew this wasn't for him. He kept everything he needed close to him as he worked and if anything he went to the glasshouse to collect whatever he'd forgotten. This was different. There seemed to be more than one person out there. Surely if anything untoward was going on Jacob would notice.

She felt sick to her stomach at the thoughts of seeing Mr. Le Blanc that evening. It had been weeks since what happened that day in his Canal Street office. She left her room and went to the kitchen for supper. When she got outside Jacob was gone, finished up for the day she imagined. The light in the outhouse was off and it looked to be vacant as she crossed the cobbled pathway to the rear of the house. Had she imagined it? Was there anyone there at all? It was getting harder to tell what was real or imagined.

Each mouthful of the food Grace plated up for her stuck in her throat.

"Are you going to the meeting tonight in the Master's study Grace?"

"No child I ain't."

"Grace…when I went to his office in town he attacked me."

"Hush now, you mustn't speak of such things. It must have been good to see your family. You never told me about it Cassy."

"Grace, please," Cassy pleaded with her to listen.

"Cassy, no you can't and you mustn't speak of such things again."

She leaned in close.

"He took my husband, he is a monster, but to survive you must silence your voice."

That struck Cassy in more ways than Grace could have possibly known. She hadn't shared with any of them her meeting in the music hall with Mr. Godfrey. This seems like an eternity ago now. It felt like a lucid dream she had.

She walked past the dining room. There was someone entertaining in there. It couldn't be Madame as she was out of town. She could see through the gap in the door that it was the men she met at Mr. Le Blanc's office. She looked across the hall. The door to his study was open. However, it didn't look like any lights were on. As she approached the door, she saw him stood by the window. Cassy was disturbed by a sound behind her. It sounded like crying but was very faint. A girl disappeared through the staff door to the second floor. She was gone before Cassy could see who it was. Mr. Le Blanc turned around and looked at her.

"Come in and close the door," he demanded.

Cassy obeyed. She couldn't see at all, except for his silhouette. He disappeared out through what she thought was the window. He beckoned her without a word. She was terrified. Whatever chance she had of any of the men in the dining room hearing her was gone.

As she walked past his desk, she was struck by a smell. She looked at his half-smoked cigar rested on an ashtray. The smoke rose from it and scalded her eyes. When she passed the window beside her, she was shocked to see Madame. The window looked back onto a room Cassy had never seen, but she quickly drew up the house layout in her mind. She remembered Beth leaving the library and taking a door she didn't know where it led to.

"Come on, she can't see you," he coaxed.

Cassy couldn't take her eyes off Madame in her drunken state panned out on one of the lounges. The night air struck her, fresh in comparison to the house. She shook all over, but this wasn't from the drop in temperature. It was the look in his eyes as he took her arm and dragged her to the nearest outhouse. She didn't scream. A swarm of lightning bugs crossed their path as they went inside the outhouse. Their light was the last thing she saw before he bolted the door behind them.

He slammed her against the mud walls. He looked at her like a predator looks at its prey. All his twisted thoughts towards her surfaced and she could see the poison in his eyes. She felt so afraid. She shook. No. No. Don't. Don't. Please. He pulled her by her legs until her head slapped off the ground. The brunt force winded her. He hoisted her up like a rag doll and sat her on the table in the centre of the hut. He leaned against the wall as if he deciding what to do next. She wet herself. He laughed and approached her with force again. Only this time he punched her over and over. She struggled to break free of him. With each punch, he called her a black bitch, a dirty black whore; over and over. She was numb to the pain. The room spun. Everything meshed into one, until she didn't know whether his fist hit her or the ground. Her vision blurred. Then a sharpness; a piercing pain in the pit of her abdomen as he tore her dress and forced himself inside her. With each thrust, she cried out, but no one would save her in this dark cesspit of pain. Her body was distorted into a position she should have never known, thrust into adulthood with each painful penetration.

The mansion seemed so out of reach. Soon this will

be over she told herself. No mama here to save her, no papa by her side, just the unending pain he forced on her young body. She had never been with Louis, not in that way. Now this act was tarnished into her psyche, so that everything from this day forward would be affected by this one heinous act. She was raped. He pulled away from her. She collapsed to the ground. He kicked her before he left. She clawed her nails into the ground and tried to get to her feet. The ground felt wet between her legs. She looked down. It was blood. The outline of his silhouette was visible as he passed under one of the gas lanterns and retreated into the house. Cassy gave way to her pain and wailed. Her cries fell dead. No one could hear her or would come to save her.

To this day, she can't remember how she got back to the mansion that night, but that night was only the start of her pain. He came to her over and over; and raped her. She could see the outhouse mirrored in the full-length mirror by her closet. The screen with the oriental pattern collapsed and fell to the ground with the force of him as he pushed his weight against her. Pain then. His body pressed against hers in a grotesque, evil union. Darkness. No escape. The echoes of that night returned to her each time he came to her room. Some part of her died.

251

Chapter 20

Louis awoke to the sound of strong winds and heavy rain. He went downstairs to where Cassy slept. She no longer wanted to share their marriage bed. He was okay with that, because he made sure to bolt the door. Once Cassy took her sleeping pill, nothing, not even a hurricane would wake her. When he saw her covers thrown back on the bed, he checked the washroom for her. It was a small house, but they had it decorated to make the most of its tiny rooms. They lived over their bookstore on Royal Street for so many years while they saved for their own home on the corner of Burgundy and Toulouse Street. Louis loved the French Quarter. It was a completely different world to the mansion he was raised in. He only had to cross over onto St. Peter Street to get to his bookstore. It was on this very street that he met Cassy again.

She was singing in Preservation Hall. He will never forget the night he saw her after years apart. She wore a long red dress with a slit just showing enough leg. Around her neck was a string of pearls. She turned them in her fingers as she sang. All eyes were on her. He was the only white man there. The stage was above the crowd, only two steps high, but it elevated her and the band so everyone in the room could see them. He waited until her song was finished and the crowd had settled down. She stood to the side of the stage talking and laughing with some of the chorus girls. He will never forget the look in her eyes when she saw him. They fell in love again and married not long after.

Louis checked the courtyard, the old servant's quarters for her. Cassy said the extra space would be useful when they had a family of their own. They suffered three miscarriages before they found out she would never carry a child full term again. He wanted to tear this part of the house down when they found out. When they were first going out she told him that she gave birth to a baby, but she died in childbirth. The circumstances of whose baby it was she kept to herself. He never asked her who the father was. Louis hoped she would heal in time, but she never recovered from the loss of her baby compounded by the fact they had no family of their own. As they settled into married life, she stopped talking about her baby. He hoped a child would heal old wounds for her, but they never got that opportunity. He took one last look back at the unused part of the house and realized she was gone from here.

Panic rose in his stomach and his heart met it with a fear he always knew would come. Cassy had been sick for some time. Controlled by medication for now, but he feared the day she wouldn't know who she was. This compounded his anxiety. He went back through the French doors that led into her bedroom, pulled back her bed sheets, and found her sleeping pill. He had watched her drift off to sleep, but remembered that he had gone into the kitchen to lock the porch door for the night. She must have pretended to be asleep. He retraced what they had spoken of that day. The parcel. She wanted to go get the parcel. He convinced her they'd wait until Monday or at least he thought he had.

The T.V. was on in the family room. He heard them talk about the storm. He went in to look at the report. The mayor and the governor issued a mandatory evacuation of New Orleans. They advised anyone that could leave, should do so. Louis switched off the T.V. and went back into the kitchen. It was then he noticed his jacket on the floor and the hook where he hung his keys for the bookstore was empty. He took one last look around their home and walked out into the storm. The sky was an electric mesmerizing blue color with low hung clouds, omnipresent; heavy with the weight of the storm. A dark presence, like a blanket over the city. There was no end to it, no escape, all encompassing storm.

As Louis walked through The French Quarter, he was bent over with the force of the wind. He leaned in close to the buildings. A bright light flashed up ahead. It blurred his vision. He tried to see in the rain what it was. It came closer. It was a cop car. The cop in the passenger side rolled down the window. He shouted at Louis to be heard with the noise of the wind.

"Sir you should not be here!"

Louis didn't answer him.

"Sir we're making sure everyone is safe before the storm makes landfall."

"I have to find my wife. She left our house on her own," answered Louis.

The cop turned to the driver of the car and said something to him.

"We really have to stress you must leave the area. No one is here. I'm sure your wife knows not to be out here," said the driver.

Louis looked around at the boarded up houses and businesses. The streets were empty.

"They've opened the Superdome for people. We can take you. Maybe your wife is there already."

255

"My wife wouldn't know to go there. She has dementia. I am going to my bookstore over on Royal Street. I need to find her."

"Sir, please get in. We'll take you to your bookstore. Which one is it?"

"Signed and Sealed, Le Blanc's Books."

The two cops exchanged looks. Louis recognized this reaction. It's the same one he got a thousand times before.

"Yes, I'm Louis Le Blanc; Le Blanc's of The Garden District."

The wind engulfed around them making its presence known.

"Mr. Le Blanc, get in we'll take you to your store."

The car swayed from the force of the wind as they sped down St. Peter Street.

The cop in the passenger seat turned around to face Louis.

"I'm Officer Earl, James Earl. And this is…"

"Officer Lee," said the driver of the car and shot the other officer a look.

"Well I think under these circumstances there is no need to be formal," said Officer Earl.

This made the driver smile. "Go on go look with him. I had better stay close to the radio. That's if it stays working for much longer," he leaned over the steering wheel and looked up at the sky. "This is your store sir?"

Louis followed to where he pointed and saw the sign for his store had fallen on the ground. Officer Earl held the door open for him and struggled to hold it with the wind. On seeing the door to his bookstore open, Louis was hopeful Cassy was inside. The short distance to the store seemed to take forever as they were whipped back with the strength of the wind. Louis looked back at Officer Lee, but he was distracted on the radio.

They stepped inside the porch. Officer Earl closed the door behind them. It was like a vacuum effect, the sound of silence that filled the hall. Louis opened the glass-paneled door that led into the bookstore. Officer Earl looked around at the books that lined the hall behind glass cabinets.

"They're all first editions. Everything, well mostly everything I have here is. Those you see in the hall are all signed."

"I see," said Officer Earl. He stood over by the window and surveyed the room. "What makes you think she would come here?"

Louis didn't answer him and went over to the solid oak desk that dominated the center of the room. It was here all the transactions took place. Money exchanged hands in return for a rare book, leather bound with gold gilding and a signature from the author or a first edition copy carefully protected in a sealed bag. Customers that came here knew what they wanted and often-waited months on end for Louis to get his hands on some rare find. He turned on the lamp on the desk. The light flickered and suspended the room in darkness again.

"Here take my flash lamp," said Officer Earl and handed it to him.

"Thank you," said Louis with shaking hands.

Items appeared in the circle of light. His box of gloves used to turn delicate pages of antique books, his magnifying glass, and his inkwell and candle wax. The roll of brown paper on top of the blade was ready to cut, the next parcel to be delivered to a customer. Some treasured books of his own that he kept on the desk at all times. He flashed the light across the table again.

"What is it you're looking for?" asked the cop.

"She came here to get a parcel," said Louis and scanned the desk once more with the flash lamp.

On the edge of the desk was the remnants of a parcel. It was open. Louis reached inside. He pulled out a lump of tissue paper, but there was nothing inside it. Whatever was there had been removed.

"Well any luck?" asked the cop.

"She was here," Louis, answered him.

"Officer Lee is flashing the lights. He's right we need to leave here. What do you want to do now?"

Louis didn't answer him.

"I'll check upstairs," offered the cop.

Louis strained to look to the rear of the store where he and Cassy spent many a lunch break together. She'd come down from where she practiced her singing in the front room that looked out onto St. Anthony's Garden at the rear of St. Louis Cathedral. Sometimes he'd hear the hum of her mama's sewing machine. She still sewed on occasion for some of the locals in The Quarter. Even when she was selling out concerts at the peak of her career, she could be found here some days sewing while he worked downstairs. She told him she loved to look out onto where they used to meet in secret, St. Louis Cathedral. He went out into the hall ahead of Officer Earl, who waited on his move. The store was full to capacity so he had to store more books out here.

"Do you want me to look upstairs for you?" asked the officer.

"It's okay," said Louis as he climbed the stairs.

He looked over the banisters at the glass cabinets that housed more books.

"Watch yourself. The staff must have been working on a delivery and left the books there in the rush to leave."

Officer Earl looked to where Louis pointed. The emergency exit sign next to the door at the base of the stairs offered little light. Louis reached the top of the stairs and shone the flash lamp back down to guide the officer.

"Do you work here anymore sir?"

"It's a while since I've worked here. I let the staff run it for me now, since Cassy's illness." His voice trailed off as he disappeared into a room. He left the flash lamp on the final step. Officer Earl reached down to pick it up. He gasped as a rodent ran across the floor.

Louis said, "I'm in here."

The officer followed the sound of his voice into the front room. It was bathed in a warm glow from the streetlights outside. Louis went to the window and leaned over her sewing machine to look out onto the street below. All the surrounding buildings were subdued in darkness. Everyone had left. Louis looked around the room Cassy used to work in. In the corner of the room was the stand with her song sheets. It was a long time since she sang. Officer Earl's radio crackled. He stepped outside the room while he spoke into it. Louis knew he was probably telling Officer Leethat there was no sign of his wife.

"That was Officer Lee. We really have to leave. He's going to insist on us taking you to the Superdome for shelter. We'll be around the streets for a quite a while, before we too will have to go there. Is there anywhere else you can think of that your wife would be? I can get him to drive by your house again on the way to the Dome."

"I don't know where she would go. She is never away from me." How bad is her memory Louis?"

"Her long term memory is perfect. It's the day to day she forgets. At least that's what the doctors say."

"But you think different?"

" There are times when she is so well, that I don't know…"

Louis looked out the window again as he spoke.

There was a loud crash. It came from the direction of St. Louis Cathedral. Two of the trees in St. Anthony's Garden fell and crashed into the ironwork fence surrounding it. Something flew from the statue of Christ the Redeemer like part of its chalk silhouette had fallen off.

"Did you see that?" said Officer Earl and whistled through his teeth as he spoke. "Right come on let's get out of here."

Louis didn't argue and they went back downstairs.

Louis looked back in at the desk where he worked for years. He used to wear a pair of white gloves as he slowly turned the pages of every book to check for rare editions. Cassy used to watch him carefully open boxes of books, which arrived from out of state. Sometimes he got books from the mansions in The Garden District. They always stirred emotion in him as he remembered the books he read as a child. As Officer Earl held open the door for him, Louis wondered what Cassy found in the parcel. The Officer leaned in against the wind and waited for him by the car. Louis pulled the door closed on his bookstore. He had no choice but to go to the Superdome to take shelter from the storm.

Chapter 21

Its midnight on August 28, 2005 when Louis joins the crowds that poured into the Superdome. This building never played a part in his life. He couldn't deal with being in such a confined space with thousands of people. He had spent the past few hours with Officer Earl and Officer Lee, but they had to help with crowd control here. Officer Lee left without saying anything, but Officer Earl delayed in leaving him.

"Are you sure you'll be okay Sir?" he asked.

"I'm in the same position as hundreds of others here," replied Louis.

"I'd say it's more like thousands. Have you ever seen this place as full? I mean it's so strange to be here in these circumstances."

"This is my first time here Officer."

"Well that is a shame. Many a game I watched here. It's very different like this with people strewn about the place. You are a fan right?"

"Of course, I support The Saints, but I always

263

declined tickets over the years. I don't like crowds Officer."

"Please call me James. I feel I know you and your good wife. Are you sure, you are okay? I mean I'm not one for crowds myself, but crowd control is part of the job if you get my meaning."

"Okay James, Call me Louis please. Once I find my wife, I will be fine. I can't help but feel being in here, is saying I've stopped the search."

"You mustn't think that Louis. You have to hold onto the fact she is looking for you. Who knows she may be only a few feet away in this place?"

The officer couldn't have known the panic that thought caused in him that she could be here searching for him; feeling alone and scared.

"I'd have more of a chance if she wasn't," said Louis, not really expecting an answer.

"Don't worry I've seen so much in my line of work, a lot of the bad, but I've seen things work out too you know. We will survive this."

Louis looked around him and wanted to believe the Officer.

"Thank you for your help James. I never asked you, have you family waiting for you?"

"I got my wife and kids out. They are gone to my

sister in Atlanta. I'll join them when we get out of here."

"I would have got her out if I could."

"Louis, it sure was a pleasure to meet you. I hope you find your wife. I've to get over there, looks like something is about to kick off. I suggest you lay low. We don't know how long we'll be in here after the storm hits or what it's going to be like either."

With that, he was swallowed into the crowd and Louis was left on his own. Officer Earl couldn't have known the impact his words had on him. Louis had to keep holding onto the belief that he would find Cassy. Whereas now, it seemed hopeless. The cops had helped him as much as they could have given the circumstances.

Everyone was the same here. They sought shelter from the storm. There was nowhere else to go. It had been decided to send whoever remained in the city here. Thousands of people were stuck in New Orleans, forced to wade out the storm. Some chose not to leave, having lived in the city their entire lives and survived countless storms before. Louis took no comfort that he was in this melting pot with thousands of others. For him this was a suffocating stadium full of strangers. He thought he knew just about everyone in the Quarter, but this was no place to strike up a conversation. It was about survival. Everyone was too busy minding their own.

Men kept a watchful eye over their families and everyone was considered a threat. The entire field was a make shift camp with many people already settled down to try to get some rest. Others walked around aimlessly on the outskirts and searched the crowd. It struck Louis that they were like him. They too were looking for a loved one. He tried to push away the recurring thought he had that by entering here he somehow ended his search for his wife. He needed to stay focused on finding Cassy, but being in here delayed this.

When he was with the officers earlier that day, they wouldn't allow him to return home. They drove past his house, checked it, and asked him to remain in the police station. It was for his safety they had said. He believed them when they said they checked his house and she wasn't there. He insisted they check the rear of the building as well, in the courtyard and the outhouse, which they did. Therefore, the only option for him was to be here in this building and wait out the storm like everyone else. He focused on his breathing until it was all he could think of. Inhale, exhale, and keep walking. The throng beside him suddenly pushed forward. Louis tried to see what was going on to cause the stir. The doors opened and more people filled the Dome. Then they were sealed in as the doors closed again. He hoped he could find somewhere to rest; if there was such a place. His body ached and his head pounded. His breathing came quicker and he had to focus on it to avoid going into a panic. It looked like everywhere was filled to capacity.

One group of people beside him broke into screams and shouts. They were trying to get the attention of someone across from them. Whoever it was ran to them and they were all reunited. The lucky ones were with their relatives and they found a place together to wait out the storm. He looked out at the sea of people who were busy setting up makeshift shelters for their loved ones. There was no comfort to be found from the fact that everyone was in the same situation. It encapsulated the hopelessness of it. He felt panicked from being confined in here with thousands of people. Someone banged into him and another. The crowd moved forward as more filled the stadium.

He looked around to find shelter. The only free space was one area left under the bleachers that no one had taken. There was a blanket abandoned on the ground. He pictured it was from someone reunited with a family member and they had found shelter together. He looked at the man next to him; before he bends down to join him under the bleachers. The man moved aside to let him in or maybe it was to avoid contact with him. He had a young

267

boy in his arms who was crying in his sleep. The man held him closer. He wrapped his arms tighter around him as Louis passed them. Louis knew there was no room for connection here, only with your own. It was very restrictive under here, but he was thankful he had somewhere on his own. He remembered what the officer told him to lay low.

A new wave of people filled the space around him. He tried to stay detached from everything he saw. Mothers tried to nurse their hungry babies. Young children clung to older siblings as they cried out for their parents. Families tried to stay together. Each new wave of people forced the crowds closer together, until the stadium was filled to capacity. Some cried out for help, while others resigned themselves to the situation. A man across from Louis stared at him intently. Louis crouched further under the bleachers until he was completely out of the man's line of vision. The smell of vomit mixed with urine filled his lungs. Someone a distance away was heaving up their stomach contents. Next to them was another urinating out in the open. The toilets were at the far side of the stadium and after hours of being in here the place started to smell. Louis closed his eyes and tried to wrap himself in the one blanket he had. He lay back, cocooned himself in his blanket and closed his eyes. His eyes felt heavy and he prayed sleep would take him.

He will never forget the look in his mother's eyes that day when he dropped out of law school. She was a stranger to him. She was completely taken over by her drinking. Louis' face flushed when Beth had to explain to his mother, "It's Louis, he's returned from college."

Even as a young boy, he knew there was a distance about his mother, something that held her back. He used to think it was because of his father. In part, that was true. Robert followed him in his ways, his distance and his drive to be a lawyer, whereas Louis never wanted that. All he wanted to do was work with books. As he sat now in the same library he'd left just two years earlier everything had changed.

There was a fear in his mother's eyes when he told them he didn't want to be a lawyer. Instead, he was going to work for Mr. Stein in his bookstore on Royal Street. His father stood up immediately and completely dismissed the idea, calling old Mr. Stein a fool of a man. Louis listened to his father speak as he paraded about the room shouting out his plans for his son, but Louis never took his eyes off his mother. When his father had worn himself out with his shouting, he flung open the verandah doors and left. Louis was left alone with his mother. He knew to expect the big showdown with his father. Robert didn't even raise his head as his brother spoke.

He told his family he loved Cassy and he was going to find her and take her as his wife. With that, Anton kicked his chair back and shouted at him, "You are no longer my son."

His final words rang in his ear. However, his mother's reaction surprised him the most. He secretly believed that somehow she knew about him and Cassy, but knew he was going to college so choose to ignore it. It looked as if she collapsed. Beth rushed over to help her. She pushed her away and went to where Louis sat and tried to hit him only her hand flew past him. He reached up to grab it as she tried to hit him again. Beth went to leave the room, but his mother asked to be taken to her room. Beth looked back at him as she closed the French doors to the library and left Louis alone. There was a look in her eyes, he would never forget. Louis felt an immense sense of fear that day as he left the mansion where he was born and raised. Memories flooded back to him like a thousand darts as he walked through The Garden District. The house still visible to him as it towered above all the rest.

Over the years, Louis felt his family haunted him. The banishment hung like a thin veil over his life. Not as much as the pain that came from not been able to have a child of their own. Sometimes the pain was so vivid in Cassy's eyes he had to look away. He didn't know how to help, but in truth, nothing could take it away. For him, she was enough. He'd stand in the doorway and watch her sew in the upstairs room up over the bookstore. He used to picture children playing at her feet. She would stop what she was working on, look up at him, and smile. He saw her now in his dreams. He promised he'd find her.

He was awoken by a loud bang above his head. It was an elderly woman lying on the bleacher above his. She slipped from where she slept and fell to the bleacher above his. She cried out. Someone came to her and helped her. They handed her a bottle of water and wrapped a coat around her shoulders. She sobbed quietly as they comforted her. She probably didn't even know her, but she was there to help her. Just then was the sound of glass breaking. There was a struggle as one man wrestled another to the ground. A third man interrupted and split up the fight. It looked to be over a portion of food. People reduced to fighting for the last bite to eat. Louis felt like he awoke to a nightmare reality. His watch read 8.55 am. He'd slept pretty much through the entire night. There was some much noise here he couldn't believe he slept that long. He must have drifted off to sleep with sheer exhaustion.

A woman next to him urinated on herself in her sleep. He tried to stretch out his legs to stand up, but they

271

were stiff and cramped. The pain was unbearable. He was in the fetal position and had to try to get up. Most of the stadium was in darkness, except for a few of the lights on the playing field. Louis pulled himself up and looked around. A little girl was throwing up and an older girl held her hair. Their papa stood and held a younger child. He had the same look on his face as everyone here, as if to say when would this torment be over? Louis kept moving. He struggled to take in the scenes of desolation that unfolded around him. Darkness closed in on him, as he felt his body break out in a sweat. His chest tightened and he felt his rib cage contract to try to grab air. Fear took hold of him. He was lost, banished and this time he didn't have Cassy to hold onto. He tried to control his breathing. Over the years, he managed to master these attacks, but the panic set in. He felt shots of pain dart through every limb.

If he was unsure about his place in life, he knew he could never be a lawyer. He didn't want to defend the guilty and rip innocent lives apart. The only peace he found was through books and his life with Cassy. He remembers growing up his father used to leave in the middle of the night. Where he went on those nights, he didn't know until he was older. He always thought they were meetings for the firm, but he was going to Klan gatherings. What he did at those meetings Louis never found out. He had to get away and start his own life. There was no justice to be served by staying and becoming a lawyer to please his father. A man he no longer looked up to. Louis' vision blurred and he fell to the ground. Someone reached out to catch him to stop him falling. He tried to speak, but he couldn't get the words out. The heat was unbearable. Suddenly the stadium was shrouded in darkness as the last of the lights went out. The blackness enveloped him.

***

When he came around there was a horrendous noise. It sounded like glass breaking. Louis never heard a sound like it. It was like the entire roof was going to crash down around them. He tried to stand up, but he couldn't. Whoever had helped him was gone. He looked up as the roof rose and fell in places. A sense of unease broke out amongst the crowd. Then part of the roof was ripped open and suddenly daylight filtered into the Superdome. It must be early morning. The rain poured in from the most tumultuous sky he'd ever seen, dark and looming, weighed heavy with the storm. He looked down to read the time off his watch, but it must have got smashed when he tumbled. He never carried a cell phone. He rang the bookstore from his house phone and Cassy was always with him now, so there was no need for it.

The wind followed a fierce piercing hollow sound.

273

No one moved in those moments. The deafening voices stilled. Everyone waited to see what their outcome would be. Again the horrendous noise; like a crashing sound. The Superdome was filled with deafening screams as another part of the roof gave way. He took his place again under the bleachers, which was a river of human waste. He didn't care. He needed to stay down here, hidden away from the enemy. As he sat under there he thought of all the times when he and Cassy used to meet at St. Louis Cathedral. It was where they went on that first night he met her back in 1959. They continued to meet there, up until he left for law school. That last meeting was emotional. Neither of them knew what the future held, but he knew he wanted to spend the rest of his life with her. He wondered if Cassy was there now. If she had gone to the bookstore as planned and sought shelter in the cathedral.

There was a loud bang like an explosion on the other side of the Dome. It sounded like gunfire to Louis, but he wasn't sure. Tensions were rising. People in a last bid attempt to get food were breaking vending machines. There were not enough food supplies to go around and they were quickly running out of water. However, amidst all the strife Louis was struck by one scene he knew would stay with him for the rest of his life. A little girl was reading from her picture book to her fluffy bunny and her papa listened to her with a protective arm around her. Her papa laughed at the funny parts and pretended to cry when the bunny didn't make it to where it was going. It was the most heartwarming thing to watch.

It was Monday August 29, when Hurricane Katrina made landfall in New Orleans. A while later word spread that the levees had broken and water rose over The Industrial Canal. The waters rose and the city began to flood. Plans for evacuation of the Superdome were in place. Louis planned to leave with the first group. He made his way to the front of the crowd. He dreaded to think what it would be like to try to leave here. Louis spent another three nights in here, in the belly of the fish.

On Sept 1, the evacuation of the Superdome began. Louis joined the line to leave. As soon as they were allowed to leave, Louis planned to resume his search for Cassy. There was talks they would be all put on buses and taken to the Convention Center. School buses were brought in and used for the evacuation He did not intend to get on one of those buses. He would make his way back through the city and find Cassy. The feeling that she was in St. Louis Cathedral drove him on in his plan.

When the line finally moved outside Louis waited for his opportune moment and stepped to one side. Nobody noticed him. Everyone was too busy looking after their own and making sure they got a place aboard one of the buses. Water was handed out as they waited. Some people had set up make shift camps outside the Dome. Louis figured by going back over to where it was he'd only reveal his plans. He needed to stay back here, hidden until they all left. They all piled onto the buses without looking back. No one wanted to be left behind. In the distance, he could see people up on the highway. They were walking up and down in a distressed state. The city he loved was reduced to a river of pain. The rain hadn't ceased. It poured continuously to meet the floodwaters below.

As he began to walk down Poydras Street he wanted to give way to his tears, but they wouldn't come. Instead, he was filled with the need to put his own upset aside and find his wife.

"Here I managed to get two bottles. I was saving one for later, but you can have it," said the man next to him.

Louis noticed he was a cop.

"Don't let the uniform throw you off. I think we're all the same here at this stage."

Louis took the water that was offered him. "Thank you," he managed.

"How come you're not getting on the buses with the rest?" asked the cop.

Louis didn't answer him and looked in the direction

of the city.

"Well the ways I see it some have to stay behind and go look for people. I heard there are people stuck on roofs and inside buildings. Don't get me wrong sir; I don't think it's all down to me," said the cop.

He held his bottle of water mid air then and said, "You're looking for someone too, right?"

"I have to find my wife," answered Louis.

"How do you know she's not here amongst all these people?"

"Because, she wouldn't have known to come here. She was on her own. She's not well."

"Sorry what is your name? I'm D.J."

Louis raised his eyebrow.

"Okay then, I'm officer Dylan Junior Howard, but my friends call me D.J."

Louis warmed to him and extended his hand. "I'm Louis Le Blanc. Call me Louis and my wife is Cassy Shaw."

"Well I be…what does it feel like to be the husband of Cassy Shaw? I mean if you don't mind me saying, your wife is my favorite singer. I grew up listening to her."

"I'll tell her you said, thank you."

"My pops was in the force too; more than a cop though, he was a detective sergeant. Wait there, you said Le Blanc. Any relation to Le Blanc's Law firm, over on Canal

Street?"

"Yes my brother Robert."

"So you're the son of Anton Le Blanc. I remember my pops knew him. Wow so you're from the biggest firm in the city and your wife is one of our greatest talents. Some house y'all got." Louis took a drink of water to avoid having to speak. The buses were nearly full and they were calling out the last few seats.

"Well Louis this is it, it's now or never. You're as sure as I am you don't want that seat?"

"I'm certain."

"Let's go find your wife."

"Why would you want to help me?"

"I'm not helping you because of who you are if that's what you mean. No as I said we all the same here."

"I'm not a lawyer. I never went into the family business. I own "Signed and Sealed", a bookstore over on Royal Street."

"Oh yes I know it. Come on let's go and you can tell me all about it. I'm intrigued Louis I won't lie."

They walked onto St. Charles Avenue crossed over at Canal Street. It was here they were met with floodwater. A face floated past them. It's pale, milky white surface had jewels where the eyes should be and a shocked theatrical expression on the red painted lips. Louis stooped down to pick up the carnival mask out of the floodwaters. A trail of wet ribbons and feathers dripped down onto his leg. He broke down crying.

"Come on Louis. We don't have much further."

Just then, something knocked D.J. off his feet. He grabbed onto the nearest lamppost.

"What was it?" asked Louis.

"You don't want to know. Come on let's keep going."

Louis looked down at the lifeless body that floated in the water. He could feel panic resurface in him, but he kept his focus on finding Cassy.

A small boat passed them with a man and two women. When they got close to them, Louis could see it wasn't a boat at all, but some driftwood tied together. Their faces were chiseled like stone. Louis noticed the woman nearest him held a dead child in her arms. A little girl in a pink coat peeped out from behind her. She beamed at Louis. They continued on their way through the muddy waters. Trees that once stood tall, now hung low with their branches snapped marking where the pressure of the water ravaged them. Mattresses and other household items all floated through the waters. Semi submerged cars with dogs stuck up on the roofs. The unbearable sound of dogs howling.

They saw unimaginable scenes of distress. People were stuck on rooftops and waited for help. They passed a makeshift grave on the sidewalk. They walked to the end of Canal Street and turned onto Royal Street.

"We're going to be okay Louis. This part of the city is on more elevated ground, so it will be easier to get to your bookstore."

With that, there was a loud bang, like gunfire. Alarms were going off from different buildings damaged by the floodwaters, but this sounded like a shot.

"They are looting. We're going to have to try and move quickly."

D.J. had pulled off his shirt and just his vest. There was the sound of a   helicopter overhead.

"Does instinct make you want to go after them?" Louis asked.

"No Louis. It should I guess, but I want to get to my family."

Louis stopped walking.

"There is something I want to tell you D.J. My wife was raped. She was raped when she worked for my family."

"Louis I don't know what to say. I'm sorry."

"It was my father. The great lawyer, Anton Le Blanc."

"Come on Louis, let's go find her."

Chapter 22

Cassy stared at her belly in the full-length mirror. It looked swollen, but then she was always bloated around this time of the month. She felt the blood drain from her face as she realized she was a month late. She was so busy with her workload that she hadn't noticed. Every morning she was sick. When she worked, her palms sweated and she had a constant dull ache in her head. Even when she brushed her teeth, she felt sick and ran into her washroom. Sometimes she missed the toilet bowl and vomited on the floor. Her taste for food was gone, but she forced herself to eat. When she got out of bed too fast, the room swirled. She just thought she was tired, but when she looked at her stomach she knew. She was pregnant. The panic set in as she wondered who she was going to tell.

Her aunt Rosalie wrote her initially, when she wasn't able to get home to visit. Jacob made sure Cassy got the letters, but she couldn't write back to her. Rosalie continued to write regardless. It helped her to hear about their lives back in Treme, which seemed a million miles

281

away. Her papa got a job in a restaurant on Esplanade Avenue playing the piano. This made Cassy smile to read, but also sad because that is where her mama dreamed of living someday. It was a beautiful part of town. Rosalie wrote how he was able to live on the tips alone. The customers loved him and the owners were so pleased with him. He is well respected as a musician now she wrote. He was making many contacts in the music business and Rosalie said in one of her letters maybe she could use it someday. Cassy closed her eyes and saw him in the restaurant and the pleased looks on everyone's faces as he played. She also saw her mama there. When she opened her eyes the letter she held in her hands was stained with tears.

Jacob was taken ill and was sent home to his son to care for him. Beth told her when she enquired to where he was. She hadn't seen him in a while. With Jacob gone, there was no one left she could talk to and no one to bring her letters. It was a while since she received one. Whether her aunt tired of writing with no response from her or whether her letters were destroyed, Cassy had no way of knowing. She couldn't trust Grace with her news. It's not that she wouldn't help her, but she had her own problems with William sent to the family plantation. There was no chance of him coming back to the mansion to work.

When Cassy was a little girl, she asked her mama where babies came from. Her mama told her that wouldn't be something she'd have to think about until she met the man that loved her and they would have a family together. Her mama told her she hoped she'd have made something of her life and have had time to pursue her dreams. Only the dreams her mama spoke of weren't to be a singer, but to work hard and become a wife. Cassy wanted all of these things, but not like this, pregnant; because she was raped.

The months wound round for Cassy. She was forced to stay in her room. The sickness passed but it was replaced with an overwhelming tiredness. Some days she found it hard to get up out of bed. If only Miss Brown would come to see her, then maybe she could get a message to her family. But then again none of the women were shown to her room anymore. She had no one to spend time with. The workload hadn't slackened if anything it increased. All the women of The Garden District were attending a ball. Beth brought their orders to her. They knew what they wanted for the ball, so they didn't need to see her and she had all their measurements. It wouldn't have mattered if one of them insisted on seeing her she wasn't told.

Madame came to her room accompanied by Beth, who looked at Cassy's reflection in the mirror. When Cassy turned around, she looked away. Madame told her that she was to let out all her clothes and conceal the baby she carried. She then asked her, whose child it was. Which of the staff was she to fire? She was practically sober, or maybe she was so used to being drunk she played the sober card well. Cassy searched Beth's face, willing her to look at her. A wave of sickness washed over her and she ran into the washroom. She didn't have time to close the door, so they heard her retching. When she stood back up, she was wrecked. She felt lightheaded.

"Can I help you Cassy?" whispered Beth.

She stood in the door of the washroom. It was the first time in a while Beth showed any sympathy towards her.

"What is going to happen to me and to my baby?"

Beth reached out for her arm and guided her into the sewing room.

"Madame is inspecting your work. You're going to have to stay on top of things you know."

"I am trying Beth."

"Try harder."

Cassy looked at her incredulously.

"No I mean it for your own sake. She will make things very difficult on you. You know that."

"What are the two of you muttering about? Beth tells me you're busy with the upcoming ball for all my friends.

I've decided I'm going to attend."

Cassy could feel herself waver again.

"Yes Madame," was all she could muster.

Beth nudged her. In the company of Madame, she couldn't be seen as a support to her. She did not intend to hinder her position in the house.

"You know Miss Brown asked to see you, but I told her you are too busy. I can't imagine she was going to the ball. She never goes to any of those things. This got me thinking then, what could she possibly want with you. I sent her on her way. Your workload is too full."

Cassy couldn't breathe. It took the strength she had not to collapse. Miss Brown was her link to her singing career. She believed in her enough to set up an audition with Mr. Godfrey and Mr. Davis, the two most influential music executives and she watched it disappear in front of her.

"Was I wrong? Sure aren't you after taking an order for me now. I don't see how you could possibly accommodate Miss Brown for whatever it was she needed sewing."

Cassy exhaled a little relieved that Madame didn't know about her audition.

"Do you not think I have a heart when one of my staff is pregnant that I wouldn't consider your needs?" She didn't wait for an answer.

"Of course Madame."

"Whose baby is it?" asked Madame.

Cassy didn't answer and felt her tongue stick to the back of her throat. Madame Le Blanc threw back her head and laughed. Beth shook her head behind Madame's back.

"It's my husband's isn't it, you filthy whore."

"He raped me, he raped me," Cassy cried out.

Beth looked horrified, but surely, she knew. Surely she knew that when she was summoned to his study that night he raped her and at every opportunity since. She pulled Cassy into the bedroom Madame followed.

"Madame she is tired, she needs to rest. The heat is getting to her. I hear it happens when you're pregnant. She didn't mean anything."

Beth implored Cassy with her eyes. Cassy lay down on the bed and closed her eyes. She listened as Madame retreated towards the door.

"Beth, come with me."

"Yes Madame," said Beth. She sounded upset, but she did her best to hide it. She looked back at Cassy before she left her alone. Cassy knew Beth had no choice, but to leave with her employer.

When Cassy mustered up enough energy to go to the kitchen to get some supper she was told by Grace she is to stay in her room and the meals would be brought to her. For the duration of her condition, she said. This made her blush. Time seemed to pass slowly, but before long, it was no longer possible to hide her growing belly. The sickness had passed, replaced with fear. Fear of what would happen to her and her baby. She hoped that she could leave here once she had the baby and was on her feet again. She could support her child as her mama supported her; even if that meant sewing for a while on the outside. All this time she didn't allow herself to think about Louis, because then she would regret her baby. The only love she had now was for her baby and this kept her strong.

Miss Brown never returned to the mansion. Cassy wondered did they know about Mr. Godfrey and what he planned for her, but how could they know. She never told anyone. She was very careful in that. There were no customers, an occasional one called for her, but Beth sent them on their way. The date passed when she was to return to St. Peter Street and start her new life as a singer. The day in the music room faded away, like a dream that can never return.

A time came when he left her alone. Then one night it started again. A light shone in one of the outhouses and she saw a shadow cross the lawn. The darkness of the night flooded into her room as he opened the door. She wept.

He forced her against him. He pressed her face against the mirror. She couldn't breathe. Further and further, he pressed her face against the glass surface. Her cried on the mirror which reflected the world outside back to her.

"My baby," she cried out and he left the room.

She made her own garments of concealment, because Madame decided she needed to be seen around the house, as the staff knew she hadn't left.But not to speak to any of them. The only ones who knew were Beth and Grace. Beth didn't speak of it. She had her own cares or freedoms, which Cassy couldn't tell. Madame was often found in the library in a drunken state. Some nights she could be heard thrashing around the house. No one went to her aid. By day, she was in her room. Cassy thought she would just send her home, banish her from here. She heard shouting some nights, but it was always just Madame. Cassy's fear grew for her baby. Unknown to the world; known only here in this dark place.

One day when she was feeling better than she had done in weeks, she left her room and went outside. She knew she was told to stay away from the other staff and about the house, but surely, that couldn't include outside as well. What did it matter now as Jacob wasn't here, so no one would see her if she kept close to her room? It filled her with immense joy to see Jacob tend to the flowers in the distance. She clutched her stomach all of sudden and wondered if anyone told him about her condition. As she approached him, she planned how she could explain her belly. Madame told her to let out her clothes that should anyone see her they wouldn't suspect she was pregnant. Though he was older than her papa, it was hard to fool Jacob he knew about things. She was drawn to him for this reason; he was so different than anyone here. He was her only confidante, so she decided immediately she was going to tell him. When he turned around from what he was planting, she saw he already knew.

"I'm so sorry Cassy. I wish I knew before I left."

This left her speechless.

"It's not your fault Jacob. Nothing could have been done. There is nothing anyone can do for me now."

He busied himself with cleaning his hands with a cloth. He never wore gloves when he tended the soil and his hands showed it. They were covered in welts from years of hard labor.

"Walk with me," he said. "I hoped you would escape. That somehow as the seamstress, it was a higher position and he would leave you alone."

Cassy stopped dead in her tracks.

"You know?" she asked.

"Come on, come to the glasshouse. The entire house

is in the kitchen. Just as we were the day, you arrived. They're welcoming more staff today."

"To replace who?" asked Cassy as she stepped in line with him.

He looked at her gravely.

"William is it and the others?" asked Cassy. She couldn't think who left that day with William.

"They plan to send you home after. Come in, I'll make us some tea."

"With my baby, Jacob?"

"That I don't know. How far along are you now?"

"I'm nearly due I reckon."

"Have they sent for the doctor for you at all?"

"At the start, but there was no complications; so Beth says they won't be fussing with me."

He made them tea. Cassy watched the steam rise out of her cup. Her mind raced ahead wondering what was going to happen to her.

"I tell you what I'll do; I'll get a message to your family."

"How Jacob!"

"I know we couldn't get the letters out before, but that was different. I'll say I'm sick again and they'll have to let me leave."

So Jacob left with a message for her family. They

decided it best he get word to them when he was home. If she wrote them a letter, they could find it. She would just have to trust him to carry this out for her. His niece would help him.

After Jacob she knew she had no one here she could trust. Madame arranged for the doctor to see her. This time he told her that her baby would be here any day and she was to rest up.

One night when Beth came to see her. There was a gentle knock on her door, but Beth didn't wait to be asked in.

"I need to talk to you Cassy."

Cassy sat up in bed. She had dropped off to sleep.

"What time is it?"

"It's after nine. Everyone is gone to bed. But don't worry about that. I need to tell you something."

"What is it? You're scaring me."

Beth closed the door behind her. Cassy reached out to turn on her bedside lamp.

"Don't bother. Here let me. I'll open the drapes."

Without further ceremony, she announced that Louis had returned home from college.

"But you said I wasn't to speak..."

"I saw y'all together; one time when I was sent to The Quarter."

"You didn't tell on us."

"For selfish reasons only; I wanted to protect my position here. So I couldn't have any part in your secret life."

"Did he ask after me?"

"You are the reason he was here. There was a huge showdown tonight."

"He was here tonight," said Cassy. Her voice went hoarse as she broke down crying.

"No need to get upset."

Beth looked out the window.

"It's not good news Cassy. There was an outburst between him and his father. Madame collapsed as per usual. I had to see her to her room. I left Louis alone in the dining room. When I returned he was gone."

"But that's okay. He'll go looking for me and my family will tell him I'm here."

" What is it?" asked Cassy.

Beth hung her head.

"He was told you moved to the plantation with the other staff and you decided to leave for a position somewhere else. You left no forwarding address."

"I can't breathe."

Beth helped her to her feet and over to the window.

"I have to look out there every day and every night

and some nights I can see him just stood watching. That is why I keep the drapes closed. Louis is my only hope. He loves me Beth."

"Can you not see Cassy they will never allow it to happen? Their son, with one of the help. It's inconceivable. They would destroy you first before they allow you to be part of their world. Do you want your baby to grow up in the house of your attacker?"

Beth shook her head.

"Beth, please tell me what to do," pleaded Cassy.

"I know they will send you and the baby away from here once the child is born. Madame is not going to keep his child here. After that, Cassy the rest is up to you. Maybe you can contact Louis somehow."

"How will I know where to find him? What will happen if he's left town? And now he won't come looking for me."

"Okay, I didn't tell you this, any of this. Louis has dropped out of law school. He plans to work for some man that owns a bookstore on Royal Street. They have disowned him Cassy."

"This all happened tonight."

"I didn't mean to upset you Cassy, but you have a right to know."

"Do you think I should just leave now, I mean I

could couldn't I?"

"You can't Cassy. She won't let you."

As if only thinking it for the first time Cassy pulled Beth towards her with both arms and asked, "Does he know about the baby?"

"Of course not. Remember you've left town as far as he knows."

"But what if he is still around and he sees me around The Quarter with my baby?"

"I don't know Cassy."

"You have to help me Beth please. Will you get my letter to Louis now?"

"A letter to Louis!"

"Do you remember I asked you before, the night you came to see me?"

"Oh that night I was upset. I shouldn't have burdened you with my troubles and you shouldn't burden me with yours."

"Beth, please," Cassy pleaded.

"I can't have any part in this Cassy."

"Please Beth. We were friends once."

"Right hurry up and write it."

"It's written."

Cassy produced a cream envelope from her skirt pocket.

"Do you carry it around with you? Right I best leave."

Beth stood up impatient, but Cassy knew she was just afraid, as she was.

With that, Beth left the room and closed the door. Cassy listened to her steps retreat down the corridor, but only after a few moments. She stood out there a while. She could see her shadow under the door. Cassy knew that any hope for her and Louis was now in Beth's hands. She held her stomach as she curled up on her bed. The hateful deed she suffered at her employer's hands returned to her repeatedly. There were times when she tried to fight him, but he used to slap her into submission.

Chapter 23

Underneath a liquid moon, the pain came strong and fast. She had the most jarring pain in her stomach. She had barely slept. She spent hours trying to get asleep. The clock in the main hall sounded out the hour. It was six. During the night, she got out of bed and opened the door to the corridor. The heat was overwhelming and she couldn't get any relief. She tried to sit up in bed, but a torrent of pain coursed through her. It was unbearable. It rushed through her in strong waves. She needed her mama. She leaned forward. She had no one. No, please little one she begged. She didn't know what to do.

"I can't help you little one," she cried out.

The next contraction came the minute the first one left. She stumbled out into the hall. Beth heard her and opened the door to her room.

"Help me the baby is coming," she pleaded.

The look of compassion on Beth's face reassured Cassy that she would help her. Without saying a word, Beth helped her into her room.

"I need to go…"

"Cassy, there is no time. The baby is coming. It's better you're in my room," said Beth and lifted her legs up onto the bed. The pain came again. Stronger and faster it took her breath.

"I'll go get Madame."

"No please Beth…" but she couldn't speak anymore the pain was too strong.

Beth left her alone.

Her waters broke. She felt the bed drenched beneath her. She screamed out in terror. She didn't want to be alone. Grace and Beth rushed into the room. Madame walked in behind them. Cassy noticed they all wore aprons like those of the staff. She realized they were waiting for this moment. Cassy's body thrust and twisted in pain. They offered her no pain relief. Grace was busy preparing towels and water at an area at Cassy's feet. While Beth sat near the top of the bed and didn't utter a word; Madame paced over by the window. They were in the room with her, but she knew it wasn't to assist her. Grace handed her a glass of water. The pain subsided, until she was taken over by it again. She left then. Beth stayed beside Cassy, until Madame called her to the window. She opened the French doors and went outside and Beth followed her. Someone else joined them.

Cassy could see the silhouette of a man. There was a car in the driveway. She recognized it as Robert's car. Cassy looked beyond the line of magnolia trees that led up to the porch with the grand pillars. She saw a woman stood there. She strained to see who it was, but she was shaded by the willow tree. Grace told her to push. She said something to her about being young, that the baby will just pop out. The doctor that saw her when she first learned she was pregnant came into the room. As soon as one contraction eased off, another rushed in.

Beth came back into the room and sat down beside her.

She whispered to her, "Rest Cassy. You're going to need your strength."

No sooner had Cassy lay down, but another pain ripped through her. The doctor came to her bedside.

Beth stood back.

"Now Miss Shaw, this baby is coming and I'm going to need you to push when I tell you." Cassy nodded. It was all she could muster at this stage. There it was an earth shattering pain ripped up through her from the base of her spine and to the core of her being. "That's it. I see the head."

Another push. Beth offered her hand. Cassy shook her head and dug her hands into the bed sheets. She closed her eyes. She pictured it was just her mama with her and the doctor, that was all. That was enough. She exhaled. Silence. She opened her eyes. Everyone was gathered in the corner of the room.

She was held up to the light by Madame, her baby. A cry. A gasp for air in the moonlight.

Cassy tried to raise her head more to see her baby.

"A girl," the doctor confirmed.

"My daughter," Cassy breathed.

She waited. Time passed in small beats of her heart. "Give me my baby. Let me hold my baby." She lay back down exhausted.

Cassy awoke in Beth's room. She was alone. It was bright outside. The sun filtered in. She managed to get off the bed. She pulled back the sheets and looked down to see they were stained with blood. As she walked across the room to see what was happening outside, the room spun. She felt weak, but mustered up enough strength to go to the French doors. She reached out for the handle of the door. There was the sound of an engine. Robert's car now stalled in the driveway. It was partially hidden by the line of magnolia trees. She looked towards the porch where everyone was gathered. The door to Beth's room opened behind her. Grace stood beside her and gently pulled her back from the door.

"What are you doing up? You should be resting."

"Grace, where is my baby?" Cassy didn't recognize her own voice. It sounded hoarse.

Grace held the drapes in her hand and dramatically let them fall to the floor.

"You need to rest now Cassy," she said, while looking out through the partially open drapes before she closed them. She guided her to the bed and helped her sit down.

"Where is my baby?" Cassy asked.

"Lie down Cassy, you're very tired."

Cassy did as she was told and hoped her baby would be brought to her.

Beth touched Grace's shoulder. Cassy hadn't noticed her come in. Grace left the room.

"Cassy, you were asleep for hours. I tried to bring her to you, but you were asleep."

Cassy cried.

"Please I can see her now," she begged.

Beth sat down on the bed, smoothed down the sheets with her hand, and didn't look at her.

"There is something I need to tell you Cassy," she said and took her hand in hers.

Cassy pulled back from her.

"Please listen. I brought her to you last night. I

wanted you to see her one last time," she said and looked towards the window.

She fell silent at the sound of the car driving down the driveway.

"No, no," Cassy screamed, but her voice wouldn't come anymore. She reached out to grab onto Beth. She started to bleed again and looked down at her blood soaked nightgown.

"You lost her Cassy," said Beth and pulled herself free of her.

Cassy cried and the most harrowing sound came from her worn out body. She buried her face in the pillows.

"I'll return later. I have to go."

When she got to the door, she turned and said, "You held her Cassy. Do you remember? I made sure of it, but you were so drained that you passed out, but you held her Cassy I promise you." With that, she closed the door.

Hours passed.Cassy tried to remember the night before. Her little baby held to the light of the moon. They were all gathered around the window looking at her. She couldn't see. Wait a glimpse of her hair. Her skin was so pink and wrinkled. She writhed, life filling her for the first time, she'd arrived into the world. Grace fussed and cleaned up the sheets. The doctor spoke to her, leaned over gave her something. Beth encouraged her to drink it. After that nothing.

Wait she played it again over in her mind. Madame looked out the window towards the balcony. She didn't hold the baby, but watched everything closely. Beth still came to her to soothe her, the doctor stalled. He stood at the window too. They spoke words she couldn't tell. Grace cleaned the sheets, but whispered something to her. She didn't want to be here. She was leaving. This place is evil. She wasn't sure. It was too much, too much blood lost, too much to understand. She followed Madame's gaze, to the balcony. Yes, there she was on the balcony. Olivia paced back and forth, a mirror image of Madame pacing in the room. She was waiting, watching. Then nothing. Darkness. The doctor stepped forward and gave her something.

Try again. Beth approached her, touched the sheets while Grace cleaned an area. Madame watched them closely. The doctor stood nearby. Grace watched from the door then, she looked upset. She had tried to say something, but couldn't they were too close to her. Beth leaned in and handed her, her baby. Madame watched closely. Cassy raised her arms to take her baby. Beth let go and allowed her full ownership of her daughter. Cassy looked into her face. Love welled up inside her. A love she had never known until this moment. She placed her finger into her daughter's palm and she responded to her touch and held her tight.

"Belle," she whispered. "You are Belle Shaw."

Beth looked away. Madame walked over and grasped Beth by the shoulder. Cassy watched a struggle. Beth left the room. The doctor intervened with the injection. Her baby's eyes, her precious face was the last thing she can remember. She was alone again.

She remembered she asked Beth to take the little gown from her closet. The one her mama gave her on her fifteenth birthday. She guided Beth to the box on the floor of the closet.   Inside was the gown wrapped in tissue. Beth took it out. Madame watched her hand it to Cassy and she looked back out the window. Belle's little body was so tiny and curled up asleep, that Cassy just rested the gown on top of her. She told Beth it was hers, given to her by her mama. Beth smiled. Madame approached the bed. She snatched the warmth of her baby from her arms. She walked towards the door. Beth followed behind her. The doctor leaned in and administered something into her arm. Darkness then.

Chapter 24

Cassy awoke to see Beth holding her case.

"I packed it for you. I didn't think you'd want to spend any longer in that room. All your sewing things will be sent to you."

Cassy looked at the clothes Beth laid out for her on the bed. The bedclothes had been changed. She had a vague memory of Grace coming in during the night.

"Am I going home today?" asked Cassy, barely able to hide the emotion in her voice.

Beth set down the case and approached the bed.

"It's better for you Cassy. I was able to get word to your papa. He is waiting for you."

"Does he know?"

"That's not my place. Come on let me help you. I'd imagine you don't want to stay here any longer than necessary."

When Cassy stood up, she felt a burning pain in her groin and reached out to Beth. Beth helped her to the chair by the window. Cassy allowed her to help put on her dress.

"Grace was in her during the night. I remember. She

put a new nightgown on me. The other one was stained."

Cassy allowed the tears flow.

"Ssh, come on now. You'll be better when you get home, you'll see."

"Where is my baby?" she could barely get the words out from crying.

"Cassy, you remember you lost her. She was buried yesterday at the plantation. Madame said it was better this way."

"Did you go with her?"

"With Madame?"

"No, with my baby. I don't want her on her own. I would want you to hold her, if I couldn't."

Beth turned her back.

"Come on now Cassy I have to get you home."

"Are you coming with me? I don't think I could make it on my own. I don't feel strong enough."

"Yes, Madame told me to travel with you. We'll ride the streetcar together, but I'll leave you at Carondelet Street. Will you be okay from there?"

Cassy nodded. She looked out at the drive where she saw the car the night her baby died.

"Who was there that night?"

"You know who was there," Beth stopped as if to compose herself. "It was Grace, Madame and I that is all;

and the doctor of course."

"No there were others. I remember seeing a man outside talking to Madame and a woman went to the car. It looked like Olivia, Robert's wife."

"Don't be foolish why would they have been here? Come on I think we should go."

"Can I say goodbye to anyone before I leave?"

"If you mean Jacob he's not here. He is still very sick Cassy do you not remember. He is gone home to his family in Baton Rouge. Is there anybody else?"

Cassy shook her head.

"Tell you what I'll give you a moment. I'll be waiting at the side entrance. Don't be long, because we don't want to miss the next streetcar."

Cassy heard her steps retreat down the corridor. When she was gone, she went across to her bedroom. Everything looked the same. She went into her sewing room. Sure enough, her sewing machine was boxed up along with anything she was working on. Everything else would remain here. As she left the room, she looked out at the outhouse where he first attacked her. The clouds parted to unveil the lawn. Such an array of color, jasmine, cyclamen, roses amidst a bountiful supply of magnolia blooms. The oak moss that hung from the cypress trees. The grandeur of the grounds combined with the opulence of the house, both equally pruned to their eloquent state. She thought of Jacob and wished she could have said goodbye. She folded her arms across her stomach and the ache she felt for her baby washed over her. She walked down the corridor and didn't look back.

Beth accompanied her as far as Carondelet Street as she said. They didn't speak for the entire journey. Cassy was thankful for this she wanted to be left alone with her thoughts. As the scenery changed for what she knew was the last time, she relaxed a little into the seat and focused on seeing her papa again. She pictured her aunt having her favorite meal prepared and her room all ready for her. Her papa would hug her and tell her how good it was she was home. Beth left her at the corner of Canal and Carondelet Street as arranged. Cassy felt she stalled on leaving her as if she had something to say, but chose against it. She watched her a moment to see would she come back to her, but Beth crossed the street and didn't look back. Cassy began her journey home.

She needed to rest so she decided to go to the little park at Margaret's Place. She looked up at "The Mother of Orphans" statue. Cassy missed her mama so much. The pain coursed through her again. She reached down into her bag for the pills that the doctor had prescribed. Beth had given her some lemonade. She washed the tablets down.

All her earthly belongings were in this bag. Beneath her few items of clothing, was the box of things she prepared over the last few months for her baby. It contained the shawl she made, a little comb and a pair of boots. Whenever she could, she kept some money aside to buy them. As she looked at them now and back up towards the statue, she thought about how she never got to use any of them for her baby. The only thing she had given her baby was the gown her mama put her in the day she was born. Now her little girl lay buried in it, at the plantation. She didn't even get to see her in it. She remembered asking could she dress her. Darkness came over Beth's face and she told her it was for her own sake she didn't see her baby like that. The only memory she had now was holding her little pink body close to her and looking down into her eyes. Then Grace took her. As hard as she tries, Cassy can't remember anything beyond this. She closed her bag and continued on her way home.

It was a different journey than when traveled these same roads to make her way to the mansion that first day; which seemed like an eternity ago. She was nervous, but also she borrowed the optimism her family felt, that somehow this could change her life. Her mama was full of optimism for her future. Her papa was wary, but he went along with it because surely it was a better life than she could have here. He hoped it would bring her the opportunity her mama believed it would. None of them knew then or could they have, the measure it would change her life.

Nothing had changed in The French Quarter. Everyone went about their usual business unawares that her life had been completely altered. She passed the turn off for Miss Lottie Brown's music hall. It was months since she saw her. She wondered did she find another girl to sing. The opportunity presented to her, seemed like a lifetime ago. So much so, she wondered did it happen at all. The pain had subsided for now, but she was exhausted.

Then in the distance, she saw her papa. He waved at her as he walked towards her.

"Papa I didn't know you'd be here."

"Cassy, it's so good to see you," he said as he embraced her. He took her bag from her. She reluctantly let it go.

"It's okay, I've got it," he reassured her.

"Beth told me you were coming home today, but she wouldn't say which streetcar, so I'm out here since six. I figured you'd have to be on one of them."

"Oh papa, you don't know how good it is to see you."

"Come on let's get you home. It's all over now sweetheart."

"You know papa."

"Let's talk at home. You'll feel much better when you've had your aunt's gumbo."

"Papa, what did Beth tell you?"

"I didn't speak to her directly at all. She left word with her mama that you had been very sick these past few months and you were coming home. That place was never for you Cassy. I always said it. Didn't I?"

"Papa that's not all. I need to talk to you."

"Once we get home we'll have all the time we need. Come on baby girl won't be long now; you'll be tucked up in your own bed."

They turned onto Congo Square. Memories of all the happy times spent her with him and her brother came to her.

"I play in "Jacques Bistro" now Cassy. I don't know if you aunt told you in one of her letters."

"She did papa and also that you haven't been back over to "The Sugar Club" since."

"That's right Cassy. I couldn't tell you when was the last time I drank and good news, I haven't gambled either. I'm making good money playing piano, although we all know that's not why I gambled."

"Do you see any of your friends from there?" she asked.

"A lot of the work dried up in these parts and it has kept most of them home or elsewhere, trying to find work. I honestly think if I was still on that building site, I'd be still drinking."

"You didn't drink back then papa."

"I did Cassy. You were just too young to remember. I think if the crew wasn't drinking the night before, maybe the accident would never have happened, but then I might never have taking my piano playing serious."

"Do you think there is a reason for everything papa?"

"Right now I think it would be wrong of me to say that to you."

Her aunt sat beside her on the sofa while her papa stood in the doorway. They listened to everything she told them. Her papa knew as she did, there was nothing they could do. Rosalie never took her hand off Cassy, while she recounted in as much detail as she could what happened to her. How he raped her and how she was closed off from the world. She promised herself that she would never speak of her baby. She looked over at her mama's sewing machine still in the corner of the room. The same cloth draped over it. She pictured the little birds painted onto its surface and then the words poured from her.

"I was pregnant," she said and looked to the floor, "but I lost my baby."

Her papa stood in front of her now and bent down to her level. He took her in his arms and said nothing. She knew he was crying she felt his tears on her shoulder.

"Oh Cassy," said her aunt. "What happened?"

She was hushed by her papa.

"She died while I slept Aunt. She is buried on their plantation on The River Road."

"Why would they do that?" asked her aunt and Amos cut her off.

"I don't want to hear anymore. Cassy is home now, where she belongs," said Amos.

"Of course," agreed Rosalie. "I'll get your room ready. Let me take that case from you."

"No," said Cassy more forceful than she meant to. "I'm sorry aunt, but I need to put it away myself."

She left them and went to her room. She removed the little box that had once stowed her little baby's gown and peeped inside at the shawl, the tiny pair of boots and comb for her baby. She lay down on her bed and decided she would show her papa. He'd know what to do. One night when Amos returned from work, Cassy told him about the memory box for her baby. He promised her that they would go to the cemetery together tomorrow and find a place to bury it. Within the safety and familiarity of home Cassy started to heal.

Chapter 25

Memories rushed at her in no particular order as she remembered life here with her family. Their voices filled the house with the gentle hum of the sewing machine in the background. When she took one last look, she saw her papa stood in the doorway. The memory of him faded again.

Tonight as the storm increased, she watched her mama fade away as it became a shell of a house again. She needed to move on from here. Her head hurt and the air felt tight as she stepped back onto the street to continue her journey to the bookstore. She looked back at the family home one last time and walked towards "St. Louis Cemetery Number One". Her parents are buried here. She entered through the narrow entrance of the rusty ironwork fence. She followed the path to the family tomb. She touched their engraved names on the marble stone. A lifetime of hopes and dreams buried with them. She stood with her back to the tomb and searched for the white brick in the wall. She remembered it was to the left of the tree directly opposite the tomb. The area was overgrown, but she could see the small wooden cross jut up out of the ground. She went over to it. It was bent at an angle from the force of the wind. She leaned down and tried to straighten it, but it was lodged against a stone. Beneath it lay the memory box her papa helped her bury for her baby, her daughter. She touched the soil, pressed her hands into it and pictured her baby's belongings. Her daughter was not buried here. She was told she had been buried at "Maison Belle". She couldn't go to where she lay, so her papa helped her bury the memory box containing the little items she should have used on her. There was part of her needed to believe that her baby was buried here, next to her parents.

From a young age Cassy had been to so many funerals. She lived in a community where everyone was there for each other and this continued in death. She can remember grieving mothers stood at the graveside of their babies, unable to leave. As she stood here tonight, she saw the day clearly when her papa carried the small white box. Her aunt Rosalie covered it in a towel until they got here so as not to raise anyone's suspicions. It was the evening and yet not too late, so there was no undesirables hanging around. Cassy remembered the sun was just gone out of sight and the sky was awash with the remains of the day. A flock of birds flew across the painted sky. She stared up at them as her papa prepared the soil. He had to dig down far enough so no rainwater could wash it away.

She walked towards her mama's tomb, pressed her hand onto its cold surface, and wished she could feel her touch her brow and tell her everything was going to be okay. She read the words on the tomb, a much loved verse of Hannah's from the book of Isaiah, "Arise, shine; for your light has come! And the glory of the Lord is risen upon you."

She watched her papa set down the box beside him on the upturned soil. He had made a big enough hole and was ready to place it in the ground. He leaned over the shovel and looked off into the distance. He took a cigarette from his pocket and lit it. Cassy watched him inhale and exhale the smoke. He pushed the shovel into the ground with his boot and walked away. She watched him walk in the direction of Eli's tomb. She wondered what Eli would of thought of what happened to her.

Her papa seemed to know what she needed and that was to do this for her daughter. This was something she had to do on her own. She knelt down beside the little white box. The wall in front of her had one white stone, which made it an obvious marker for the burial so she could always find it again. This area wasn't sold as plots for tombs, because there was no space with the trees on either side of it. She held onto the lid and delayed opening it. The smell of her baby and the little curl in the centre of her head came back to her now. Her palms sweated. She opened the lid and lifted off the layer of tissue that covered the items. She didn't want to disturb the way they were arranged so she just ran her hand across them gently. She touched the shawl that she sewed in the lead up to the birth, sewn in secret in her room when all her days' orders were completed. She ran her finger across the comb and gently touched the boots with ribbon laced through them. She saw one of the laces were open. She reached in to tie it. Tiny steps in tiny shoes that her baby never took. A comb that would never contain a strand of her hair. A shawl that would never cover her. Whenever she had saved enough, she bought these things for her baby. All the rest of her wages she brought home to help her papa. She closed the lid of the box. It wasn't much to mark her daughter's entry into this world, but it was all she had. She placed the box into the freshly dug grave. Rosalie gave her a pen and she wrote across the box, "Belle Shaw, my baby girl forever, love…" The tears came as she finished writing "Mama."

Cassy felt at sixteen a burden thrown upon her that she had to force her family to carry. She had left them with all the hopes and dreams of a change of life for her. Sent off with their best wishes and had returned baring a dark secret they all had to carry. No one knew the absolute emptiness she felt. She saw her papa walk towards her, so she touched the lid one last time and stood up. Her face was awash with tears and her neck felt heavy as if it couldn't hold her head anymore. Amos stood a distance away, close enough for her to see the pained expression on his face. He held the shovel by his side and looked awkward, as if he didn't know when to come back to her. He stared off into the distance and rubbed his brow. She knew he had cried and didn't want her to see. Cassy looked down at the little box. Nothing could have prepared her for the overwhelming sense of loss she felt.

The wind howled around the tombs tonight as the storm strengthened. She needed to leave here and get to the bookstore. She stood up. She looked down at the soil embedded under her nails. She looked over at her parent's tomb. It was shrouded in darkness. She remembered the day of her papa's passing and Louis placed his arm around her and told her everything would be okay. The wind clipped through the tombs and made a strange sound. She needed to leave. She looked down at the ground one last time and pictured her baby nothing could take away the memory of her. As she walked towards the exit, she looked back. Her papa helped her that day when she didn't want to leave. Even though she knew her daughter was buried on the plantation, she found solace to have something of hers here. She was told by Beth she would never be able to go to the plantation to see where her daughter was buried. Here was the only place she had that proved her daughter lived.

Amos never spoke of the awful deed that brought Cassy's baby into the world. She felt summoned into silence. Her papa stood in the doorway and cried as he heard his daughter recount what happened to her. Her aunt held her what seemed like hours as she broke down and cried. Rosalie helped her into her familiar bed and brought her some tea. Cassy sunk down into the bedclothes and closed her eyes. She pictured her mama still lived here and her time at the mansion was a nightmare that never happened. She heard the front door close and watched her papa walk past her bedroom window. Her aunt came into her room. She didn't want her papa to know the awful deed that brought her home. She fell asleep that night with her aunt by her side. Neither of them spoke. Cassy just wanted to sleep. Her belly ached and her head pounded, but she was exhausted and fell asleep.

Tonight she looked back at the gate where her papa once stood. She looked down at her hands, older, veined and covered in soil. She left the cemetery with the same grief she did all those years ago as a sixteen-year-old girl.

Chapter 26

Tonight she passed Lottie Brown's music hall. The storm had strengthened. It was an effort for Cassy to walk. She didn't know if she could go on. She thought about that day when her papa brought her here. Rosalie had moved back to her own house, but still visited when she wasn't busy with her family. Amos had a piano at home. Something Cassy wondered would her mama have allowed. He sat down to play. He settled the music sheets.

"I'm going to play you a number I've been working on."

Cassy closed her eyes and listened to him play. It felt so good to be at home. When he finished she clapped enthusiastically. He turned around to face her.

"I told you where I'm playing now Cassy didn't I?"

"Yes you did papa."

"Well that finishes up about nine and I go on over to the music hall. You may know it. It's on St. Peter Street."

"You play in Miss Brown's place. Do you remember when I went for the audition during Mardi Gras?"

"How could I forget? I came back and you were

319

gone.

Maybe you'd feel like coming with me one of the nights."

"Oh papa, that would be amazing. And Miss Brown is she well?"

"More than, she's the helm of the place. Cassy to think, no more of those old haunts I used to play at."

"Papa that day when I auditioned, it was for Mr. Godfrey. He came from New York. He planned to make me a singer. He chose me as his lead act…"

She broke down crying.

"Let's see what tomorrow brings. I know Lottie will be delighted to see you. I've met Mr. Davis he runs the place with Lottie. I told him you are home. He's keen to see you."

"And Mr. Godfrey?"

"He's in New York mostly. I haven't had the chance to meet him yet. You need to rest," he said and walked her to her room. "Goodnight Cassy Belle."

***

She heard the music drift out from Miss Brown's Music Hall as she walked with her papa. They could hear laughter, cheering and a loud whooping noise as they stepped inside. The main hall had smoked glass windows. That was where all the merriment came from. They climbed the stairs to where she had auditioned. Cassy looked around at the same peach walls she had seen that first day, now wall to wall with customers. She looked up at the tiny raised stage, the same one she stood on with anticipation waiting to sing for Mr. Godfrey.

"Cassy, it's so good to see you," said Miss Brown.

Cassy turned around in recognition of her voice.

"Miss Brown," was all she could manage.

"We've been over this sweetie, its Lottie," she said smiling. "Your papa tells me you still want to sing. I hoped this was true."

Cassy looked to her papa.

"He's here tonight Cassy. Mr. Godfrey," said her papa and pointed. She followed where he nodded and saw Mr. Godfrey sat at the same table she sat with him that day. The man that wanted, to make her a star. She looked back to Miss Brown with a worried look on her face.

"It hasn't been that long Cassy, that he's forgotten your voice. Not much has changed here," Miss Brown reassured her.

Her papa took her hand.

She took to the stage when the set was over and looked down at the crowd. They all waited for her to start to sing. She found the same crack on the wall she did the day of her audition. She was accompanied by Miss Brown

321

on the piano, but the music stopped. She looked down at Mr. Godfrey for the first time since she saw him all those months ago. She watched her papa walk through the crowd and go to the piano.

"Carry on Miss Shaw," said Mr. Godfrey with a smile.

She sang her heart out. That night she was given something that was taken from her, her voice. It was at Miss Brown's music hall that her career took off. From that night on, she performed there and grew in popularity. She sang accompanied by her papa and the band. Every night she was on stage it was a full house.

***

Louis recognized her voice drift out onto the street from the music hall. He looked down at the flyer in his hand.

"Cassy Shaw, New Orleans' most celebrated act."

He waited for her to finish her set at the bar. He attempted to come up to her during the break, but there were too many people around. They all wanted time with her. Cassy was told a man waited for her by the bar. She expected it be another admirer of her voice. Nothing could have prepared her to see Louis. Two years had passed since they said goodbye. She'd given up all chance of seeing him again. They spoke for hours that night. Cassy told Lottie she'd lock up after her. Louis asked her if she'd like to go to

Café du Monde before he walked her home. He told her how he was banished from his family for dropping out of law school. That he opened his own bookstore. The owner Mr. Stein died and left it to him, as he had no family. He taught him everything he knew about first edition books and how to source them. Louis told her how he was told she'd moved on to another job out of town and had left no forwarding address. How his father shot himself not long after he dropped out of law school his mother still drank and she was adamant not to have a relationship with him. Cassy told him about the audition here that first day when she still worked at the mansion, but how her papa arranged for her to meet with Mr. Godfrey and now she has a sellout show most nights. She told him she wrote him. He never got the letter. He asked her if she could remember what she said. She said it didn't matter now. They got married and moved into their first home together up over the bookstore.

Chapter 27

Tonight the force of the wind pushed Cassy's frail body along. She was scared for the first time since she left her house back on Burgundy Street. She wished Louis was here to help her get to the bookstore. She knew he must have been looking for her. Every morning he had to give her, her pills in case she forgot. How could she forget the size of those pills and the taste? They had a back taste that rose in her throat. However, they calmed her and helped her get through the day. Some days she felt she didn't need them at all. She listed out everything she remembered, to prove to him that she was okay. She hated the look of pity in his eyes. She had always been the strong one, they both knew that. How strong she really was he would never know.

When she listened to the phone call about a parcel for her from the River Road, she knew it was about her baby. She had no idea what time it was; perhaps morning. There was no way of telling. The sky was dark. One thing she did know was this storm wasn't leaving any time soon. Despite the strength of winds, she continued on her way to the bookstore, nothing was going to stop her. She looked across the street at the dark green shutters of the bookstore and remembered times spent there. This was their first home together. She looked up at the wrought iron balcony, which led to their former living quarters. It was heavy laden with blooms of every color. The flowers were interwoven with ribbon, which gave the building a distinct charm. The ribbon was symbolic of Cassy's work as a seamstress and remained long after she stopped sewing. It was a pretty addition to the building. Some memories faded as she looked at the shutters on the front of the store.

The sign up over the door said, "Signed and Sealed." They came up with the name together one night sat in Lafayette Bar on Bourbon Street. They were so excited. A young couple full of dreams and plans. The name was scrolled in gold letters. Another sign hung over the downstairs window from the balcony in the same gold letter, 'Le Blanc Books.' Louis slowly built it up over the years to become what it is today, the city's best bookstore for first edition books. As Cassy stared up at the sign now she gasped for air. She felt weak and dizzy as she crossed the street. She had a dull ache in the pit of her stomach.

The bookstore was originally built as a townhouse, which retained much of its original charm. Its lace sheers concealed the books inside and protected them from the glare of the sun. She pressed her face against the glass. Inside was in total darkness. The storm probably had knocked off the power. She turned the key in the door and stepped into the porch. The rainwater from her nightdress pooled on the floor. Her hair was soaked and clung to her face.

The lines around her eyes crept down her face to meet the curve of her once full lips. The inky blackness of her eyes had lost the deep of their blue youth. She pushed open the door. Her eyes adjusted to the dark. She looked at the staircase, which ran in the opposite direction to her; lined with books on each step. There were a number of boxes at the base of the stairs. Orders ready to be shipped out to customers. Against the wall that led into the bookstore were more boxes. Probably a delivery the staff didn't get around to completing before they left. All along that same wall were glass cases that housed the store's first editions, safely locked inside.

Cassy looked through the glass paneled door that led into the bookstore. She pushed it open. It dragged against the carpet faded with wear and tear. There was something timeless about this room. The years of history it carried in its books, probably lent to this; but the antique furniture Louis had imported over the years helped create it also. The familiar smell of books surrounded her. The dizziness she felt outside had passed. She walked over to the desk in the middle of the room. It was the most dominating feature with its hand carved design. She ran her hand along its surface. The dizziness returned, so she sat down in the chair and put her hands on the desk to wait for it to pass. It was a losing battle. The medication made her tired, but without it, she was sick and dizzy. It had been yesterday evening since she took the last pill. She skipped it last night, so she wouldn't be tired. She honestly believed she remembered more without them.

Just behind her was the little area she used to sit and eat her lunch with Louis. It was here he sat the day she rushed through the door to tell him she was going to be singing on the radio. He jumped up and down with excitement for her and made such a fuss the whole store looked. She burst out laughing and apologized to everyone outside. She gave out to him then in the next breath for not looking after the plants. They looked like they needed water. He told her to stop fussing and wrapped her in a hug.

The dizziness came back stronger, that the ground

rose up to meet her. She leaned forward for the phone and held it to her ear. The line was dead. She rubbed her head. She couldn't bare the intense pounding and pain. She tried to call out, but nothing came. The dizziness stopped after a while of just lying still. She touched whatever it was on the desk in front of her. She came here for the parcel. Her name was written on the front. She turned it over and sure enough, it had a return address of Maison Belle, The River Road. It was bound in twine. She couldn't open it. She searched for a scissors or a knife something to open it with, but couldn't find either. She pulled at the corner of the parcel. The twine slipped off on one side and there was more packaging. It was a document of some sort. She opened the page.

She saw the name she's played repeatedly in her mind all these years.

'Belle'.

At the foot of the letter was a line marked with an X, where a signature should be. This was what Cassy marked on that heinous day in 1960. She thought it was a birth cert, but this letter revealed it was adoption papers. Above where she marked was the signature of Anton Le Blanc, who granted custody of her baby, her daughter to Robert and Olivia Le Blanc of "Maison Belle Plantation, River Road, Louisiana." The letter was dated December 1960.

The words were written in her employer's scrawl, Frances
Le Blanc.

> *'I hereby grant sole custody of my daughter 'Belle',*
> *to the care of Robert and Olivia Le Blanc on this date*
> *December 6 1960.*
>
> *Born December 5 1960.*
>
> *Named Sara Jane Le Blanc from this date.*
>
> *Signed X."*

Cassy stared at the words in disbelief. She looked at
the parcel. There was something wrapped in tissue inside.
Her hands shook as she opened it and saw the little gown
her mama gave her on her fifteenth birthday. There was an
envelope attached to it in her handwriting. The letter was
addressed to Louis. It was the letter she wrote him. She
couldn't move. She pressed the little gown against her face,
breathing in the smell of her baby. She wept.

It seemed like hours passed since she opened the
parcel. She needed to leave here and go find her daughter;
all the years of heartache and of closing off what happened
to her. She believed the only piece of her daughter she had
lay in a cemetery; when all along her daughter was alive.
Her Belle was alive. She tried to speak her name, but
nothing came. Before she left the room she placed the
letter to Louis beside the telephone. She closed the door to
the bookstore and headed in the direction of Jackson

Square. She held the gown to her chest and tried to walk against the force of the wind. Her daughter hadn't died as she had been told that night. She lived and she was going to find her.

The walk up Pirates Alley was difficult. It felt like the walls of St. Louis Cathedral closed in on her. She got to the steps of the cathedral and the dizziness came at her in waves. Her breathing was shallow. She looked out onto Jackson Square it was deserted. She pushed open the cathedral door and was surprised to find it open. She walked past the angel statues either side of the aisle. The only light was from the night-lights, which were permanently lit from patrons of the church. There was a painting of Jesus and His followers above her head. She walked towards the altar. She thought she saw a candle, a flicker of light next to the pulpit, like someone stood there.

Then a piercing sound like a wail. She hid down behind one of the pews. There was a book on the seat in front of her. It was a book of Psalms. She held it as it sounded like the walls crashed in around her. There was a loud bang behind the altar, then a second one. She could hear a crashing noise. It sounded like the trees had fallen in St. Anthony's Garden, to the rear of the cathedral. Then another bang, but it came from overhead. A hole appeared in the roof and the rain poured in. She was safe in here, once that hole didn't get any bigger.

She looked at the little gown belong to her baby all those years ago. How she had rested it on her tiny body, but never got to dress her in it. She thought of how proud her mama was when she gave it to her. It was for when she was much older and would have a baby of her own. Her mama would never have imagined that a year later she would hold it against her baby. Cassy needed to find her daughter. She thought of Louis and he surely would be searching for her. She wondered where he was. If he was still at their house waiting her return or had he left in search of her. The storm had hit and its rain battered against the cathedral. She was exhausted. All those years trying to piece together that night brought her here and finally led to the truth of her baby. She had blocked out the pain of losing her baby and mourned her. And tonight to find out she lived was overwhelming. She looked up at the altar again and at all the candles, they soothed her as she shut her eyes.

Belle's tiny hand flayed helplessly up in the air and searched for life, for her place in the world. Cassy was brought back to the room again the night her baby was born. She held her baby so close and didn't let go. She knew where she was. She was safe with her. Then she looked down at the bloody sheet in her hand and she was pulled away from her baby. She couldn't breathe. She tried to call out. She opened her eyes, the rainwater poured in still, but the sound outside had ceased. The storm had passed. She prayed for the rain to wash away the stains of the past; to give her that night back. All she had for years was a memory box buried in an unmarked grave. She pressed the little gown to her chest and walked towards the door. The rain still fell, but she knew she had to keep going. In that moment as she stood there she wished she could tell Louis that she believed she didn't have dementia. She would find a way to tell him about her daughter.

All of a sudden, Cassy forgot where she was. She didn't know how much time had passed since she took refuge inside the church. She stepped out onto Jackson Square. It was completely deserted. Alarms were sounding off in different buildings. There was no one around. A sense of fear crept over her and she wished Louis was here. The hurricane the city of New Orleans feared had hit and its aftermath seeped through the streets as the levees burst their banks. This area had escaped the floodwaters, which made it possible for Cassy to keep going; though she was exhausted.

**

Louis and D.J. arrive at the bookstore. He checked the parcel again on his desk."

332

"Have a look make sure there is nothing else inside," said D.J.

Louis checked. All that remained was the brown paper and some cord. He pushed it aside in frustration. D.J. looked around at the books that lined the shelves. He made a comment to Louis about all the years of history are untouched from the storm.

"I should have known she'd come here to get this. I told her she had to wait."

"That wasn't your fault Louis. At least you know she was here."

"But where is she now?" demanded Louis.

"I'm going to take a look upstairs Louis, just in case."

Louis broke down. He had stayed strong in the Superdome. Just then, he saw an envelope with his name on it on the floor. He recognized it as her writing. He bent down to pick it up. He opened it and began to read.

He found out that she became pregnant when his father raped her. She was about to be sent from the mansion, but her baby died. She named her Belle Shaw. She was to return to live with her father back home in Treme. She hoped this letter would reach him, so that he could know she loved him and never wanted this and that she loved her baby.

Louis thought of all the failed attempts over the

years to become pregnant and the many miscarriages they suffered.

He put his hands onto the desk in front of him and let out a lowly cry.

When D.J. returned from upstairs, he saw the look on Louis' face.

"What is it?"

"I don't know how to say this…"

"It's okay Louis, go on."

"It's Sara Jane, I mean Belle…"

Louis dropped the letter to his side.

"Do you want me to read it?" offered D.J.

"No it's okay. Remember I told you Cassy was raped by my father. She had a baby back then, but she died. In the letter she tells me she loves me and that they are sending her home to her family in Treme."

"Louis I'm so sorry. What do you suppose the parcel contained then?"

"I don't know. That's it, I don't know. I have to find her D.J."

He took one last look around the store and asked D.J. "What happened here?"

They were back out in the floodwaters. Louis stopped walking and looked up at the cathedral in front of him. As he got closer to the wrought iron fence, he could see where the tree had blown down from the hurricane and part of the fence was broken. Christ the Redeemer statue was missing two fingers. He thought of all the times he and Cassy met behind its walls. D.J. was already on Pirates Alley. He was eager to get to The Garden District. Louis followed him and stared up at the Cathedral with its chalk white walls.

"Come on Louis, we need to step it up a notch, they're going to sweep the streets and expect everyone to evacuate. We're not going to get away with staying out here much longer."

The noonday sun was beating down. He called back to D.J. to wait that they should check inside the Cathedral, to make sure Cassy wasn't there. Reluctantly D.J. doubled back. It was here that Louis and Cassy came to seek refuge, to meet in private all those years ago, before they got married.

They entered the Cathedral. The roof had collapsed on top of the organ. Louis walked up the aisle. He sat at the seat they always sat near the altar, which was hidden by a pillar. The flags, which surrounded the altar, had collapsed and one was draped across the pew in front of him. He noticed a piece of paper out of the corner of his eye on the floor. It was yellow and faded. He picked it up and read it. He felt D.J. touch his shoulder. Louis wept. He handed the paper to him.

"My wife's baby is alive. This is her adoption papers to my brother and his wife. Her baby is my niece," Louis said.

A thousand thoughts flashed through his mind. He explained to D.J. that the girl he knew to be his niece was his wife's daughter. He had no relationship with her as his brother prevented any. He did when she was a baby, but he never saw her again after his father cut him off from the family. His brother Robert had nothing to do with him and prevented any contact with Sara Jane. As a result, any possibility of having a relationship with her was removed.

"Louis, we need to focus on the fact she was here. Your wife is alive. We can be sure of that now."

"What if she was here days ago and something happened to her in the hurricane?"

"Well I'm no detective, but I am a cop and something tells me that parcel has led your wife to her daughter.

"Didn't you tell me your brother and his family moved back to The Garden District after your father died?"

"Yes they did."

"Come on let's go there. I believe Cassy will be there."

"What about your family?"

"I had to force them to leave New Orleans and go to Baton Rouge for safety. They'll be waiting for me. Once I see you safely to your family's house. I'll be on my way."

"D.J. how can I ever thank you?"

"Don't forget Louis we came through this together. We have a bit of a walk ahead of us, but I'll get you there."

Chapter 28

Cassy walked up the drive of the house she had left all those years ago as a young girl. She began to walk past the house and take the staff entrance, but she saw Beth on the front porch waving at her. She couldn't see anyone else. So she opened the nearest gate and walked across the lawn. The grass was overgrown. She couldn't help but think of Jacob and all the years he tended to it. Beth came down to meet her.

"Cassy, how are you?"

"I'm fine Beth. You haven't changed."

"There is so much I want to know Cassy," she said as she linked her arm in hers. "First of all how does it feel to be back here? Strange to see the place after all these years I bet."

Cassy was about to answer her when she saw a woman with long dark hair on the verandah. As she got closer, this woman smiled at her. The blanket that was around her shoulders fell to the ground. Then Cassy saw the wheelchair. She looked to Beth.

"It's Belle. She has so much to tell you Cassy."

Cassy ignored the monstrosity of the house, which made her draw her breath still today and fixed her eyes on her daughter. She crossed to where she sat. The younger woman had tears in her eyes. Cassy clasped her chest. To come face to face with her daughter after years of thinking she had died here in this very house was overwhelming. She reached out her hands for her daughter's. Cassy held her daughter's face in her hands and pressed her lips to her cheek.

"Belle...sorry Sara Jane I should say.

"It's Belle."

The two women embraced. Cassy didn't want to let go now she'd found her. Belle offered her a seat. Cassy sat across from her.

"There is so much I want to know mama and so much I want to tell you. It is okay I call you mama?"

"Yes of course. I've waited a lifetime to hear those words."

"You don't have other children?"

"No myself and Louis were never blessed with children. But first I want to hear all about you."

"I was married and we lived at the plantation, but he left me some years ago. So I moved back in here with my grandma, father and Beth."

"What happened to your mama?"

"She died in a car accident. Before she died she gave me the gown you had for me as a baby. Beth helped me send it to the bookstore. I am sick and confined to this chair."

"I'm sorry this happened to you and your mama."

"I had father and Beth here with me. It must be years since Louis saw him."

"Yes it is," said Cassy.

"Jacob was here also until he passed away. All the other staff left and found work elsewhere. Nobody could tolerate grandma for long."

"He was very good to me when I was a young girl here," said Cassy.

"He spoke of you often mama," reassured Belle.

"And your grandfather?" asked Cassy.

"Oh I thought everyone knew about that, he shot himself on the plantation. Sorry I thought you knew."

"I must have forgotten," said Cassy, annoyed at her inability to remember certain things.

"We knew that," said Louis from behind her.

"Louis, you found me," said Cassy.

They embraced and he said something to her and she hugged him.

"You must be Sara Jane," said Louis.

"I want to tell you both; I have gone by Belle since I was fifteen when my mother told me I was adopted."

"Is that when you found out about me?" Cassy asked nervously.

"It was only through Beth that I found out years later. Father didn't want me to find out, but when he saw how much I've gone through he changed his mind."

Louis took his wife's hand.

"Louis, I never knew about you until Beth told me everything. I never knew I had an uncle. Beth explained to me that she was forced to keep up the lie you were dead, that was until my grandma passed."

"Is my brother inside?"

"He didn't want to intrude on us," she said and took her mama's hand in hers.

Cassy drew in her breath and held out the gown.

"I wanted to know who the initials H.S. was belong to. Beth told me that was my grandma's signature when she made a garment."

Cassy clasped her hand to her mouth.

"Beth told me as much as she could, but I want to hear it all from you, mama. I want to know about my grandparents and my uncle Eli. I want you to know even as a little girl I knew there was something different, something hidden. I could feel it."

Cassy fought hard to keep the tears at bay.

With that, there was a disturbance from inside the dining room.

"Come out," Belle called. "I want y'all to meet your grandma. This is Isaac, Jackson and Hannah."

With that, two boys and a girl came out onto the verandah to meet Cassy. Beth stood behind them.

"Are they yours?" asked Cassy overcome with joy.

"Louis, I'm sure you read the letter. So you know now that I had a part to play in keeping Belle from Cassy. I want you both to know I am truly sorry and I know there is no way I can ask for forgiveness."

"It is not my wrong to forgive..." began Louis.

But Cassy stopped him.

"Beth, I have lost out on years with my daughter, but I was there and I know you had no choice or say in the matter. You were like me then forced into situations we wanted no part in. So yes I do forgive you."

"Thank you Cassy... You will never know how much that means."

With that little Hannah jumped up onto Cassy's lap and hugged her.

"Will y'all come inside I've prepared lunch for us?" asked Beth.

Cassy never planned to set foot inside this house

again. She knew it was the same for Louis. He took her hand as they went inside. There were suitcases just inside the grand hall.

"We waded out the storm here, but we're leaving for my house on the River Road. Will you come with us," asked Belle.

"We will," said Louis.

"Mama, the main house is just a shell. I built my own house on the land after my divorce. You'll be safe there. We all will, until they say we can return."

"Belle, I'd love to come," said Cassy.

Her daughter squeezed her hand. The children were running around. Belle told them to go into the dining room.

"Beth, please join us," said Louis as she went to leave.

He followed the children into the dining room, with Beth trying to get them to calm down. His brother stood up when he entered the room. He reached out for Louis. Robert wept as Louis hugged him back.

Cassy stood in the grand hall with her daughter by her side.

Belle said, "I know all your songs, but I don't have a note in my head. I love the sound of your voice."

Cassy whispered to her, "You are my voice, my reason to sing, Belle."

Made in the USA
Middletown, DE
05 March 2017